DEAD SHOE

SOCIETY

A Short Story Collection

by

Mark Souza, Stephen Penner, Kate Cornwell, Jonas Saul, Christi Craig, E. Victoria Flynn, and Lori Gordon

PUBLISHED BY

Imagine Press

ISBN: 978-1468081428

Title copyright ©2011 by the individual authors

This is a work of fiction. All of the characters, organizations, and events portrayed in this novel are either products of the author's imagination or are used fictitiously.

All rights reserved. No part of this publication may be reproduced, stored in a retrieval system or transmitted in any form or by any means without prior written permission from the author.

Neath Lily Pond

by Mark Souza

November 14th, 1648

Blow after rhythmic blow, metal on metal, reverberated from the blacksmith's anvil while Mary Johnson listened, trapped and on display in the stocks at the foot of the Hartford Town Hall. Walter Woodward had taunted that he was beating out her death knell. Earlier in the evening, before the rain started falling, chilling Mary like the icy hand of Lucifer, Constance Taylor had stopped by long enough to spit in Mary's face. Constance didn't utter a peep, and didn't need to. Mary knew why she was angry.

Hands trapped, and helpless to wipe the glob of mucus away, Mary could do nothing but let it slowly slide down her face, thick and warm. Mary said nothing - how could she? She just watched Constance waddle away down the street, skirts hoisted a few inches to keep the mud off. By the time the spit finally dripped from her chin, the mayor's wife was safely indoors, snug and warm. And what a happy home that must be: stony silence, accusing stares, bitterness fouling the air. Of all the charges leveled against Mary, adultery was the only one that she couldn't deny. She felt for the woman, but how could she say no to Constance's husband? Mary needed the money - she had children of her own to feed.

During the night, a November wind pushed sleet sideways and drove a frigid spike of pain into Mary's skull. She came to long for the warmth of Constance Taylor's spit on her face. Part of her hoped she'd die before morning, depriving the town of their spectacle. She envisioned her lifeless body sagging in the stocks at first light, and the disappointed spectators realizing there would be no execution; that her death had come in darkness without witness, and the day would be ordinary, unrecognizable from any other in the week. She prayed for this, though God had grown deaf to her prayers long ago.

***

Damn TV reporters always had the upper hand. Jim Woodward watched the story play out again on the flat screen at the front of the Hartford Herald newsroom. Images hit the airwaves within an hour of the tragedy while Jim's story wouldn't hit the streets until the evening edition at 5:00. It was the top story on a slow news day. The local television stations kept replaying tape of a fireman carrying a tiny swaddled body from Lily Pond amid a scrum of police struggling to hold back onlookers and obscure cameras from getting a clear view. Even CNN had picked up the story.

The who, what, where, when and how of it had already been broadcast to all of Connecticut. The *who* was Maggie Perkins, twenty-four, college educated nanny, now in police custody. The *what, how, when and where* was that Perkins had drowned Zach Taylor, her four year-old charge, in Lily Pond on an otherwise lovely summer day - a day that lured businessmen from their offices to take lunch in the park under the shade of a tree, a day for teens to throw Frisbees around, a day for children on summer vacation to play in the grass. Witnesses, and there were plenty of them, reported seeing Perkins sprint toward the bank with the child in her arms and hurl him like a caber into the water at the south end of the pond. The child went straight to the bottom. Bystanders tried to help, but their efforts were thwarted by murky water and a thick layer of loose mud. The question that remained unanswered was *why*? And that's what Jim hoped he could get to the heart of before the television prima donnas.

From what Jim had uncovered, Maggie Perkins had driven seventy miles to throw the boy into Lily Pond, passing a score of lakes and rivers along the way. Why? Jim had five-hundred words to tell the story, maybe more if he could put enough juice behind it to get an editor's green light for more column space.

He decided to focus on the human element, to convey the sense of a mother's loss. Joyce Nickerson Taylor had lost her only child just months after her husband was killed by a hit-and-run driver. Zachery's death signaled the end of the Taylor line, a family with a long, rich history in Connecticut extending back centuries. Mrs. Taylor was alone now, the last of her family. Jim wanted an interview with the woman to make the story more personal, but there was a roadblock. Taylor's mother-in-law was screening calls and shielding Joyce from the press.

Jim had a small son himself and could imagine what Joyce Taylor was going through. He had almost lost his son and wife during childbirth. The pregnancy had turned toxic. Jeb had to be delivered eight weeks early. Both Lucy and Jeb nearly died during the procedure. He remembered the hours of waiting, how it felt when the nurse ushered Jim out of the delivery room and advised him he might want to pray. The grief, the vast emptiness prematurely felt, and the fear of facing the future alone, consumed him. The experience tested his faith. Doctors warned that another pregnancy might kill Lucy. Jim had taken steps to make sure that could never happen. They had decided any future children would be adopted - a decision they both felt good about.

It was that experience that allowed Jim to understand Joyce Taylor's anguish. He'd been there himself, if only for a few hours, and he wanted to make sure that emotion was captured in his story.

Jim had sent a summer intern from UConn to the scene to ferret out more information. Though Crystal Olnick was green, she was bright and eager, qualities that would serve her well as a reporter.

***

An ambulance had cut across the manicured grass of Bushnell Park in a sweeping arc flattening parallel swaths from a service road to the shore of Lily Pond. Crystal Olnick followed the tracks down the slope on foot. It felt like stalking an animal. This animal was a news story - real honest-to-God news, not another lame congressman trying to make himself look good for an upcoming run for governor, not another library closing, not another plea to raise the state income tax, but real blood and guts news. Until today, the UConn undergrad would have characterized her internship as a total bore that had her wondering whether a degree in journalism was a mistake.

The ambulance crouched beside the water, lights spinning, looking like it was ready to roll. A crowd had gathered and a ring of uniformed police kept them at arms length while the divers and EMTs finished their work. Camera crews representing the three major networks were still among the throng. Crystal fiddled with the press credential hanging from her neck to make sure it was visible.

Crystal's path to the lake took her past the rear of the ambulance. She peered inside through the back windows. The small form of Zach Taylor rested on a gurney under a blanket. It was her first dead body. She hadn't arrived in time to see the boy pulled from the pond, which was just as well. As encounters with death went, this one was as sterile as it could be. The body was a motionless lump under a blanket. She knew it was a child, but she didn't have to see it. She didn't know how she would feel the first time, and though his face was hidden and she didn't have to look into his lifeless eyes, she felt an ache in her chest and sadness; sadness at a future stolen away, the times and experiences the boy would never know.

A few yards from the bank, bubbles rose in steady streams through water turbid as lentil soup. Plumes of mud roiled the surface, kicked up by the divers below, unleashing the fetid stench of rotting vegetation putrid as a pig's wallow. Why were divers still at work though Zach Taylor lay in an ambulance? It seemed odd. What else was there to do?

Crystal noticed a fireman eying her from the shade of a maple. She'd caught him leering, but he didn't seem to mind that she'd noticed. He appeared to like what he saw. Though Crystal was not tall and leggy, her curvy, athletic build held charms of its own. She smiled. The fireman smiled back "What's your name?" she asked.

"Mike."

"Crystal," she said.

He tapped her press credential. Crystal's name was spelled out in capital letters. "Yeah, I got that."

Crystal blushed. "I'm new at this. I guess I missed all the excitement. If the body is in the ambulance, why are the divers still in the water?"

Keeping his voice low, Mike said, "They found another body down there while they were looking for the boy."

"Why haven't they brought it up?"

"It's a skeleton. It's been there a long time. They're marking its position and waiting for a forensic anthropologist."

Crystal's eyes drifted toward the nervous surface of the pond. She was about to walk away when she caught sight of Tina-Around-Town from the Channel 3

Eyewitness News Team. Tina didn't usually do hard news, but must have been recruited because she was nearby when the call came in. Crystal turned back to Mike. "Is there anything you can tell me that they don't know?"

Mike glanced at the camera crew and grinned. "When they found the boy, he was wearing metal boots."

"Metal boots?"

"Weirdest things I ever saw - handmade, crude, kind of like they were constructed a thousand years ago. The kid didn't stand a chance. He went straight to the bottom. He's still wearing them inside the meat wagon. We couldn't figure out how to get them off without cutting them, and the cops want them preserved." He stared at the camera crew, his face stern. "The divers covered him up so those vultures wouldn't splatter his image across all of New England. It's going to be hard enough on his family without that."

Crystal nodded, unsure whether Mike had also lumped her into the vulture category. She turned to leave and Mike called after her. "Oh, and one more thing. One of the divers said the skeleton down there is wearing the same kind of boots."

She stopped and turned. "Mike, can I get your phone number?"

A grin spread across his face. "Sure."

Jim was deep into his research on the nanny, Maggie Perkins, when his cell phone rang. Caller ID showed Crystal Olnick's name and relief washed over him. He needed details. The story sorely lacked them and the clock was ticking. Crystal's excitement flowed through the phone though her voice was barely loud enough to hear. It was as if he was back in high school exchanging dirty gossip in study hall. He assumed there were other reporters nearby, the television hoard and other papers as well, and Crystal had something they didn't.

"The divers are still in the water," she said. "I heard they found another body while searching for the boy, and don't want to disturb it. They've called in a forensic anthropologist. What do you think that means?"

"I don't know? Does anyone else have this?"

"I don't think so. One more thing - I talked to one of the firemen who helped move the body. He says the kid had on metal boots."

"Did I hear that right? Metal boots?"

"Yeah. He said they were made out of iron."

"Do you have confirmation on that?"

"No, not yet. It's tightlipped down here. Do you want me to head down to the police barracks to see if I can get a statement from the nanny?"

"No. She's either lawyered up, or is still being interrogated. Either way, they won't let you near her."

"I don't think that's going to be a long interrogation. From what everyone is saying, she left here screaming, *what have I done, what have I done.*"

"You'd be surprised how a good lawyer can twist that. Trust me, they'll take their sweet time with her. Stay where you are and get me that confirmation."

After hanging up he looked at the clock. Less than three hours to finish the story if it was going to run in the evening edition. Doubt nestled into his stomach like a porcupine. This was the stuff ulcers were made of. Could Crystal corroborate the facts in time, or would the story go as is? He reread what he had so far. It sounded as flat and lifeless as a shopping list, and full of holes.

***

They took the handcuffs off Maggie Perkins as soon as she cleared security screening in the Justice Center. She wasn't dangerous and they all knew it. The room they put her in was small and stark. Three metal-frame chairs, a metal table from the same manufacturer, a small video camera set high in the corner near the ceiling, and a mirror in the wall. Maggie knew from watching too many episodes of Dateline that the mirror was fitted with two-way glass.

She was sobbing when they found her at the pond and slapped her in cuffs. She cried again when they escorted her up the steps of the Justice Center and she realized she was going to jail. They left her alone for a while in the room. Whether it was a kind gesture to allow her emotions to settle, or a calculated move to let the enormity of her situation press onto her shoulders like an exhausted pachyderm, she did not know. All she was sure of was she was being watched.

Two detectives came in bearing weary expressions and slumped into the empty chairs on either side of her. The older of the two placed a manila folder and pen on the table and did most of the talking. He made introductions. He was Detective Sowders, his partner, Detective Laveen.

Sowders' crew cut and heavy jowls reminded Maggie of a cartoon bulldog. A roll of flesh bulged above his collar. He rolled his sleeves up over pudgy forearms, perhaps to foster a more casual atmosphere. While Sowders questioned her, Laveen, a lanky, sad-looking man, would pat her hand from time to time as if to convey it would all be okay.

"We just want to get your side of the story, and let you have your say," Sowders said. "Why don't you start from the beginning? When did you arrive at the Taylor house?"

"Nine, same as every morning." It was an easy question and the answer came tumbling out without much thought. Maybe this was the way smart detectives worked. Ask the easy questions first; get the suspect lubed up to follow questions with answers - sort of a patterned response. That's how they tripped people up. She had heard about false confessions, about how the police got people so mixed up and bewildered that they would say whatever the police wanted them to say. Maggie resolved to take her time, to consider what was being asked and what the implications were. She wouldn't be one of the unfortunates who had to spend the rest of their lives in jail because they got confused.

"What happened after Mrs. Taylor left for work?"

"Nothing. I finished feeding Zach breakfast and did the dishes. It was an ordinary day." In her head it seemed as if she was pleading to get them to believe her. She didn't like the way it sounded, the mewling tone of it. Sowder's eyes bored in on her, and as she finished her response, the corners of his mouth lifted slightly. He wasn't buying it. Only twenty minutes before, she'd been in handcuffs. Clearly it wasn't an ordinary day.

"So when did you decide to drive to Hartford?" Sowders asked.

Maggie glanced from one detective to the other. This was the hard part, the part they wouldn't want to hear. The part they wouldn't believe. "I never decided to come to Hartford. I don't remember the drive or even getting into the car. It's all a blank. The last thing I recall is people screaming at me beside the pond. I didn't know how I'd gotten there or what was wrong."

Sowders raised an eyebrow and gave his partner a look. He then shook his head side to side and set his jowls aquiver. "Maggie, may I call you Maggie?" She nodded and he continued. "We are trying to get to the bottom of a very serious matter, and this isn't helping you at all. Have you ever heard the old saying, *the truth will set you free*?" He didn't wait for Maggie to acknowledge. "It's true. All the worries about keeping your story straight, all the pressure you feel; it disappears once the truth comes out. We have a whole host of people who saw you throw the boy in the pond. That's not in dispute. What we need to know is why you did it. Perhaps if you can tell us that, we might be able to help you."

Maggie recognized Detective Sowders' clever little trick. Providing an explanation for her actions acknowledged the first part of his statement was true, the part he'd presented as fact - that she had drown Zach. It was tantamount to a confession.

"I don't remember throwing Zach in the pond, and I don't remember driving to Hartford. I have no idea how I got here."

Sowders looked frustrated. He sat back in his chair and raised his hands as if to say *what are we going to do with you,* and let them fall to the table with a loud smack.

***

Jim searched online for more information on Maggie Perkins. He found her Facebook page. There was nothing out of the ordinary there, no signs of compulsive behavior, no signs of unbalance or a recent change in demeanor. She was just an average twenty-four year-old, engaged, and making wedding plans. Not the type to hurl a child into a pond. What had gotten into her? The more he learned, the less likely it seemed. But there were witnesses who had seen her do it. Lots of them. What had made her snap? Even if there had been no one in the park, she was the last person with the boy, and the first person the police would have looked at. She had to have known the police would come for her. What possible reason could she have to kill Zach Taylor?

He jotted down the fiancé's name from Facebook and searched the Internet for more information on him. He got hits for half a dozen men in Connecticut with the same name and weeded through them old-school style, dialing each number until he got his man.

Todd Winslow was at work when Jim called. He hadn't seen the report and had no idea what was going on. When Jim broke the news, Todd stammered for words, completely flummoxed while the enormity of it overwhelmed him. His fiancée was being held for murder. "It can't be true. Maggie loves children. She wouldn't hurt a soul, let alone a child."

Jim would use the quote in his story, but Todd had nothing else significant to contribute and wanted off the phone to help Maggie. Jim didn't have the heart to tell him there were over a dozen witnesses, and the fact that she had done it really wasn't in dispute.

Maggie's friends repeated what her Ben Winslow had said; Maggie wasn't the type. Some had already seen the story on the news and still couldn't believe it. A few were caught unaware. None of them had noticed any change in Maggie's behavior or demeanor and all were surprised.

***

The forensic anthropologist arrived at the pond in an old Ford station wagon. The car settled heavily on its springs and an old man stepped out. To Crystal, the anthropologist looked close to becoming a part of the fossil record himself, diminutive, white haired and leather skinned. He emerged from his car dressed in a wetsuit. In a matter of minutes he had unloaded his scuba gear and assembled it on the bank. A policeman updated him on the situation while the old man donned his equipment. He entered the pond with a large, mesh bag in one hand and a flashlight in the other. The muddy water quickly swallowed the old man, leaving nothing but a trail of filthy bubbles.

The ambulance bearing little Zach Taylor's body rolled slowly toward Elm Street with its lights flashing. The crowd parted to make room and started to disperse as there was little to see. An unsettled patch of water and a string of bubbles popping at the surface wasn't much of a show.

When the old man finally emerged from the pond, he was flanked by a pair of police divers. He struggled up the bank, walking backwards, and dragged the mesh bag behind him with both hands. Inside, Crystal could make out a skull and curved rib bones stained black from decades in the mud, and something else dark and unrecognizable. It wasn't until the old man crossed the pedestrian walkway on his way to his car, and she heard metal scraping on concrete, that she realized what it was and why the bag was so heavy. Inside was a pair of metal boots with lower leg bones jutting out from the tops. They were just as Mike the fireman had described. She raised her phone and snapped a photograph.

***

Jim had worked reactions from family and friends into the story. It was starting to come together. He checked the clock. Time was getting short. His cell phone chirped. It was a text message from Crystal. *Check your email - you're going to love this.* He brought up his email. A new message titled "BREAKING NEWS - Intern Deserves Mo' $$$," had just arrived from Crystal bearing an attachment.

He opened the file, and saw an image of an old man in scuba gear pulling a sack along the ground. The quality of the photo wasn't great. He wondered what about it was so important. What was he supposed to notice? He read the email, a single sentence - *It's in the bag, Boss - bones from another body and metal boots like on the kid.* He looked again and shook his head. How had he not seen it before? The photo would run with the article. For the first time since he'd been assigned the story, he felt good about it. If forced, the piece was good enough to go out now. He still had an hour and a half to add a little more meat, and he'd use every second.

He glanced up at the television. It had returned to regularly scheduled programming. Either the television crews didn't realize what was in the diver's bag, or the decision had been made that old bones weren't worth breaking into *Health and Living with Mark and Laura*. He had a scoop on his hands. He called Crystal for an update.

Crystal's voice was muffled and indecipherable, as if she had her hand over the microphone. Jim heard a man speaking in the background. "Hold on, Boss. I'm working it. Give me a second." A moment later she was back on the line. "I was just talking to one of the police divers. He wouldn't confirm the Taylor kid was wearing metal shoes. When I pointed to the ones on the skeleton they just pulled out of the pond and asked if he'd seen anything like them earlier today, he said *no comment."*

"You tried, and that's all you can do."

"The police are wrapping up here and pulling out. Do you want me to head down to the morgue to see if I can get a picture of the shoes?"

"No. You would need consent from the police and family, and I don't see that happening. Follow up on the bones. Dig up whatever you can. Snap a few more shots of the boots and bones and email them to me. We need more visuals to go with the story."

***

November 15th, 1648

Mary Johnson's teeth chattered between bouts of unconsciousness. Flickering candlelight appeared in nearby windows and smoke rose from chimneys at the still, dull gloaming of morning. The town slowly stirred to life. A new day was dawning in Hartford, Mary Johnson's last. She wondered if there existed enough will amongst the doubters to halt her execution. She thought not. Those who wanted her dead were powerful men who would prefer to bury their sins by committing another. To them, it was a better option than admitting what they had done. Charging her as a witch was a calculated move aimed to prevent dissent, lest the objectors risk being accused of being in league with the Devil.

People stumbled from their homes to fetch water or bring wood inside for the fire, and pretended not to see Mary. To look at her and acknowledge her presence was to acknowledge their part in the injustice they were permitting. Before they admitted she existed, they would first gather at church, and upon convincing themselves they were good and righteous Christians, they would come for her as a group. Guilt can be parsed thin among a mob such that no one feels responsibility.

Long shafts of sunlight filtered through the trees and provided meager, yet welcome warmth. The church bell sounded the call to service, and a torrent of people washed into the street as if they'd been waiting impatiently at their doors until the beckoning of the clarion released them.

They wore their best clothes. They sang hymns, voices raised to heaven as one, and they prayed to their God, knowing full well what they planned to do that day. Though Mary could not hear the sermon, she knew the topic would be wickedness and the need for the lambs of God to cast out the evil in their midst. Reverend Parker would work the devout into frenzy until those with doubts would cower to the will of the mob.

After service, the town-folk milled about the steps until those in power, the men of influence who decided for those too weak to decide for themselves, emerged and took control. They came for Mary as a congregation, united in its purpose. And soon, she would learn how they had decided she would die.

***

Sowders blew out an exasperated sigh that hissed off the interrogation room walls. It felt exaggerated to Maggie, for affect. If he was trying to manipulate her, he should have consulted Maggie's mother. The detective could learn a thing or two.

"Okay then," Sowders said. "Let's go over this step by step. What happened after dishes?"

"Sesame Street. Zach pitches a fit if he doesn't get his Oscar the Grouch fix." Maggie covered her face with her hands at her mistake. She had referred to Zach in present tense as if nothing had happened - as if he was still alive, and she could just walk out of the interrogation room and go home. Tears filled her eyes and traced warm tracks down her face. She felt Laveen's hand on her shoulder trying to comfort her and reflexively pulled away. He was a stranger and his touch disturbed her almost as much as the thought that he felt entitled to lay his hands on her without asking.

"Do you watch television with him?" Sowders asked.

"Sometimes. Sometimes I use the time to clean up or to get a head start on lunch."

"And which was it today?"

Maggie tried to recall. What was the last thing she remembered?

***

For back-story, Jim did a search on other drownings at Lily Pond. He wasn't prepared for what he found. Lily Pond had a long and storied past where drownings were concerned. Many people had met their end in the pond over the years. Records went back more than three centuries. Jim skimmed the information and concentrated on those with suspicious or criminal circumstances. Over the centuries, there had been a string of young victims recovered from Lily Pond shod in metal shoes. Perhaps no one noticed the trend because they happened so many decades apart. But it was there for anyone to see if they cared to look.

This was the part of the job Jim loved. His story was coming to life. History, and the pond itself, were becoming characters with prominent parts to play. A story from 1932 included a photo of the metal shoes taken from the body of little Melvin Huff, drown by his mother. Jim saved the article off to his hard drive.

There was another case in 1909, John Putnam, four years old, was thrown into the pond by the family maid. He, too, was weighted down with a pair of metal boots. An artist's drawing of the boots accompanied the article. Two days earlier, his older sister tried to throw John into the pond but was interrupted by a bystander. The sentence and its implications stopped Jim. When one killer was thwarted, another cropped up with a new pair of metal boots the very next day to finish the job. It was as if the child was being hunted by some unrelenting malevolence.

Jim was not one who believed in the supernatural, but the story about the Putnam boy gave him the creeps. It reminded him of the movie, *Fallen*, where an evil entity hopped from person to person to avoid being caught, making it unstoppable. It was as if little John Putnam's fate had been predetermined and there was nothing that could be done to stop it.

He found five more stories spanning more than two hundred years, all involving metal boots and Lily Pond.

The victims were all boys. How had no one seen this trend? How could the same crime be committed so many times and not noticed? They were so similar. There was no way it was coincidence, they were too bizarre and had too much in common. But it all happened over such a vast stretch of time. How could any one person be behind it?

Jim wrote a single question on a note pad. *Who is making these boots?*

***

The old doctor was nothing like Crystal imagined. Dr. Clark Howard was funny and charming. She got the impression that, although well into his seventies, the good doctor still entertained thoughts of a carnal nature. There was something about the way he looked at her and the way he smiled. Initially, Crystal thought she'd have a fight on her hands gaining entrance to his lab and access to the bones, that the doctor would be more bureaucratic and protective of his find. Instead, Dr. H, as he liked to be called, was very welcoming.

"Why aren't the police all over this?" Crystal said. "I thought they would try to keep me from seeing you."

"What for? Whatever happened occurred centuries ago. Even if it was foul play, the perpetrator is long dead. There's nothing left to prosecute. Whoever did this, got away with it. Wouldn't you agree?"

"And you don't have a problem with me being here?"

The doctor eyed her up and down with a leer. When he grinned, every crease in his weathered face found its place. "No, of course not."

He pulled the dark bones from his sack one by one and laid them out on a long table, each one carefully placed like a puzzle piece, as he tried to reconstruct the skeleton.

"From the condition and amount of mineralization, I'd guess the bones are 300 to 400 years old."

"Mineralization?" Crystal asked.

Dr. H glanced up and grinned. "Over the years, as the skeleton sat at the bottom of the lake, dissolved minerals in the water gradually replaced the organic compounds and calcium in the bones. It's like what happens to petrified wood. The process isn't complete here, but it's on its way. It occurs at a predictable rate, and that allows me to date the bones to a reasonable level of accuracy."

He placed the iron boots down at one end of the table with the tibia and fibula pointed toward the skull. Crystal stared at the boots. Strips of black metal coated with algae, arced layer over layer like the armor of an armadillo. They appeared to have been fashioned from the metal bands of wood barrels.

Doctor H pulled the pelvis from the sack.

"Will you be able to find out who this is?" Crystal asked.

Doctor H furrowed his white brows and set the pelvic bone in the center of the table where it would have been in relation to the body. "There's always a chance, but records from this time period are spotty." He pointed at the table. "From the pelvis, I can tell the remains belong to a female, and that she bore children. I can measure the leg bones to get an approximate height, and from the growth zones, an approximate age. But that likely won't be enough to put a name to her."

"So what happens then? Do the bones go into a museum or something?"

Doctor H grimaced and shook his head. "She'll likely be cremated as a Jane Doe and the ashes buried at a potter's grave."

"That's so sad."

The doctor pulled a small curved bone from the sack and stared at it confused. He glanced at the skeleton spread out on the table and back at the bone in his hand, his mouth agape.

"What's wrong?" Crystal asked.

***

Hoping to find a link, Jim typed the drowning list he'd compiled into Google along with *Hartford, Connecticut*. Google returned pages of possibilities. At the top of the list was the title *Hartford Witch Trial of 1648*.

His phone rang.

"What have you got for me, Crystal?" he answered, the annoyance in his voice tangible. For a moment there was no response.

"Who is Crystal?"

It was his wife. "I'm sorry, honey. Crystal is an intern. She's working on a big story with me. Maybe you've seen it on the news."

"I haven't had the TV on. Did you order something recently? We just got a package."

"No, not that I recall. What is it?"

"I don't know. It's heavy and there's no return address. Are you sure you didn't order something? I don't want to be surprised by an overdraft fee because this didn't get into the check register. It's addressed to you."

"I swear, I didn't order anything. Just set it aside and I'll take care of it when I get home."

After he hung up the phone, Jim returned his attention to the results of his search. Most of the hits featured one, and sometimes two, of the names on the list. Only the Witch Trial of 1648 listed them all. The names included the judge, jury, prosecutor, and prosecution witnesses against Mary Johnson, who stood accused of witchcraft. His family name, Woodward, was among them, but there were several dozen Woodwards in the greater Hartford area.

Jim checked Ancestry.com for family histories. The first thing he noted was how quickly those on the list, prominent families in good standing, dropped in social status over the generations. The other was the similarity in the shape of the family trees. They had been healthy, growing and branching out prior to Mary Johnson's execution. Then afterward, they started dwindling to nothing. Each time, the last male child in the family line was a name on his list. Each had died in Lily Pond with metal boots on their feet.

***

John Taylor, who served as mayor and judge, led the crowd to the courthouse steps. Taylor unlocked the stocks with a key he kept about his neck, and two men took hold of Mary's arms in case she had thoughts of flight. And though she fantasized about breaking free and fleeing through the woods, her limbs were not fit to carry out an escape. She nearly collapsed without the support of the stocks, and only managed to stay upright with help.

The crowd was silent at first, and Mary thought they might be sympathetic to her, seeing how weak she was and imagining what she must have endured the previous night. She searched the crowd for her children and thankfully didn't spot them. She didn't want this to be their last image of her. Someone must be caring for them. Would they still care for her darlings after she was gone?

Taylor tied Mary's hands under the watchful eye of his wife. He cinched the rope down until Mary winced, and knotted it fast. Then a boy near the edge of the crowd screamed, "Witch!" The rest of the mob picked up the call, chanting in unison. They started to move, and Mary was swept up with them like a dinghy caught on a wave speeding toward the rocks.

They surged up a trail that led to the Connecticut River, but soon veered onto another leading into the Bushnell Wood. The path was carpeted in yellow maple leaves the size of skillets, and oak leaves tinged the color of blood. The air was redolent with the fragrance of syrup. Under other circumstances, Mary might have considered this a beautiful autumn day.

Within minutes, they stood at the edge of Lily Pond. The lilies were gone for the year, rotted and sunk to the bottom to join the mud. Mist rose off the glassy surface as if the pond was close to a boil. But nothing could be further from the truth. The water was frigid as it could be without turning solid. Soon the pond would be frozen over for the winter.

Walter Woodward, the blacksmith, dropped a canvas sack at Mary's feet. The contents clanked as it hit the soft earth. He pulled out a metal boot and removed a rear panel. This was what he had been working on, what he'd been so proud of the night before. He took off Mary's shoes and slid the icy boots over her feet, affixing the rear panels back in place with metal pins.

When he finished, he cast a rope over the thick bough of a maple leaning out over the water. He tied a large loop in the line and dropped it over Mary's head. He pulled it down over her shoulders and tightened the loop snug to her chest. Judge Taylor stepped forward and in a loud resonant voice announced, "Mary Johnson, you have been found guilty of the crime of witchcraft by a jury of your peers. May God have mercy on your soul."

A group of men pulled the line taut and raised Mary off the ground. "Please," *she pleaded,* "you know not what you do. I have sinned, yes, but I am not a witch. I am guilty of adultery, but only that, which I did to provide for my children. I beg your forgiveness as good and righteous Christians."

Woodward shoved her in the back. She swung out over the water. When she reached the apex, she held her breath and waited to fall. For a moment she felt weightless, then the rope came tight again and she arced back toward shore. "Please," *she begged,* "there is innocence within me. Condemning me is condemning innocence."

Woodward pushed her again and she swung out further over the pond. She realized then that they would not change their minds. There were too many on shore who thought their problems would end this day at the bottom of Lily Pond.

The blacksmith pushed Mary harder, lost his balance for a moment, and nearly fell in. Mary knew he wouldn't risk it again. "I shall never forget what you have done this day," *she screamed,* "I will strike from the grave at thee till none is left."

The line went slack. Mary plummeted, her hair whipping behind her. The icy water hit her hard as stone, stunning her momentarily as its frigid fingers squeezed her chest. The metal boots propelled her to the bottom where she embedded in the muck like a spear. She thrashed to free herself. The foul taste of mud filled her mouth and stung her sinuses. Above her, through the wavy surface of the pond, golden maples framed a cloudy sky tinged orange by her last sunrise. On the shoreline stood those who had condemned her to hide their own sins.

She would never forget them.

"What's the matter, doc?" Crystal asked again.

Doctor Howard dropped the bone he held and lifted the mesh bag, spilling the remaining contents onto the table. He fished through the pile, pulled a bone from the jumble, and held it in his hand. "My God, I thought this was a vertebra when I plucked it from the muck."

Crystal couldn't make out what he was staring at, she just knew that what ever it was, the doctor thought it significant. He turned it toward her. A tiny pair of empty eye sockets caught Crystal in a vacant glare.

"There wasn't just one extra body down there. There were two," he said. "She was pregnant when she died."

Crystal glanced at the clock. Maybe there was still time to get this into today's edition. She pulled her cell phone from her purse and pressed the speed dial button for Jim's desk.

***

Detective Sowder's dark eyes bored in on Maggie. "Well, which is it?" he insisted, "Did you watch Sesame Street with the boy or not?"

"I don't remember."

Sowders rolled his eyes. He looked to his partner, Laveen. "Does it feel like we're getting closer to the truth to you?" Laveen wagged his head slowly. "Me either," Sowders said. "It feels to me as if we're tap dancing all around it but not getting anywhere." He turned his eyes on Maggie. "The sooner you tell me what happened, the sooner you can move past this."

"I'm not lying!" she yelled.

Sowders looked to Laveen and shrugged. "Okay, what's the last thing you remember?"

Maggie stared at the camera in the corner near the ceiling, the eye that gazed back without ever blinking. In her mind, she tried to put herself next to Zach on the sofa, tried to hit PLAY as if her mind was a DVR that could wind flawlessly forward and back. But it wasn't perfect. It captured chunks, and skipped others of its own accord. She closed her eyes and tried to relax.

"The doorbell," she said. "I remember the doorbell ringing."

"Who was it?"

"No one. The Taylors have a window next to the door and I always check just to be safe."

"Someone had to have rung the bell."

"I know," she said. "But when I got there, there was nothing but a box on the stoop."

"A box?"

"Yes, wrapped in plain brown paper."

"Who was it from?"

She shook her head. "It only had Mr. Taylor's name on it, and he's been dead for months."

"What did you do then?"

"I brought it inside. It was heavy."

"What then?"

"I called Mrs. Taylor and asked her about it."

"And what did she say?"

"To leave it, she would take care of it when she got home."

"And did you - leave it?"

"No," she said, her voice trailing off. "I couldn't. I put it on the foyer table and tried to walk away, but it was like it was calling to me and wouldn't let me go. So I opened it."

"And what was inside?"

Maggie's eyes fixed on the camera in the corner as if she was in a trance. "A pair of boots, metal boots. They looked ancient - like maybe they came off a suit of armor."

"And then what did you do?" Sowders asked.

"I tried to pick them up. They were cold - like ice. The cold seemed to creep up my arms. It hurt. I wanted to let go, but couldn't. It was like my hands and arms didn't work anymore."

"And then what?"

Maggie looked away from the camera and stared at Detective Sowders. "I don't remember. I think I passed out. The next thing I knew, I was next to the pond being tackled."

"Tell us about throwing Zach Taylor into the pond."

"I already told you I didn't. I would never hurt Zach."

Sowder's eyes pinched into a glare. "We have witnesses who say you did. If you didn't, why did you keep repeating, *what have I done?*"

Tears streamed down Maggie's cheeks. "Because they said I did it. I didn't know how I'd gotten there or where Zach was. I just knew I wouldn't leave him all alone. I assumed they were right. But I'm telling you, I would never do it. Not in a thousand years."

Laveen and Sowders exchanged a look - they didn't believe her, she knew it.

"So let's go over this again," Sowders said. "Pick it up from when the package arrived."

They were going to beat questions down on her until she yielded, just like the blows that curved the metal bands that made up the boots. They were made of much tougher stuff than she, but if pounded on long enough, even metal would relent. They weren't going to stop until she said what they wanted to hear.

***

When Jim picked up the phone, Crystal sounded excited. "The skeleton in the pond is a woman, the doc doesn't know who she was, but she was pregnant when she was thrown in."

"I did some digging on my end," Jim said. "I think her name was Mary Johnson. She was executed as a witch in 1648. See if the doctor can confirm that. Take a few more photos and then come on in. I'm going to ask Lou for more column space. Good work Crystal. I'll see about that raise while I'm at it."

Crystal's excitement was infectious, as if Jim needed any more adrenaline in his system. What had started out as a story lacking details had grown beyond his dreams, and come together so quickly. The historical links would push it way over the top. It would be up for awards, he knew it would, and not just in Hartford, and not just in Connecticut. This story had national legs.

The door to the editor's office was closed, which was unusual. Lou Parsons had an open-door policy. Jim could hear voices inside. He knocked and it went quiet. Lou's voice beckoned him in. As he entered, Lou switched off the television. It was a replay of the Lily Pond story. Sam Boselli sat in a chair beside Lou's desk looking sheepish.

"I'm going to need more column space in the evening edition," Jim blurted, "about eight more inches. This thing has really come together. There's a string of these killings going back a couple centuries. No one else has made the connection. They fished another body out of the pond about two hours ago, an old skeleton, actually. It had the same kind of metal boots on its feet. The bones belonged to a pregnant woman I believe was executed as a witch in 1648. Can you believe it?"

Jim glanced at Lou and then Sam. Where was their enthusiasm? This was the story of the year, no, maybe the story of a lifetime. Something was wrong. "Did I miss something here?"

"Sit down, Jim." Lou sat on the corner of his desk, a somber expression on his face. "I'm giving the story to Sam. He'll finish up and bring it home."

Jim felt dazed for a moment, like he'd been cuffed upside the head. "You're what? I couldn't have heard that right? Did you just say you were giving my story to Sam? *My story*? The thing I've been breathing life into for four straight hours?"

"I'm sorry."

"Sorry? Sorry doesn't begin to cover it. Stories like this don't come along every day. You can't."

Lou nodded for Sam to leave, and spouted off his marching orders. "The story is on the server. Check over what Jim has so far. I'm sure it's first rate. You have less than an hour to make deadline. Run the story under Jim's byline, and get in touch with that intern - what's-her-name."

"Crystal Olnick," Jim said.

"Yeah, that's it. See if she has anything else."

Sam closed the door behind him. Jim felt befuddled and angry. "What the hell is going on here? Why would you pull this away from me?"

Lou raked his hands through his hair and let out a sigh. "Have you been following the news lately?"

"Yeah, enough to know we have something no one else does. We have a scoop here. It may not be Watergate, but it's not far behind. There won't be another story like this in Hartford for as long as I live. You can't take it away from me, Lou."

Lou gazed at Jim, eyes bloodshot and stripped of any morsel of humor. "Sit down. There's been another drowning at the pond."

A wave of excitement swelled inside Jim. "Then Sam is going to need help or we'll miss the evening edition." Jim thought about how to work this newest revelation in, and whether there was still time to do it properly. It was risky revising this late. It could drag down the quality of the article.

"Sit down, Jim. Sam has got this."

"But he's going to need my help."

"It's your son, Jim. Your son is at the bottom of the pond. Your wife threw him in half an hour ago."

It took a moment for the words to sink in. "What?" he sputtered. At first he thought it was a joke, a very sick joke. The expression on Lou's face said it wasn't. He remembered Sam's demeanor when he first entered Lou's office, his inability to look Jim in the eye. Jim originally thought it was guilt. Now he realized it was profound awkwardness at not knowing what to say. Jim felt dazed and numb, like only a small part of him was still in the room. Lou kept on talking.

"Divers are searching Lily Pond for him now. Your boy had metal shoes strapped to his feet, like the Taylor kid. Your wife is in police custody. I've had our people confirm it. I'm sorry."

***

The inspiration for this story by author, Mark Souza:

Before I wrote Neath Lily Pond, I wrote another short story titled *Witch Apples* set in Salem, Massachusetts. While researching the Salem witch trials, I noticed there were similar trials in Connecticut almost fifty years earlier. And while the Salem witch trials became a vivid part of American history, I had heard nothing about those in Connecticut before my research for Witch Apples.

In the seventeenth century, a common test for witches was dunking. It was accepted fact at the time that water, being pure, would reject something as evil and impure as a witch. In a most ironic Catch 22 twist, if the accused drown, it was evidence they were innocent of witchcraft; and if they survived, it was because they were witches and the water rejected them. Dunking survivors were burned at the stake or hanged.

When I joined the Dead Shoe Society and was asked to write a story themed around death and shoes, I thought of how shoes could be linked to death. Metal boots and drowning came to mind. Drowning reminded me of witch executions, and with that, I had a basic story premise.

Hartford was the site of some of the Connecticut witch trials, and as luck would have it, Lily Pond is just mere blocks from the Capitol Building. One of the women found guilty of witchcraft in Connecticut was Mary Johnson. For the sake of accuracy, no record of how she was executed exists, and she was tried in

Wethersfield, Connecticut, a few miles from Hartford and Lily Pond, so it is unlikely that body of water played any role in her fate.

If you would like to know more about the Connecticut witch trials, read Walter Woodward's, "New England's Other Witch-Hunt: The Hartford Witch-hunt of the 1660s and Changing Patterns in Witchcraft Prosecution," or John M. Taylor's "The Witchcraft, Delusion in Colonial Connecticut, 1647-1697," or John Putman Demos' "Entertaining Satan: Witchcraft and the Culture of Early New England." The fact that characters with names similar to these authors appear in this story is purely coincidence.

High-Heeled Killers

by Kate Cornwell

Jason walked into the lunch room, a cup of coffee in his hand. His boss, Mr. Ashlock, lay face-down on the floor, a pile of vomit beside his head. Jason dropped his cup. Coffee shot in an arc up the wall like arterial spray. He shut the door before anyone else could see. He dropped to his knees, crept forward and leaned over.

He couldn't hear any breathing. His own breath stopped. He leaned closer. Nothing. He nudged him, but there was no reaction.

He hadn't expected this. "Fuck!"

His heart pounded in his chest, wanting to escape as badly as Jason did. *What am I gonna do now?*

Jason grabbed Rick's shirt and rolled him over. He definitely wasn't breathing. "Fuck!" Louder this time. "Fuck shit fuck!" He performed CPR on him, as well as he could remember. He opened Rick's mouth and made sure his airway was clear. Jason gave him mouth-to-mouth. No change. *Oh shit, oh shit, oh shit. I'm dead. No, he's dead. Oh shit, oh shit, oh shit.*

He moved to the door and listened. The girls were working in the front office. It was tax season so they wouldn't be stopping for a break anytime soon. He was usually the one to bring *them* coffee. He enjoyed the grateful smiles they gave him as the only nice male, and the youngest in the office.

The lunch room was pretty much a closet. It had a counter, a mini fridge and a coffee maker. There wasn't a table or even a chair for comfort. Mr. Ashlock, Rick, didn't believe in niceties for his staff.

Jason heard one of the girls coming down the hall and he panicked. He grabbed the handle of the door and held tight. The knob wiggled in his hand a few seconds later, but he wouldn't let it turn.

"Hey," he heard from the other side of the door. It was Ashlee, the cute blond that turned every client's head. That's why Rick put her at the front desk. It was like putting out candy laced with roofies. They'd smile while they were being fucked.

"Jason? Are you playing a joke on me?" Ashlee asked in her sing-song, breathy voice, that made men instantly think of…

"Jason. Let me in." Ashlee giggled. He knew she had a huge crush on him. Lots of girls did, but he was least interested in Ashlee. She was exactly the kind of girl who set his teeth on edge. All cotton candy with no substance. Too much eventually made you want to puke.

When Jason didn't reply, Ashlee moved away from the door. He could hear her calling for Janet. His hope soared. If anyone could help him, Janet could. She was the no-nonsense Office Manager who hated Rick as much as he did, maybe more.

Jason heard Janet moving down the hall. Her shoes had a solid *pock, pock* sound, while the other girls had the light *tick, tick,* of stilettos. Rick insisted on the younger girls wearing stilettos even though they weren't practical. He only gave way for Janet since she had back problems. Jason had to agree that stilettos looked sexy on women, but it should be their choice what type of shoes they wore to work.

"Jason?" Janet was there.

"Are you alone?" he whispered.

"Yes, but not for long. Let me in."

Jason opened the door in a flash, pulled Janet in and then shut it quick. He turned her to face him, so she wouldn't see the mess on the floor just yet. "Look at me," he commanded.

She looked up at him, way up, her eyes wide with surprise. She probably hadn't heard that tone from him before. Jason would have laughed at the look on her face if he wasn't about to throw up.

"What's going on?" She moved her eyes away from his face, but he grabbed her chin and wouldn't let her move.

"Wait. I have to tell you what happened."

She rolled her eyes down and gasped. "Is that Mr. Ashlock?"

"Yes. It's Rick. I've killed him."

Janet reeled back, jerking her chin from his grasp. "What?" She fell back against the door.

"It was an accident."

"Well, why didn't you call someone?" She moved toward the door. That was her way. Action was the answer to everything.

"Because they will blame me."

"Why?" She tried peering around his body, so Jason shrugged and moved.

There was no stopping it now. *I'm a dead man.* Every bit as dead as his asshole boss, whom he hadn't meant to kill. Maim yes, give some very intense pain to, but not kill.

"Why?" Janet asked again, her eyes on the corpse.

"Because I put Ex-Lax in his tea."

"You what? Why did you do that? And how would that kill him anyway?" Janet's voice got steadily louder.

"Please. Shush."

Janet looked up at him, eyes wide. Her already wiry hair stuck up like a bottle brush. "Explain everything to me, please."

Jason looked down at his feet. "Okay, I was pissed. Rick was being his asshole self as usual so I decided to get back at him. I knew that Ex-Lax would give him an unpleasant day, but I'd never heard of it killing anyone. I put a little honey in so he wouldn't notice the taste, but..."

"What?" Janet's eyes went huge and a funny look crossed her face. It made Jason wonder if she was going to be sick. "You put honey in his tea?"

"Yes, why?"

Janet squeezed her eyes shut and massaged her temples. "You wouldn't know," she mumbled, "but he's deathly allergic to honey."

Jason stumbled backward as he felt the room tilt. He caught himself up against the wall and stared at Janet. "No, I didn't know," he whispered. "So the Ex-Lax didn't kill him, but the honey did?" Jason paced the tiny room, thinking. He looked up at Janet, bleakness washing over him. "It's still manslaughter, isn't it?"

"Well, maybe not. I didn't even think a food allergy could kill someone that fast."

She thought for a minute more. Jason felt like he was in front of a tribunal, about to decide his fate.

"Okay. We have to fix this," Janet said.

"How? There's no fixing this. I'm dead. I'm fuckin' dead."

Janet glared at him. "This is no time for swearing." She sounded like a school teacher.

"On the contrary, Janet, I think this is precisely the perfect time for swearing," Jason said as he slid down the wall opposite the body. He stared at Rick, the now wonderfully silent Rick, and let out a few more expletives to punctuate his feelings.

Janet straightened up, adjusted her skirt and smoothed down her hair. Hope lit in Jason's heart despite his despair. When she got that look, shit happened. She got things done.

"This is a horrible situation. But, what's done is done."

Jason raised his head, eyes wide.

"So, we're going to fix this. You're not going to go to jail after everything else he did to you." Janet looked towards the cupboards and got that funny look on her face again. Then she shook away whatever thoughts were going through her head. Janet gave him a glance that was almost soft. "We can't let the girls know. So, I'm going to send them home early. Then you and I, we'll deal with the cleanup."

Jason struggled to stand up. His legs were trembling like a groom on his wedding day. "What? Why, Janet? You don't want to be associated with this."

"I don't have any choice, dear boy. I'm not going to let you take the fall and you're in no condition to handle it on your own. Look at you." She waved an arm at him, taking in his disheveled clothing, his shaky legs and his likely bloodless face.

"Now," she continued. "You clean everything up." She glared at the offending corpse messing up her perfect floor. "I'll be back as quick as possible. I have to get the girls to leave. Ashlee will be easy, but Emily, she'll know something's up."

Janet opened the door, turned to him with what was, for her, an encouraging smile and said, "Hold it together, partner. We have a big job to do." The door closed. He could hear her no-nonsense shoes tapping down the hallway.

Jason slumped against the wall again and clutched his stomach. It felt like the acid was trying to eat its way free. He moved to the body and felt his lunch move toward his throat. He grabbed a towel from the counter and threw it over Rick's face. Feeling much better, he found a cloth, soaked it in the sink and started to clean up the room.

***

The front office area was empty. Emily sat in her office, door open to the front desk where Ashlee sat with her nail file. Janet bit her tongue. She had told that girl umpteen times not to file her nails at her desk. She was sure Rick had hired her for looks alone. The balloons swelling her too-tight blouse must have sealed the deal.

"Ashlee."

The twenty-something and no more, turned in her chair, ultra slow. She never showed the deference an office manager should receive and which both Emily and Jason gave freely. Rick had always stepped in when Janet tried to discipline the girl. She was probably not just his receptionist, but his floozy.

"Yes?" Ashlee said with a fake drawl. She tried on a new accent every other month. The flavor of the week was Southern Belle. Too bad Ashlee didn't have the manners and soft ways to go along with the drawl.

"I'm closing up shop early. You can go home."

Ashely's eyes widened and she leapt out of her chair with speed that would have shamed every Belle in Georgia. Without another word, she grabbed her purse and bolted before Janet could change her mind.

"What's going on, Janet? Or did you forget it's the beginning of tax season?" Emily asked, eyebrows raised.

Janet grimaced. She never got anything past that girl. *What am I going to say?*

"Nothing's going on, Emily."

Emily snorted.

Very unladylike.

"What's going on, Janet? Where's Jason?"

"He's in his office. Now, I'm tired, Emily. I want to go home."

Emily folded her arms and studied Janet. "No. There's something going on. I can help."

Janet's lips thinned. It would endanger them all to let more people in on the secret. She could handle it with Jason alone. But, how would she keep Emily from figuring things out? She'd never met a smarter girl. She couldn't have been much older than Ashlee, but her IQ had to be three or maybe four times higher.

"Come on, Janet. Let me help."

Before Janet could react, Emily shot out of her chair, raced past Janet and down the hall. She burst into the lunch room and yelped when she saw Rick.

"Holy hell!"

Janet finally gave in to the urge and slumped into Ashlee's chair. They were all doomed.

The front door opened and Janet jolted. *I forgot to lock the door!* She stood up from the receptionist chair and turned with a smile. It was one of their frequent customers. One the staff called a BYT, *bite your tongue*. He was arrogant and didn't care if they had work to do. His problems were always the most important.

"Hello, Carl." Janet smoothed her sweaty hands down her skirt.

"Janet. Where's Rick? I need to add a few more of my investment certificates. I forgot to give them to him." Carl approached the desk and slammed his briefcase on it.

Janet winced.

He clicked both locks open with force. It sounded like twin guns going off. Janet allowed herself a quick glance behind her, but didn't see either Jason or Emily. Hopefully they would stay hidden until she got rid of Carl.

"I'm sorry, Carl. Rick has gone for the day."

Carl looked at the clock over the desk. "It's only three p.m. He never leaves this early." He narrowed his eyes at her. "And his truck is outside."

Janet bit her tongue. "Be that as it may, Carl, he has gone for the day. I'd be happy to give him the certificates."

"I need to explain it to him," he snapped.

"Well, I am sure he can give you a call when he's back and you can explain it then." Janet held out her hand. It hung in the air while Carl studied it like she was offering him a germ-covered sandwich. A moue of distaste crossed his face.

"Fine. Here." He slapped the papers into her palm with his usual force.

Janet bit her tongue again. "Thank you, Carl. Now, we're closing up early, so I'll just get the door after you."

Carl gave her a suspicious stare. It made her glad for just a split second that Rick was dead. He would have heard all about her behavior and torn a strip off her.

The door slammed behind him and Janet breathed a sigh of relief. She locked it and closed the blinds.

***

Jason came out to the front office and peered around the corner at Janet. "Who was here? I heard voices."

"It was Carl."

"That asshole?" Jason said.

"Jason," Janet had on her schoolmarm face.

"Sorry," he said. He loved it when she chastised him for swearing. She didn't know it, but he did it on purpose around her.

"How's Emily?"

"She's okay. As okay as anyone can be with a dead body in the lunch room. What are we going to do?"

Janet smoothed down her hair and put on her 'let's get shit done' face. "We have to move him. We can use my car."

"Why yours?"

Janet moved down the hall and spoke over her shoulder. "Because I'm the oldest."

"That makes no kind of sense," Jason muttered.

"I can hear you."

Janet stood in front of the lunch room door and put her hands on her hips. She shook her head, then entered the room. Jason went back to his office where Emily was.

She sat in his chair, her head back, eyes closed. His heart stuttered. His body didn't care what they were going through or what he'd done, reacting as soon as he saw Emily. She was the most beautiful woman he'd seen in his life. Her long dark hair flowed over her narrow shoulders and halfway down her back. His fingers sometimes itched with the longing to touch it.

Her body was slight, but strong-looking. Emily seemed so capable and yet vulnerable. Especially now as she sat in his oversized chair. He hated that he'd caused her distress with his actions.

Emily never seemed to notice him. She was direct and serious at work. She was a hard worker, another thing he loved about her. Once in a while someone would say something that would cause her to laugh. Jason lived for that laugh. He hoped one day he'd get a chance to be the one to make her smile every day.

Emily opened her eyes and looked right at him. She didn't ask him why he stood there staring at her. Their eyes locked. She dropped her face and leaned forward in the chair.

"You okay?" Jason asked quietly.

She looked up at him, not moving from her position, leaning her arms on the desk. Her mute response was a small shrug.

"I'm sorry, Emily. Real sorry."

"I know," she said. She got up and stood to her full height.

Jason had secretly measured it, standing as close to her as he'd dared. She reached just under his nose. He was a tall man and liked a woman to be tall too. He realized he was staring again and turned away, his cheeks warm.

"Let's go help Janet. I presume she's got a plan?"

"What?" Jason turned back, shock kick-starting his heart. "You're not going to call the cops?"

Emily smiled a sad smile. "Oh, Jason," she said. And that was all. She walked past him and joined Janet in the lunch room. Jason bowed his head for a moment, humbled by the women who were willing to protect him. He wondered what he'd done to deserve them. A good man might turn himself in, refuse to get them involved. He might insist they go home while he took care of things.

Jason squared his shoulders. Maybe he wasn't a good man, but he was definitely one who didn't look a gift horse in the mouth.

***

They all piled into Janet's car and took triple deep breaths, letting them out in unison. Jason sat in the back. He'd insisted on Emily sitting in the front seat. His heart felt like a bongo drum that kept losing its rhythm. The entire day seemed unreal, like he was caught in a nightmare of his own making. They'd pulled the car up to the back of the building where no one would be able to see them. Together they'd wrestled the body into the trunk. *Who knew a body would be so awkward to carry?* They'd each worn latex gloves. Janet kept a box in the office for cleaning the bathrooms in between the janitor visits.

Janet sat with her hands clenched on the wheel.

Emily leaned over and put her hand over Janet's.

"You okay?" she asked, her voice soft.

Janet turned and gave Emily a grim smile.

At least she tried, Jason thought.

"Let's do this," Janet said. She started the car and put it into gear.

Janet told them they could keep Rick in the huge deep freeze in her garage. They both agreed with the plan while trying not to picture a body amongst the roasts. Jason wondered how long it would be before he ate meat again.

He sat back and tried to calm his pounding pulse. He remembered Emily talking a few weeks back about deep breathing and how it could calm a person no matter the situation. It had been on a particularly busy day when they were all trying to cope with not only the pace of the job, but their boss.

Mr. Ashlock, *Rick,* Jason reminded himself, rode them all hard. But, he was the hardest on Jason. As the only Certified General Accountant of the group, Jason had the sole responsibility of making sure the files were perfect. He was the only one who could sign off on a year-end other than Rick himself. Rick liked to keep his workload light and that meant Jason was stuck with the raw end of the deal.

Emily did her best to help. But, as a junior accountant, she could only complete a file and submit it for approval. Jason still had to go through every detail before signing off on it. Rick went through every fucking one of his files just to make sure Jason hadn't made a single mistake. One, just one, and he was raked over the proverbial coals. *Fuck, I hate that man!*

Then, he remembered where they were and what they were doing. The heavy pounding came back. He realized the deep breathing had helped. Emily was right. Although, he didn't think she quite meant a situation like this.

Lights came on behind them, strobing blue and red. Jason almost shit himself.

Janet pulled the car over in a smooth manner right up to the curb. She sat staring straight ahead while Jason went into a full blown panic. The body was in the fucking trunk and a cop was coming up to the driver's door. *Fuck shit fuck!*

Janet rolled down her window. She reached for her purse and whispered, "Don't say a word," just before the cop reached the car.

"Good afternoon," the cop said, with a smile that didn't reach his eyes.

Jason felt sweat trickle down his back. He settled into the seat and put on a nonchalant look.

"Hello, officer," Janet said with a calm voice. She sounded like she didn't have a care in the world.

Fuck, she's good, Jason thought.

"License and registration please," the cop said.

Janet handed them over.

He studied the documents without saying anything. Jason felt more drops of sweat join the rest pooling at the base of his spine. Before long he was going to be pissing himself.

The officer handed everything back. "Did you know your rear tail light is out?"

Janet's head snapped up in surprise, the first moment she'd shown any tension. "No, I didn't. I'll get that fixed first thing tomorrow, officer." Jason could hear a little strain in her voice, but figured you'd have to know her well to notice it.

"Well," the officer said, "it didn't look like the plastic was cracked or anything. It might just be the bulb. I can take a look at it if you like."

"Uh," Janet stalled and Jason clenched his fists. He could see Emily's face turn white.

"We're kind of in a hurry, officer. Thank you, but I'll take it into the shop tomorrow."

Wrong answer.

The cop's face got thoughtful. "It won't take long for me to check. Please step out of the vehicle, Ma'am."

Janet took off her seatbelt and got out of the car. Jason groaned and leaned his head back. Now his stomach joined the revolt and he was sure he was going to puke any minute. Why? Why did he go along with this, bringing Janet and Emily into it as accomplices? They were now as guilty as he was.

"Jason?" Emily whispered.

"Yah?"

"He won't look in the trunk will he?"

"Well, he can't unless Janet lets him. I think he'd have to have a warrant to search the vehicle. But, if he wants to look in there and she refuses, that will be noted when they start looking for our boss."

Emily moaned. "Oh, God."

"I think he stopped listening."

Jason craned his neck to see what was happening behind the car, trying not to look too interested. The cop was bent down behind it, obviously fiddling with the light. He could hear them talking, but there were no harsh sounds. It was all light conversation. Jason didn't feel relieved. Relieved was as far away from his state of mind as freedom to a death-row inmate.

Janet appeared at the driver's-side door. "He wants to know if I have tools in the trunk." Her voice shook. *What do I say?* her face asked.

Jason grabbed his cell phone. "Act like you're going to open it, then I'll call your cell. Answer it and act like you're mad and then frustrated. Your husband wants you home now because some relatives have arrived and you're not there yet. Go," he commanded.

Without a word, Janet grabbed her keys and headed to the back of the car.

Just as she reached it, Jason hit send on his cell phone.

Janet was fumbling with the keys in the trunk lock when he heard her phone ring.

Jason could hear Janet answering the phone and then get into an imaginary argument. The cop raised his voice to be heard over Janet's strident tones.

"It's okay, Ma'am, you can go. I don't want to keep you from your family."

Janet yelled into the phone. "I'll be home in a minute, Dave," and slammed it shut.

"Thanks, officer, sorry about this," Jason heard her say.

"I won't ticket you, but please get it fixed tomorrow."

"Thank you so much," Janet said, and raced back to her door.

The cop got in his car and drove off. They sat in stunned silence with how close they had come to being arrested for murder.

"Holy blue fuck!"

"Jason!" Janet shook her wiry head and started the car. "We need to get rid of the body and fast."

***

They pulled into Janet's garage and she hit the remote to close the door after them. She turned off the car while they all took a second to breathe.

"Now what?" Emily asked.

"We bag the body and put it in the freezer." Janet no longer sounded in control. The encounter with the cop had obviously shaken her almost beyond what she could handle.

Jason sat in the back, his eyes wide and a sick look on his pale face.

Emily unhooked her seatbelt. "Well, I for one want to get this over with. Where are your garbage bags, Janet?"

The other two stared at her. "What?" Jason said.

"Garbage bags. You have heard of them I presume?"

Janet gave her head a little shake and got out of the car, forgetting to unlatch the belt. Her forward motion was halted with a jerk and a cry. She reached with a shaky hand, undid the belt and carefully hauled herself out of the car.

Emily got out and pulled the seat forward so Jason could climb out too. He stood beside her and leaned on the car for support.

Emily shook her head at them. "Come on, you two. If we have a hope of getting away with murder, you better pull yourselves together."

At the word, *murder*, they both snapped to attention.

"That's better," she said. "Now, Janet, the garbage bags."

They spent the next few minutes finding bags and debating about how they would fit Rick's rather large body inside.

Emily finally opened the trunk and prodded them all into action. Once they had the distasteful job done—she insisted on triple-bagging the body--they stood back. They all had sweaty, red faces.

"Now let's get him into the freezer," Janet said.

***

Emily locked her car and moved with reluctant steps to the front door of Ashlock and Company. She had slept all of three hours the night before and was surprised she even got that much. After putting Rick in the freezer, they drove back to the office, picked up hers and Jason's cars and all went to their respective homes. They decided not to do anything until they'd had the night to sleep on it. She could still call the police and report it if she wanted, Jason said, and she would get nothing more than a slap on the wrist. *As if I'd send the man I love to prison, even if he doesn't know I love him.*

Emily pulled out her office key and unlocked the front door. She was the first one to arrive as hers was the only car in the lot besides Rick's truck.

What are we going to do about his truck?

She wondered how Jason and Janet were doing. She also wondered, with a pitch of her stomach, how Ashlee was going to react to everything. How would they hide Rick's disappearance from the one who focused every molecule of her being on making him happy? Emily's groan was in tune with the snapping of the lock.

She moved around the office, turning on lights and her computer. She also turned on Rick's computer, since his truck said he was in the office. She knew Janet had the keys to every office (and Ashlee didn't), so she locked and closed his door, planning on telling Ashlee he was working on an important file and was not to be disturbed. She ignored the little voice telling her that it would last all of twenty minutes before Ashlee would be suspicious. They all knew Rick wasn't a hard worker. It was probably going to be a necessity to fire her. Emily decided she'd talk to Janet about it as soon as she got in.

Emily made coffee, all the better to soothe Janet's ravaged nerves. They were going to have to be on top of their game. And tax season was just beginning. At that thought, Emily nearly spilled the carafe of water. *Don't think about it! Not just yet. One thing at a time.* She steadied her hand and continued to pour the water.

Glass and water spilled all over the counter as she jerked and smashed the pot against the cupboard when the front door opened and slammed with a crash. *Who the hell is that?* Emily dropped the carafe handle into the sink amongst the broken glass and went to see who had come to work.

Ashlee stood beside her desk, muttering to herself as she rummaged in her purse. Emily stood in the doorway, her arms crossed, and glared at Ashlee. It frustrated the hell out of her how inconsiderate Ashlee was. It didn't matter what was going on in the lives around her, she was always the most important person. Her feelings mattered more than anyone else's.

"Lose something?" Emily asked, crossing her arms tighter and leaning against the door frame.

Ashlee glanced up, her pretty face pulled into an expression of concern. "My phone. I think I, like, left it at home. Jim and I had a fight and I think I, like, left without it."

Emily grimaced. Ashlee used *like* at least once in every sentence.

"Is that why you slammed the door?" Emily asked.

Ashlee looked up with a frown. "Did I?"

"Yes, you scared the crap out of me and I smashed the coffeepot."

Ashlee giggled.

Emily gritted her teeth and left the room. Getting Ashlee to care was a battle lost before it started.

Emily cleaned up the broken coffeepot, sure that steam was coming out of her ears. She normally didn't get upset about fairly minor things, but the tension at her core had been building since the day before. She would be happy to see Ashlee go and hoped Janet would agree with her.

The office was a mess. Files were stacked on the cabinets, and the waste baskets overflowed. The janitors only came on Fridays and Janet kept the office clean the rest of the time. She felt it was her duty as Office Manager. She didn't want Emily and Jason helping as Rick rode them hard enough as it was. Ashlee? Janet didn't even ask Ashlee. She might break a nail or smudge her makeup.

Emily looked around and found a spare coffeepot. The relief was palatable. If Janet didn't have her coffee first thing…well, Emily had never seen it happen, but she had a good imagination.

She filled the pot, careful to keep it away from the cupboard. Just as the last of the water was draining into the top of the reservoir, the door slammed again. Emily's hand jerked, but this time only a few drops of water spilled. She clenched her teeth, placed the pot onto the heating element and hit the on button. She turned to confront the newest offender and walked straight into a very large chest.

Laughter rumbled in her ears as Jason's arms came around her, a little more snug than necessary. "We have to stop meeting like this, babe." He was mimicking someone, but Emily had no idea who. She realized his bravado when she looked up into his eyes. They were red-rimmed with worry. He hadn't slept either.

He gave a quick shake of his head and then said, in a slightly louder than necessary voice, "We have a few files we need to go over. Is eight-thirty okay for you?"

"Yes. I'll come to your office."

Jason gave her arm a quick squeeze just as Janet swept in.

Her eyes took in everything with a glance. Emily was always amazed at how quick Janet was. She could walk into a room, assess the situation, take over and have everyone marching to her orders within five minutes.

She moved close to Emily and Jason. "How are you guys?"

Emily shrugged and Jason winked. His attitude was starting to irritate her. Why couldn't he show that he was as upset as she was?

Janet's eyes found the coffee. "Hey? What happened to the pot?"

"I broke it." Emily hoped Janet wouldn't be upset with her. The coffee was sacred. "There was a spare pot, so I used that."

Janet studied Emily with her dark eyes, then watched Jason move to his office. He didn't do well with confrontation and usually got out of the vicinity of any impending explosion. That could be translated as, whenever Janet's feathers got ruffled, he took off.

"You okay?" Janet's voice showed unusual concern for that early in the morning and without coffee.

"I'm fine. We have to act like everything's normal." Emily lowered her voice even more. "Maybe we should have a quick powwow in your office. There are a few things we need to decide."

Janet gave a quick nod and an uncustomary squeeze of Emily's arm and stepped into her office. Emily wondered if everyone thought she was falling apart. The concern was unnerving.

***

Janet's office was perfectly ordered. Emily let her eyes roam while Janet got settled and picked up the phone. She spoke to Jason briefly and then turned back to Emily.

"As soon as Jason gets here, we'll discuss the situation."

"You don't think that Ashlee will overhear us, do you?" Emily asked.

"The walls are pretty soundproof, so no, I don't think so. Rick," Janet winced a little as she said his name, "was always worried about privacy for the clients, so he made sure to soundproof everything."

Emily settled back in her chair, willing her stomach to calm. "Well, all I can say is we better figure out what to do quick because Ashlee is going to get suspicious. I'm surprised she's not already wondering what we're up to. I think she's smarter than she lets on."

Jason entered the room and shut the door. "I think you're wrong. She's just as dumb as she looks. In fact, she embodies the dumb blond jokes."

He sat opposite Emily with a brave grin. She didn't smile back.

They were sitting at the round table opposite Janet's desk where she sat. Janet picked up a legal tablet and her favorite pen. "I'll make notes while we talk. We're going to need a plan."

Jason leaned back in his chair, his hands behind his head, looking as relaxed as if he were on a beach studying the girls in bikinis. Emily bit down so hard on her tongue, she tasted blood. Sometimes he drove her crazy, but never more so than now. He was putting on a brave face, she knew, but she wanted him to be real.

"I agree, Janet," Emily said. "We need to plan what we're going to do, and say, when clients call. Also, what are we going to do with Rick's truck? It's sitting out in the parking lot, looking to all the world like he's here for business. How are we going to explain that he never goes home? And his body? What are we going to do about that?" she ended in a fierce whisper.

Janet put up a hand to stop Emily's tirade. "One thing at a time, Emily, okay? I know you're getting worried," she rolled her eyes to the ceiling. "No, you're well beyond worried by this point, but trying to solve everything at once will only muddle our minds and then we'll start making mistakes."

Jason smirked. "You go, Janet."

She turned to him with a glare.

"This is no laughing matter, Jason. I'm surprised at you. Why are you acting so casual when our lives are on the line here?"

He sobered instantly, looking like a chastened boy. "I'm sorry." He turned to Emily. "Sorry, Emily. I didn't mean to make you two think I'm not taking this seriously. I'm feeling guilt way beyond my ability to cope. I guess that's how I cope, but I don't want my way of dealing with this to hurt you, so I'll try to be more sensitive."

Jason leaned over his legs and stared at the floor. "I can't believe I got you involved in this. I really think I should turn myself in."

Janet snorted. "And how do you think that would help?"

Jason looked up at her, surprise on his face. "It would put the blame where it belongs. Me."

"We helped you move the body, Jason, which is now residing in my freezer, in case you forgot. The law doesn't gloss over something like that. Like it or not, we're fully involved now. As guilty as you might be, although that's still up for debate since you didn't mean to kill him, but putting anything in someone's drink that causes them to die would probably be manslaughter." She shuddered and looked sick. "So, since none of us want to go to jail, I think we should develop a plan."

As Janet finished speaking, there was a knock on the door and Ashlee poked her head in. Her eyes scanned the office and then lit on Janet. Emily realized what fools they were. There was not a file in sight. Why would they be having a meeting, excluding Ashlee, if it wasn't about their files? *We are already in big trouble and we haven't even come up with a plan. Must be why so many murderers get caught. No brains, all panic.*

"Do you know how long Rick will be in his office?" Ashlee asked. "Craig Dunsmore is on the phone."

Emily could see Janet's groan, although she didn't let it out.

"I don't know how long he will be, but he expressly said he wasn't to be disturbed. Put the call through to me and I'll deal with him."

Ashlee smiled. "Thanks Jan! You're the best." She turned and banged the door shut behind her. The phone rang a few seconds later.

Janet grimaced as she picked it up. "Hello Craig, how are you today?" She listened for a few minutes and then went into her story of how Rick would be unavailable for most of the day and that she would personally see to it that he returned his call as soon as possible.

Jason turned to Emily. "I'm sorry Emily. So sorry I got you into this." His eyes showed his true feelings despite his earlier attitude.

"You don't have to keep apologizing, Jason. I know you're sorry. I just get bothered when I think you're not taking seriously the situation we're in." A thought occurred to her. "But then, maybe I'm the one who's wrong."

"What do you mean?" He was obviously surprised.

"Well, the more serious we take it and the more stressed we get, the harder it's going to be to cope."

He tilted his head, considering her words.

"Maybe if we relax a little and try to calmly figure our way out of this, we might actually succeed. I don't like that we're in this trouble any more than the rest of us, but the fact remains, we're fucked," Emily said.

Jason's head rocked back with her vulgarity, but he didn't comment on it. He had never heard her use that word before.

"Well, I can't deny that. I think you're right though. I don't know how we'll accomplish the calm part, but we can try. No matter how relaxed I may look, I'm shitting myself on the inside."

Emily cracked a smile. She realized in that moment why she was so drawn to him. He said things no one else was brave enough to say. And he always made her laugh.

Janet hung up the phone and looked at Jason and then Emily. "Okay, are we ready to make a plan?"

***

Jason slipped into Rick's office, closed and locked the door and breathed out a sigh of relief. He'd gotten in without Ashlee noticing. Emily had called her to her office to discuss something so he would have a clear path. He figured it would be good to make a little noise in the office so Ashlee would really think Rick was in there.

His mission, which he'd chosen to accept, was to find Rick's keys to his truck. He would come back around midnight and drive the truck to the airport. Hopefully that would keep the police off his real trail for a while. If they could keep the body from showing up, they just might be clear.

Who'm I kidding? We should blow the fucking thing up! Rick treated the damn thing better than any of us. Asshole—

Jason stopped short, his thoughts frozen as he glimpsed his name on a piece of paper on Rick's messy desk. It was partially hidden underneath a file folder. He pushed the folder aside and sank into Rick's chair to study the document.

Fuck shit fuck!

The rage built and nearly vibrated the air around him. The need to keep up the masquerade was the only thing that stilled Jason's tongue. *The fucking bastard was stealing my money!*

The report he held in his hand detailed his investments. Rick had been handling them, but the report Jason received monthly was not the same as this one. Rick was using Jason's money to make more and pretending the investments were only growing slowly.

Back when Jason was naive about his boss and excited about the new position, he had asked Rick's advice on investing his newly inherited money from his grandmother's estate. She had given him a tidy sum, not one he could retire on, but an amount that would be a good spot to start from. Rick said he had a few ideas for turning his money into a great retirement plan. Jason trusted him.

There was one point about a year into his employment with Rick, that he was told the stocks had taken a huge hit, so nearly half of his nest egg was gone. Devastated, Jason wanted to withdraw what was left, but Rick persuaded him to leave the money where it was, promising him he would be more careful. After that the reports had shown a small monthly increase, but never dropped again.

Five years into his employment and Rick had a stranglehold on him. Looking back, Jason didn't understand how it had happened. In his life, he'd always stood up to everyone. He wasn't afraid of confrontation. But, with Rick, it was all different. Killing him was like being released from prison. Ironically, it was also the thing that could put him into a more real prison than he'd been in before. *Is a prison of the mind any easier to escape, though?*

Jason tapped his finger on the report as he thought. *Who was doing up the phony reports?* It wasn't Rick's style to take the time. Besides, he could barely use a computer. Someone had to be helping him.

Jason took a closer look at the report and saw he was a wealthy man. *What good would money do me in jail?*

He fished around on the desk and found the envelope the report had come in. It was addressed to Ashlock & Company, but had Jason's name on it. Ashlee handled all the mail, so why did this report never make its way to his desk?

Jason ground his teeth as the truth dawned. Ashlee was helping Rick. She may be a dumb fluff bunny, but she knew how to use a computer. She could easily have done up a fake report and placed it on Jason's desk with his mail.

Fury broiled up in Jason's chest as he tore apart Rick's office looking for other evidence. Ten minutes later, he sat on the floor, papers strewn about him while he checked his pulse. It was racing so hard, he was worried he was going to burst a blood vessel. *How could I have been such a fool?*

The phone on Rick's desk rang with the interoffice tone. He saw it was coming from Janet's office so he picked it up. "Are you almost done in there?"

"Did Ashlee act suspicious?"

"Not really. I told her you went into Rick's office for a meeting with him. What have you been doing in there? We heard a couple of bangs. I told Ashlee you guys were probably fighting again. She gave me a funny look, but didn't push."

"Okay, I'm almost finished. You won't believe what I found out."

"We can talk about that later. Did you find the keys?"

"Shit!"

"Jason," Janet growled at him, "the keys are what you went into there to find."

"Sorry." He reached his hand into Rick's jacket that hung over his chair and felt metal. "Got them. I'll be out in a sec."

"Okay, give me about three minutes to get Ashlee distracted." Janet hung up with a solid click.

Jason grabbed the keys, the reports, and waited by the door. Once he felt he'd given Janet enough time, he cracked open the door, stepped out and closed it. He tested the knob to make sure it was locked and hurried to his office. He could hear Janet talking to Ashlee and was sure neither had heard him come out.

Jason slumped into his chair, head on his desk, and thought about the new facts. Rick had been keeping his money from him. It didn't look like he'd taken any of it yet, but he must have been planning something. Otherwise, why make up phony reports?

He banged his head a few times on the desk a little harder each time. *Think, think, think.*

"What are you doing?"

Jason's head shot up. Emily stood in the doorway, a quizzical look on her face.

"You okay, Jay?"

"Yeah, I'm fine. I've got Rick's keys. I'll come back tonight and move the truck after dark."

"Sounds good." Emily glanced around as Ashlee went by with some files. Ashlee stared into his eyes as she passed. It was almost as if she was trying to tell him something. *Weird.*

"Jason?" Emily shook her head at him. "You sure you're all right?"

"I will be as soon as we have the body and that damn truck moved," he whispered.

"When are we meeting again?" Emily asked.

"I'll come by and pick you up at about ten and we'll drive over together. It should be full dark by then. You're still sure you want to use your car?"

"Of course."

"Make sure you wear black like Janet suggested. Once we're done with that," Jason swallowed hard at the thought, "I'll come back here and move his truck."

"Do you need help?"

"No, it's okay. I can do it myself."

"Okay, I'm going to head home and see if I can get some sleep."

Jason glanced up at the clock, surprised Emily was leaving for the day at noon. She never did anything like that. Never even took a sick day. *I've never killed anyone before, either. I guess we're all doing things out of character.* "Okay, take it easy. I'll see you tonight. I'll text you once the truck's moved. I won't call and wake you."

Emily turned away, paused and then turned back. "No, you can call if you like." Jason was surprised to see her face go pink. She hurried away. Soon after he heard the front door open and close. He reflected on her comment for a long time after.

***

"Hey," Jason said. "I just thought of something. In Dead Body Disposal, Necro says to put pepper spray on the bags so police dogs can't find the body and animals won't tear the bags open."

Emily stared at him. They were all standing in front of the freezer, preparing themselves for the next step. They were dressed head-to-toe in black and wearing gloves as Janet had insisted. She didn't want them to leave any trace of DNA behind. They even wore black ski hats. Jason had a few extra which he'd shared with the women. They didn't ask why he had so many.

"What on earth is Dead Body Disposal?" Emily asked.

"It's a song."

"That's a song?" Janet snapped.

"Well, it's pretty famous," Jason sounded defensive. "It still sounds like a good idea, don't you think."

Emily sighed. "Yes, it does." *And I've learned more about you today than I ever imagined I would know.* "I have pepper spray in my purse. I always carry it. We can spray the bag just before we dump it. Uh, Janet, where are we dumping it?"

"The dump."

"Oh," Emily and Jason said in unison.

"We can sneak in. They don't have anyone there after it closes."

"And you know this, how?" Jason asked.

It seems we're learning a lot about each other today, Emily thought.

"I've had to dump extra garbage and I didn't want to pay for it," Janet said, in a prim voice.

Jason whistled. "Janet doing something illegal, who would have thought?"

Janet glared at him.

"And what would you call dumping a body, Jason?" Emily asked.

Jason dropped his head, shamed. "Sorry, ladies. I don't know why you're helping me, but I do appreciate it."

"Okay, let's get to it," Janet said.

They spent the next half hour wrestling the frozen corpse into Emily's trunk. By the time they were done, they were all sweating.

Janet slammed the trunk shut.

They drove to the dump in silence with Janet giving Emily the directions.

Emily turned onto a dirt road. The area was dark and there were no other cars. Her stomach felt like it held a coiled snake, ready to strike at any minute. She was terrified they would be pulled over again or someone would see her car and report their activity as suspicious. There were so many things that could go wrong. The trees were dark silhouettes and she tried not to imagine the many things lurking behind them. Emily didn't like the dark.

They approached the gates and Emily groaned. "Now what? I didn't know they locked the dump at night. Who would steal from a dump?"

Jason swore, but Janet said nothing. After Emily parked in front of the gates, Janet got out of the car. Emily's mouth dropped open as she watched Janet unlock the gates and swing them open. She came back to the car, her lips a grim line.

"What the hell?" Jason sputtered. "How do you have the key?"

"An old boyfriend." Janet's prim voice didn't fool Emily.

"He just happened to give you the key to the city dump? Come on Jan, what gives?"

"I stole it," she admitted, her voice hardly above a whisper.

Jason let out a bellow. "Who would have known you had so many secrets Miss Janet?"

Emily could almost see Janet's wiry hair bristle at Jason's taunts, but she didn't retort. She directed Emily to drive the car around the service building and to the nearest dumpster in the row.

They all got out of the car and looked down into the dumpster. It was half-full of garbage, mostly bags.

"This looks like the best place to toss it," Emily said.

She took the pepper spray out of her purse. They hauled the body out of the trunk and put it on the ground near the edge of the dumpster.

"Okay, you should both step back. You don't want a whiff of this," she said.

Emily kept her gloved hand over her mouth and nose while she sprayed it all over the bag. When it was empty, she tossed it into the bin.

"Wait until the air clears a bit," Janet said when Emily stepped back and took a deep breath.

While they waited, Emily looked at Jason. She couldn't stand the thought of sending him to jail. She could claim collusion. That he'd talked her into helping. She could get out of charges, but he wouldn't be able to. She pictured him with an orange jumpsuit and a hopeless expression. Tears came to her eyes and she reached out a hand, patting his shoulder. Oh, yes, it was wrong what they were doing. *I'll probably go to hell for this.* But, she couldn't blame Jason entirely for what he did. He didn't mean to kill Mr. Ashlock and he shouldn't pay for that for the rest of his life. It was done and there was no going back.

"Okay, ready?" Janet asked.

They picked up the body and stood at the edge of the dumpster.

"Let's swing together and toss it in. Ready?" Jason asked.

They swung in unison and let go, all watching while the body dropped into the pile of garbage and sank out of sight. They stood and stared at the spot, none of them seeming ready to believe it was over.

"Now, let's hope no one ever finds it." Janet said. "Let's get out of here."

"Hey!"

The voice came from behind them, near the service building. They whirled around, the flashlight beam just missing Janet's face. She ducked down behind the car, Emily and Jason right behind her.

"What are you doing?" the voice yelled, coming closer.

"Shit!" Jason whispered. "We can't let him see us!"

"Well, he's going to see us if we don't get out of here," Janet shot back.

The flashlight lit on the car. "I see your car," the man yelled. "I have a cell phone and I'm calling the police right now."

All three of them panicked and they scattered into the dark. Emily ran down the incline and behind the dumpsters, hoping Jason and Janet were behind her. *I can't believe we got caught. They're going to see my car and know I'm involved. Shit! What am I going to do?*

Emily looked wildly around, but couldn't see either of them in the dark. She turned back toward the car, but heard the man coming closer, the flashlight bobbing and weaving in the dark. She heard a sound behind her and then Jason was there, grabbing her hand.

"Come on, we have to go this way."

She held tightly to his hand and ran with him in the dark, trusting him to lead her to safety.

They reached the fence at the back of the property and she saw Janet there waiting for them. Emily gasped in relief that they were all together again, then she looked at the fence, her heart sinking. She'd never been good at climbing fences. She turned around and saw in the distance that the man was at her car. The flashlight was playing around it. She squeezed her eyes shut, too terrified to even formulate a prayer. So much for good ideas. *We were crazy to think we could get away with this!*

"Come on, Emily, you have to climb," Jason whispered in her face, his voice desperate. He leaned down and cupped his hands. "Use my hands, I'll boost you." She stuck her foot in his hands and squeaked when he practically threw her to the top of the fence. She grabbed and hung on for all she was worth, glad she had gloves.

It was a chain-link fence, with sharp bits at the top, but at least it wasn't barbed wire. She stuck the toes of her shoes in the holes and climbed.

Janet was next. She was surprised when Janet reached the top and climbed over with ease. "Hurry, Emily!" Janet hissed at her. She could feel the fence shudder with Jason's weight as he came after her.

Icy dread hit Emily as she clung to the fence. A dog barked; a ferocious sound. She looked back toward her car, but the flashlight was gone. Maybe the man had gone back for his dog. *Do they have guard dogs at dumps?*

She felt Jason grab the back of her sweatshirt and push her onward.

"Come on Emily, we can't wait around for that dog."

So she wasn't just imagining it. Terror lit a fire under her and Emily scrambled to the top and climbed over. She could feel the fence cutting her arm, but ignored the pain in her desperation to get out of there. Jason flipped over the top and jumped to the ground.

She hovered near the top, but on the other side now, afraid to jump.

"Come on, baby, I'll catch you," Jason said in a stage whisper.

She shook her head, but of course he couldn't see her. She swallowed hard, squeezed her eyes shut and jumped.

She hit Jason hard. She could hear his gasp and his breath leave in a rush.

Emily rolled off. "Are you okay?"

"Come on, let's go!" Janet said. "We have to get out of here before the police arrive."

Emily and Jason clambered to their feet.

"This way!" Janet said. "I've walked this area before and I think I can lead us back in the dark."

They could hear the dog coming closer.

"Come, quick," Janet said, and set off through the thick brush.

"I'm so sorry about your car, Emily," Jason said from beside her. "I feel sick about it."

"Not now, Jason," Janet barked. "We have to focus; we'll decide what to do once we get home."

They followed Janet the rest of the way in silence. All Emily could think about was a small concrete cell. She didn't kill anyone, but who would believe that now?

***

The parking lot was dark when Jason got back to the office at midnight. They had made it to Janet's house only a half hour before. They were scratched up and exhausted, but safe. For now. Even though Emily's car left at the scene changed everything, they still had to do what they could to cover their tracks. He'd kissed Emily goodbye and told her he loved her. If their lives were over, then he was going to do and say whatever the hell he wanted to.

At least she returned my kiss.

The streets were pretty much empty, especially in the professional district of the city. Their office was isolated, with a huge plot of empty land on the one side and their large parking lot on the other. He didn't want someone driving by and seeing his distinctive red Mustang, so he parked a few blocks down in an apartment parking lot and walked the rest of the way. He approached on the empty lot side. He thought the office was dark until he came around the front of the building. A light was on. It was in Rick's office. *Who the hell would be in there?*

Jason's heart went into a triple-time stutter and he rushed to the parking lot. But, there was no vehicle other than Rick's. He had no idea who it could be. They had a good alarm system, so it wasn't likely to be a burglar.

Shit. I'm fucking done with this shit.

Jason exploded into the building and caught Ashlee just coming out of Emily's office. He skidded to a stop and stared at her. Then his financial reports flashed back into his mind and rage followed.

"What the fuck do you think you're doing in here?" he demanded, his voice nearly a roar.

Ashlee's eyes were huge pools of shock. "I...uh...uh," she stuttered. Then her hands came up over her face and she started sobbing.

Jason felt immediate guilt, then more anger followed. "Don't start that shit, Ashlee. Explain to me what you were doing in Emily's office and how did you get in there anyway? How did you get into Rick's office? What the fuck is going on?"

Ashlee mumbled something, but her sobs drowned it out.

"What?"

She mumbled something again. It sounded like, "I did it for you."

Jason stamped forward, grabbed her arm and pulled her into Emily's office. He pushed her, none too gently, into the visitor's chair in front of the desk. He'd had a tough night and all the manners he may have had were gone.

"Now, stop the *fucking* crying and tell me what's going on, Ashlee," Jason said as he dropped into Emily's chair facing Ashlee.

Ashlee lowered her hands from her face and stared at him with huge watery, blue eyes. "I did it for you, Jason. I love you."

Jason stared back feeling like someone must have slipped acid into his drink somewhere along the way.

What the fuck?

"I came back to put the poison in Emily's desk and find the reports. Now that we'll be free of her and Rick, we can go away together. I love you, Jason, and I know you love me too."

Jason couldn't speak. He kept trying but his brain couldn't seem to find the words. *What the fuck is she talking about? Free of Emily and Rick? Go away together? She's lost her mind.*

Jason leaned back in the chair and tried to organize his scrambled thoughts. "Okay, Ashlee," he said, willing his heart to slow its crazy speed. "Why don't you tell me everything."

In that instant, he had perfect clarity. He knew what she'd done and why. And he knew what he needed to do.

She opened her mouth to speak, but he lifted a hand. "Hold on, honey, let me get you some tissue. I haven't been very nice to you and I'm sorry. It was just a shock to find you in here and I've had a rather bad day."

Ashlee gave him an adoring, but still wobbly smile. "It's okay. I understand, baby."

Jason reached across the desk and grabbed Emily's box of tissue. He got up and held it out to Ashlee. She plucked a few and began mopping her eyes. Jason pulled a couple himself and began mopping his sweaty face, turning his back to Ashlee. In the few seconds it took, he pushed line one on the phone, while coughing loudly, then pushed mute and 9-1-1. He casually dropped his few tissues over the red light and pushed Emily's inbox in front of the phone, blocking Ashlee's view.

He stepped around the desk and sat in the chair. Hoping the operator had answered by this point, he said, "So I think we need the police," his voice raised a little.

"Oh, no, Jason," Ashlee pleaded. "We don't want the police. I've got it all set up. You just have to give me time to finish and then we can call them together."

"I'm confused, Ashlee," Jason said. "Why don't you start at the beginning?" He gave her a gentle smile, trying to keep the rage out of his eyes. She seemed to accept that he was going along with her. Jason clenched his fists underneath the desk and struggled to look calm.

Ashlee tossed back her long blond hair and dabbed at her nose. She sniffed and began, "Rick was forcing me to sleep with him."

Jason interrupted. "Please speak louder, my ears are a little plugged from an oncoming cold. Did you say you were sleeping with Rick?"

She raised her voice. "I'm sorry, Jason, I didn't want to. He forced me. He also forced me to do up the fake reports about your money. We're rich, Jason, really rich. I had to stop Rick before he could take your money. It's all still there." She gave him a proud smile. "I know lots of people think I'm dumb, but I'm not. I just let them think so because then I can find out stuff. I know how Emily has been chasing you and even Janet likes you. It makes me sick." Ashlee wrinkled up her pert nose. "I don't know why they couldn't see how you love me and only me."

Jason didn't speak, he couldn't. He just gave her another endearing smile.

"I did my research," she continued. "Since it's so hard to kill someone without being caught, I knew we needed someone to pin it on."

We? Fuck!

"So I learned about a plant called Monkshood. It grows all over North America. I found some and put the leaves in Rick's salad. You know how he's been on this health food kick lately. He didn't even notice." Ashlee leaned back with a proud smile. "He ate the salad and then died."

Jason leaned back in his chair, mouthed, "Wow," and gave her a big grin. "And then…"

"Well, then I put the leaves in Emily's desk, so the police would find them. I even went by her house tonight and planted a few of the plants in her back flowerbed. They'll think it was her for sure."

Jason widened his eyes like he'd just thought of something. "Hey! Emily told me her car disappeared tonight and she is going to report it stolen. You took her car, too, didn't you. So you could get rid of the body."

Ashlee shook her head.

"Who helped you move his body Ashlee?"

"What? No one…"

The front office door opened with a crash. "Police. Is everyone okay in here?"

Ashlee jumped to her feet with a little scream.

Jason gave her a lazy smile. "In here, officers. She's here."

Ashlee stared at Jason. "You called them? How?"

He lifted the tissue off the phone and shoved the inbox back. She could see the red light on the phone. Jason reached out and pressed the disconnect button, now that the police had her recorded confession.

Two officers burst into the office just as Ashlee launched herself at Jason. One of them grabbed her arms and pinned them behind her back, whipping out his cuffs. The other started reading her Miranda rights.

Ashlee thrashed and screamed invectives at Jason. Just as they were hauling her out of the office, she pivoted on her heels and thrust her right leg toward Jason. One red stiletto flew off her foot and missed Jason's head by a fraction. The heel stuck into the drywall like a knife. Jason stared at it, glad it hadn't connected with his skull.

After the officers took his statement and left, Jason sat back in his chair with a huge sigh of relief. He was glad he'd thought of planting the stolen car idea. He'd let the police figure that one out, but at least Emily would be in the clear. He picked up the phone.

Janet answered on the first ring. "Did you deal with it?"

"Oh yes, oh yes," he said.

"What? Why do you sound so happy?"

Jason told her what had happened. She gasped when he said Ashlee had killed Rick. "It's all done. You just need to get Emily to call her car in stolen in the morning, and we're clear."

"No, Jason, Ashlee didn't kill Rick, or at least didn't kill him all the way."

"What? Yes, she did, she told me."

"Emily and I watched a news story tonight. It was about a local farmer who'd been arrested for selling honey made from Oleander flowers, which makes the honey poisonous. I bought some of that honey from the farmer's market and put it in the cupboard of the coffee room. It's the honey…"

"I put in Rick's coffee," Jason said.

Fuck shit fuck!

***

The inspiration for this story by author, Kate Cornwell:

I was inspired to write this story quite some time ago after working for a difficult boss during tax season. Of course I would not act on thoughts of murder, so I came up with a story idea where a man accidentally poisons his boss and then has to cover it up. Originally, it was a novel idea, but when I was asked to join the Dead Shoe Society I realized I already had the perfect story mostly written. It even had shoes in the title.

High-Heeled Killers was a lot of fun to write. It's the first story I've written mostly from a man's point of view. Jason is a fun character and I enjoyed the challenge of writing from his perspective. The twist at the end with the Oleander flowers came out of my research into different poisons. I like the idea that the boss had been poisoned pretty much three different ways. I have now expunged all animosity from those days of working horrendous tax seasons.

Thanks for reading!

Lady Justice Wears Heels

by Stephen Penner

Assistant district attorney David Brunelle looked down and admired his new shoes: three-inch, red leather stilettos.

"Nice shoes, David," laughed Kat Anderson, the county medical examiner, as she strutted past him toward the drug-den apartment they had both been called out to. "Try not to get any blood on them."

Brunelle admired the retreating figure of the shapely coroner. Then he sat down again in the passenger seat of Detective Chen's cop car and popped off the stilettos.

"Forgot to change back," he shrugged at the gumshoe as he pulled his wingtips back on. "Those things are surprisingly comfortable."

"Just admit it, Brunelle," joked Chen. "You like 'em. They make you feel pretty."

Brunelle stood up and tugged exaggeratedly at his suit coat. "I am pretty. And with those babies I'm gonna win that 'Prosecutors in Pumps' fundraiser next month."

"Next month?" Chen laughed. "You got 'em a month early? Oh yeah, you like 'em."

"Just need to break them in so I don't get blisters," Brunelle assured as he slammed the car door. "But enough about shoes. Let's see what we've got inside."

What they had inside was a homicide. A murder. And a messy one. It was going to be hard for anyone to keep blood off his shoes. As they stepped inside, Brunelle fought back a gag at the metallic stench of blood.

Anderson already had it all over her gloved hands.

"Massive sharp force trauma to the anterior neck," she reported. When no one responded, she simplified. "Someone slit her throat. And bad."

Brunelle and Chen didn't really need the medical examiner to tell them that. The victim lay face down on a ratty mattress, her head in the center of an enormous pool of thick arterial blood. Given the position of the body, the only other explanation would have been a gunshot wound to the face.

The professionals fanned out to do their jobs. Anderson returned to examining the body. Chen rounded up officers to seal off the crime scene and begin identifying potential evidence. And Brunelle watched for all the little mistakes everyone else might make which could lead to a key piece of evidence being suppressed by some defendant-loving judge.

It was a typical addict's shithole. Windows blocked off by blankets and furniture. Dirty dishes everywhere. Filthy bathroom. Needles and pipes on every flat surface.

And a framed school picture of some smiling eight-year old kid whose mom loved him almost as much as she loved the crack. Or the heroin. Or the meth. Or whatever garbage filled his mom's veins and made her forsake everything else in the world for her next high.

This particular mom--the one whose blood was all over her bedroom floor--had been into heroin, judging by the tracks on her arms and legs and even the bottoms of her bare feet. Not to mention the half dozen needles sitting on the bedside table like so many ballpoint pens.

"Found the murder weapon!" one of the officers shouted from the squalid bathroom. Brunelle and Chen rushed over.

"Where is it?" Chen asked as he approached.

"Don't touch it!" Brunelle ordered.

"I know that," the officer sneered at Brunelle. "I'm not a rookie. It's behind the toilet."

He stood up and let the other men get a better view. It was a simple kitchen knife, serrated. A nicer home might have had a knife block with this one single knife missing. Not this dump. The only thing that differentiated it from all the other cutlery strewn across the apartment was the still wet blood glistening on its blade.

Forensics rushed in, put a numbered placard next to it and started shooting photographs. Brunelle and Chen backed out of the closet-like room and stepped outside for some fresh air.

"So whattaya think?" Chen asked, content to let his officers handle this part of the investigation.

"Robbery?" Brunelle suggested. "Drug-rip gone bad, maybe? I'm not sure. That's a pretty violent way to kill someone."

Chen nodded. "Pretty personal too. Gonna get your hands bloody."

"And your feet." It was Dr. Anderson. She'd followed them outside. "The boys found a bloody footprint on the bathtub edge and another on the bathroom window sill."

Brunelle scanned the outside wall for the bathroom window and in a moment all three of them were leaning over a series of bloody footprints leading across the parking lot to a nearby patch of neglected grass.

"Barefoot," Chen observed. "And small. Probably a woman."

"She could've used those stilettos of yours, David," Anderson joked.

"Naw," Brunelle shrugged. "They're size thirteen. It takes a man to wear shoes like that."

**

Thirty-two hours later, Brunelle watched through the two-way mirror at the main precinct as Chen and a junior detective brought the prime suspect into the interrogation room.

Brunelle immediately frowned. She was too small. The jury would take one look at her and start doubting, thinking she couldn't have done it. Doubting, as in reasonable doubt. One more damn thing Brunelle would have to convince them of.

Then he smiled.

He'd have to call the M.E. to explain it to them. Another excuse to talk to Kat.

"Have a seat, Ms. Flowers," Chen said, steering her into a chair and sitting down opposite her. "We just have a few questions. This shouldn't take long."

Virginia 'Ginny' Flowers. Tiny, frail drug addict. She had scabs all down her face, which meant meth. She'd probably been up for days, and no doubt her brain was fried. It wouldn't take Chen long at all. As long as they remembered to Mirandize her, Brunelle would have a confession to go along with her fingerprint on the knife and the expected match on the bloody footprint. A judge had already signed the warrant to sample her footprint, but that would come after they extracted the confession. Brunelle looked at his watch. He had a court hearing in 45 minutes. He looked again at Ginny Flowers. He'd make the hearing, no trouble at all.

"Do you understand each of these rights as I explained them to you?" Chen was asking as he finished going through the Constitutional rights form.

Ginny nodded--a jerky, wide-eyed nod--and signed off on the form. Brunelle smiled. He'd just won the confession suppression hearing.

"Can I get you something to drink, Ginny?" Chen asked. "Or eat?"

"We have some candy bars somewhere, I think," the other detective offered. It sounded nice, but it wasn't. Meth addicts crave sweets like fish crave water.

"A c-candy bar would be nice," Ginny Flowers stammered, trying not to sound too desperate. She picked anxiously at the sores on her face where the meth made her scratch till she bled.

"We'll be happy to get you a candy bar, Ginny," Chen smiled, before letting the smile drain away. "Right after you answer a few questions."

Ginny fell back in her chair. She was crashing, Brunelle knew. This would almost be painful to watch. Almost.

"You knew Theresa Hastings," Chen started. It wasn't really a question. He added her street name to be sure. "Curly."

Ginny's eyes were fixed, unblinking, on the detective. "Yes," she finally admitted.

"You did drugs with her," Chen went on.

Ginny ran a hand through her dirty hair.

"We don't care about the drugs, Ginny," said Chen's partner. The good cop.

"Curly's dead," Chen announced. "Murdered."

Ginny still didn't say anything.

"We know you were there, Ginny," Good Cop went on. "Just tell us what happened."

"I--I wasn't there," Ginny tried, but it was weak. "I swear. I don't know nothing--"

"Your prints were on the knife, Ginny," Chen said. "You better come clean. It's not gonna look good if you keep lying to us."

Ginny's brow creased as her meth-addled brain raced. "Okay, s-sure. Sometimes me and Curly did drugs together. She liked her heroin and I liked my crank. But that don't mean I was there--"

"Prints, Ginny," Chen interrupted. "On the murder weapon."

"That don't mean nothing," Ginny snapped back. "I coulda touched that weeks ago."

Chen stared at her for several seconds. Good Cop leaned back and shook his head sadly. Ginny looked up, down, and all around while her hands twisted and twirled and wrung. Then Chen reached down and slammed a paper bag on the table. He stood up and pulled out the contents: a clear plastic bag, sealed with evidence tape, containing a pair of blood soaked women's tennis shoes.

"You left your shoes behind, Ginny," Chen said. "The only pair of shoes in the whole damn apartment. Your shoe size, not Curly's. And your DNA is all over them."

Brunelle knew that was a bluff. They hadn't DNA typed the shoes yet. But Ginny Flowers didn't know that.

"We know you were there that night," Chen barked. "And we know you killed her. This is your one chance to tell us what happened."

"If it was self defense, Ginny," offered Good Cop, "please tell us. We'll understand. But no one's gonna believe it was self defense if you don't tell us that now."

Brunelle was impressed. These two sure knew how to get a person to admit to murder. He waited to see if it would work.

Ginny Flowers' eyes darted around the room, a trapped animal looking for an escape. But there was none. The only question was whether she was going to realize it.

She did. The words came in an amphetamine-fueled flood.

"Oh my God, I don't know what happened. There was so much blood. Blood everywhere. And the knife. And it was bloody. And oh God, she's dead. Curly's dead. And I did it. I didn't mean to do it. It was an accident. Or self-defense or something. I panicked and I don't remember what happened next and I didn't know what to do and I so I just ran and ran and ran. And oh my God, Curly's dead. I killed Curly."

She dropped her head into her hands and started sobbing. Brunelle was curious about the details, but he could get that later from the transcript. He had his defendant and he had his confession. He stepped out of the observation room and headed back to the office to draw up the charging documents for Virginia Flowers' arraignment that afternoon on charges of murder in the first degree.

It would be several days before Brunelle regretted his decision to leave the interview early.

***

"Manslaughter," was the first thing Flowers' attorney said when Brunelle answered the phone.

Brunelle smiled. "Well, hello to you too, Jessica. And no way. Did you see the autopsy photos? That's not manslaughter."

Jessica Edwards was one of the top attorneys at the public defender's office. Good for Flowers, but bad for Brunelle. He'd been hoping the case might get assigned to someone less talented, or at least who cared less. But Edwards was a 'true believer'--every client was innocent and every cop was crooked. Now Brunelle was gonna have to work for the conviction.

"Your confession sucks," Edwards countered. "No details. Just blacked out and woke up with a bloody knife in her hand."

Brunelle cringed at the truth of that assessment, but he wasn't about to give Edwards the satisfaction. "Pretty convenient," he scoffed.

"She didn't do it, Dave," Edwards pressed. "But she'll plead to manslaughter. Save everybody the trouble of a trial."

Brunelle had to laugh at that. "I like trials, Jess. You know that."

"Yeah, I know that," Edwards admitted. "But you know what else I know? Ginny didn't murder her friend."

"Then who did?" Brunelle challenged.

This time Edwards laughed. "Why don't you check out the victim's boyfriend? I think you might remember him. Goodbye, Dave."

Brunelle hung up after her and tapped his chin for a moment. Then he pulled the police report binder off his bookshelf and flipped through looking for the identity of Curly's boyfriend/drug-dealer of the week.

It took until the seventh report, some lower level officer identifying potential contacts from the victim's cell phone.

'Lawrence Carrington.'

"Fuck," Brunelle whispered through his fingers. "They were supposed to warn me before they let him out of prison."

***

"We the jury," the foreman had stood up and read the first verdict form aloud in the crowded courtroom, "find the defendant, Lawrence Carrington ... *not guilty* of the crime of murder in the first degree."

Brunelle had managed not to flinch at the verdict, but he had squeezed his pen tighter. The victim's mother had started to cry behind him in the gallery.

No big deal, Brunelle had assured himself. *It's always hard to prove a murder was actually premeditated. They'll convict him of the intentional murder two.*

"We the jury find the defendant, Lawrence Carrington ... *not guilty* of the lesser crime of murder in the second degree."

Oh, fuck, Brunelle had thought. He had set his pen down. The crying had turned to sobbing, accompanied by murmurs of consolation, disbelief and rising anger.

But the foreman hadn't finished.

"We the jury find the defendant, Lawrence Carrington ... *not guilty* of the lesser crime of manslaughter in the first degree."

Even the judge had seemed surprised by that point.

"We the jury find the defendant, Lawrence Carrington ... *guilty* of the crime of manslaughter in the second degree."

Involuntary manslaughter. For shooting a man in the back. Sure, it had been a bar fight. Those were always hard cases. And Carrington had taken the stand and claimed self-defense. But four shots to the back? That wasn't manslaughter. That was murder.

The jury had disagreed, though, and Carrington had been looking at only a three year sentence instead of the twenty-five to life he'd been facing on the murder one. At the sentencing hearing Carrington had been all smiles and giggles until Brunelle asked the judge to give him an exceptional upward sentence of ten years despite the verdict. Ten years--the maximum for second degree manslaughter. And the judge had done it too. Just because the jury bought the self-defense story didn't mean the judge did.

Carrington had gone from smile and giggles to yelling and threats.

"I'm gonna get out one day, Brunelle!" he had yelled as the guards had dragged him out of the courtroom. "And when I do I'm gonna put four bullets in your back too! And another one in that fucked up head of yours!"

Brunelle shook his head as he finished recounting the memory.

Chen considered for a moment. "And he's out now?"

"Been out for about six weeks," Brunelle answered. "Went right back into the drug culture."

"Got a girlfriend right away," Chen observed. "Guy works fast."

Brunelle grimaced. "Great. Let's hope 'Kill the prosecutor' is still a ways down his 'to do' list."

Chen grinned and stood up from his desk. "Don't sweat it, Dave," he said as he slapped Brunelle on the back. "I'll go interview him. Let him know we're watching him."

Brunelle thought about arguing, thought about insisting on tagging along. To confront Carrington. To show him he wasn't afraid.

But he knew he wouldn't be able to show him that.

"Sounds good," he said instead. "That's *your* job anyway. I ask people questions in the courtroom."

"Where there are armed guards," Chen pointed out.

"Yeah." Brunelle didn't laugh. He thought for a moment. "Do what you can to eliminate him as a suspect. I don't want Edwards to be able to argue to the jury that Carrington did it."

Chen slapped his friend on the back. "And you don't want to have to call him as a witness either, armed bailiffs or not, right?"

Brunelle shrugged, but didn't answer the question. "I know: find something to arrest him for. He's probably got a gun somewhere. Arrest him for felon in possession."

"I bet he doesn't let me search his apartment," Chen laughed. "But I'll tell you what. For you, I'll plant one on him."

Brunelle finally laughed. "Thanks, pal."

Chen threw his hands wide. "Hey, what are friends for?"

***

"Here." Kat yanked Brunelle's hand out. "Hold this."

'This' was heavy, reddish-brown, and gooey solid. Mercifully, it was also in a sealed plastic bag, so he didn't actually touch whatever it was--or had been.

She looked up from the freezer drawer she was rearranging to examine Brunelle's face. Then she laughed in it.

"What's the matter, David? Don't like liver?"

Before he could think of a witty response, she lifted the organ from his repulsed palm and set it into the freezer compartment.

"So what was your question again?" she asked as she rubbed her cold hands on her thighs.

Brunelle was more distracted by the thought of her thighs than any harvested cadaver organ. He shook the thoughts out of his head--for now--and managed to recall the question he'd interrupted her with.

"Could the injuries in the Hastings homicide have been caused by someone smaller than the victim?"

"Sure," Kat shrugged as they walked into her small office off the examining room. "Anything's possible. Like if she was sleeping or something."

That would have been a terrible answer in front of a jury, Brunelle knew. That's why he always interviewed witnesses before trial.

"What if she was wide awake?" Brunelle countered. "And able to resist?"

Kat considered, then shrugged. "Seems less likely. It was a clean incision, no ancillary injuries. With a struggle I would have expected additional lacerations to the throat and neck, as well as defensive injuries on her hands."

Brunelle just stared at her.

"But like I said," the medical examiner finished, "anything's possible."

"Wow," Brunelle laughed. "I'm not sure I should call you as a witness. You could really screw my case."

Kat smiled. The way she used to smile at him before they agreed to call it off and put their careers first. "Oh, David. You know it's not your case I can screw."

Brunelle could feel himself blush. He hated that she could still do that to him. But it made him remember what else she used to do to him. Lately he'd been wondering why they had ever called it off in the first place.

All that thinking led to another non-response by him.

"Pretty quiet for a lawyer," Kat teased. "Just send me a subpoena and I'll be there for you."

"Great, Kat," Brunelle managed to say. "Will do. I guess I better get going. I'll make sure I ask my questions carefully so you can tell what answer I'm looking for."

"Don't worry, David," Kat felt bad for the teasing. "I won't screw you in court."

Brunelle figured he'd better at least try to keep up. "Where will you screw me then?"

A deep laugh escaped from Kat's throat. Then she patted the metal examining table with a clank-clank. "Sturdy."

Brunelle laughed too, but couldn't think of anything else to say. So he kissed her on the cheek and left with a quick, "Thanks."

Kat watched after him. She waited until he was out the door before touching her cheek and chuckling, "See you in court, counselor."

***

"You may call your next witness, Mr. Brunelle," boomed the judge in that officious voice all the lawyers knew was fake, but the jurors were supposed to take as solemnity.

The trial had gone well so far for Brunelle. His opening statement seemed to be well received. He'd told the jury about the confession, then explained why Flowers would have claimed a black-out, namely to avoid reliving the crime and give herself wiggle room for later. The only tricky part was motive. Brunelle knew he didn't have to prove motive--*why* someone commits a given crime is never an element of that crime--but he also knew the jury would want a motive anyway. So he went with drug-fueled rage following a drug-fueled argument that escalated into a drug-fueled fight. The apartment was in enough disarray to support a fight scenario. He didn't have to tell the jury that drug addicts live like that all the time.

"Mr. Brunelle?" the judge prodded.

Brunelle swallowed. "The State calls Lawrence Carrington to the stand," he announced calmly. No one could tell he was scared to death of the homicidal maniac.

Unfortunately, Edwards' opening had been pretty good too. And she was going squarely with the S.O.D.D.I defense: "some other dude did it." And the some other dude was Carrington. So even though Chen had been able to place Carrington at home across town based on his cell phone records and cell-tower pings, Brunelle had been forced to call him anyway, just so the jury could hear him actually deny the murder.

Not just proof, but proof beyond any reasonable doubt. Pretty damn high standard. The ironic thing was that Carrington knew all about that high standard. It had saved his murderous ass from life in prison.

Carrington stepped into the courtroom. One look at him and Brunelle had to suppress a smile. Carrington knew the game too. Rather than the latest in urban hoodlum fashion, Carrington was decked out in a new suit. A cheap suit, but still, a suit. And he was a good looking guy, so even the cheap suit looked sharp. More importantly though, he looked sad. Mournful even. He and Brunelle knew he'd just used Curly for drugs and sex, but to the jury he was The Grieving Boyfriend.

After the initial introductions--name, rank and department of corrections number--Brunelle got right to it.

"Did you know Theresa Hastings?"

Carrington hesitated, the words apparently caught in his throat. "Yes," he rasped.

"How did you know her?"

"She," he paused at the tense of the verb, "*was* my girlfriend."

"When was the last time you saw her--" Brunelle gave a dramatic pause himself before adding, "--alive?"

Carrington nodded and bit his lip. He looked down. Brunelle was even starting to believe he might actually have cared for her. "The day she was--" But he stopped. "The day *it* happened."

"The day she was murdered?" Brunelle offered. He wanted the jury to hear the word 'murder' in all its variations as many times as possible.

Carrington nodded, and then raised his chin. Stiff upper lip and all that. "Yes, sir. The day she was... murdered."

So Brunelle took him through the day. They had separate apartments, but sometimes he stayed overnight at her place, sometimes she stayed over with him. The night before the murder they'd stayed separate because they had different plans.

Then Carrington knocked it out of the park when he admitted his plans were to hang out with some homies and smoke crack.

Regular people think you shouldn't tell a jury bad things about you, but Brunelle had learned that the best thing a witness can do is admit the stuff he shouldn't have been doing. When Carrington told that jury he smoked crack the night before his girlfriend was murdered, they knew he wouldn't say that if it weren't true. And if that was true, then everything else was Gospel too.

As a result of this rule, Edwards' cross examination fell flat.

"Where were you when Theresa was murdered?" she demanded as soon as she stood up.

'Theresa,' like they'd been friends or something.

"I was hanging with some homies," Carrington answered calmly.

"Who?" Edwards' voice was mixed schoolteacher and angry wife.

"Torch and Lil Maxie."

Edwards narrowed her eyes. "Are those street names?"

"Yes, ma'am," Carrington answered with a polite nod.

"What are their real names?"

"Don't know their real names," Carrington explained. "That why we got street names."

Edwards smiled just a bit. "Do *you* have a street name, Mr. Carrington?"

"Yes, ma'am."

"What is it?"

"Rifle, ma'am."

"Rifle?" Edwards repeated slowly. Nice and violent. She thought she had him. She didn't. "Why Rifle?"

This time it was Carrington who smiled. "Because I shoot straight, ma'am."

Brunelle bit back a smile. One of the jurors actually laughed.

Edwards narrowed her eyes again and tossed her hair over her shoulder. She only did that when she got frustrated.

"All right, Mr. Rifle--" she started.

"Just Rifle," Carrington corrected.

"All right, Rifle--"

"Objection," Brunelle complained.

"Sustained," said the judge. "Use the witness's correct name, Ms. Edwards. This isn't the street."

"Fine." She was flustered now. That was never good for a trial lawyer. "What were you doing with 'Torch' and 'Lil Maxie'?"

Carrington hesitated. He looked up at the judge. "Do I have answer that?"

She looked down from the bench. "Yes, Mr. Carrington."

Carrington pursed his lips and nodded. "I was selling them some weed."

And it was all over. Carrington had just admitted to a class B felony. No way the jury didn't believe him now. Edwards tried to push him around some more but she got nowhere. When he started to tear up at not even getting a chance to say goodbye, Edwards decided to cut her losses and sit down.

"No further questions, Your Honor."

"Mr. Brunelle," the judge inquired, "any redirect examination?"

"No, Your Honor. Thank you."

Carrington stepped down from the witness stand and started for the door, right past Brunelle's counsel table. He couldn't wait for that murderous--but helpful-- thug to be out the door.

"May the witness be permanently excused?" the judge asked.

"Yes, Your Honor," Brunelle answered.

"No objection," Edwards huffed without looking up from her papers.

Carrington stopped and leaned onto Brunelle's table. "What does that mean?" he whispered.

"Uh, it means you won't be recalled as a witness," Brunelle explained. He was pleased with how the testimony had gone, but that didn't mean they were friends. Or homies. Or whatever. "So, you can leave now."

Carrington thought for a moment. "Can I stay? Can I watch the rest of the trial?"

Not a question Brunelle wanted to hear, and not one he'd expected. But then--as his desire to win the case overcame his fear of Carrington--he was delighted. There was nothing quite like grieving family attending the trial day after day to put the pressure on the jury. "Sure," Brunelle said. "Of course."

Carrington thanked Brunelle and took a seat in the back of the courtroom for the rest of the afternoon.

However, the rest of the afternoon was just a couple of cops. Officer First-On-The-Scene and his friend, Sergeant Put-Up-The-Crime-Tape. Brunelle had actually forgotten Carrington was still there as the judge excused the jury and the guards took Flowers back to the jail. But as Brunelle headed for the door, Carrington jumped up from the otherwise empty gallery and stopped him.

"Mr. Brunelle?" Carrington extended a hand. "You probably don't remember me, but you prosecuted me a few years back. Uh, for, well… homicide."

Brunelle hesitated, but then took Carrington's hand. He tried to squeeze it forcefully. "Oh, I remember, Mr. Carrington."

Carrington laughed just a bit as they released hands. "Yeah, I guess you would." He didn't need to say why; they both remembered his outburst. "Sorry about that. But now, well, I just wanted to thank you."

Brunelle nodded, still hoping to end the conversation as quickly as possible. "Just trying to get justice for Curly--" he started.

Carrington smiled again, this time wide enough to see the silver crowns he had on most of his teeth. "No, Mr. Brunelle. Thank you for prosecuting *me*. For sending me to prison."

Brunelle's eyebrows shot up. He wasn't sure what to say.

"I learned a lot in the last ten years," Carrington explained. "Not everybody changes in prison. Hell, most of them don't. But it opened my eyes. I used to be a thug, always carrying, looking for a fight, trying to show everybody how bad I was. But that ain't no way to live. It's a way to die."

"Ah. Well. Glad to hear that," Brunelle stammered.

"Yeah, that road's only got one end," Carrington went on. "And I'm too old for that shit now. Ten years is a long time. I ain't a kid no more. Now, out on the street, I get respect. I did time for murder--"

"Manslaughter," Brunelle corrected with a grimace.

Carrington laughed right out loud. "Yeah, manslaughter. Damn, I almost beat it, didn't I?"

Brunelle smiled tightly. "Yeah, almost."

Carrington slapped Brunelle on the shoulder. "You all right man," he laughed. "But yeah, I got rep now and no one hassle me. Sure, I sling some dope on the side, but no more guns, no more thugging, no more looking for a fight to prove I'm the biggest and baddest."

Carrington looked down and shook his head. "You almost got me, man. Life without. But I got lucky. God wants me to do more. So I did my time, and I ain't going back to that lifestyle." He looked up. "And I owe it all to you, Mr. Brunelle."

Carrington stuck his hand out again.

There were times when Brunelle wondered why he did what he did. When he looked at his classmates from law school at the big firms, with their gold watches and luxury SUVs and golf course homes, and he wondered why he spent his days looking at autopsy reports for half the money. Okay, a third of the money.

And then there were times like this. When he remembered why gold watches and luxury SUVs and golf course homes were for suckers.

"Glad to hear it, Mr. Carrington," Brunelle shook Carrington's hand, this time gladly. "It's nice to know the system actually works sometimes."

Carrington smiled again. "Sometimes," he repeated. Then he shook his head and laughed again. "See you tomorrow Mr. Brunelle."

Brunelle smiled at his former adversary. "See you tomorrow, Mr. Carrington."

***

"Please state your name and title for the record," the judge instructed.

"Catherine Anderson. Medical Examiner."

And Brunelle's date for that night's fundraiser. As he approached the witness stand to question her, he offered her the smallest twitch of a near-wink--with the eye opposite the jury box of course. Kat reacted by raising a 'don't do that again' eyebrow and the direct examination commenced.

The last two days of testimony had gone exceedingly well. A parade of shiny polished patrol officers, followed by Chen, who was perfect as the gruff but admirably competent detective. Now Brunelle was down to his last witness. The medical examiner. Cause of death equals slit throat and rest the case.

The final nail in Flowers' coffin, so to speak.

Brunelle started with her credentials, education and experience. Then a general description of what an autopsy entails. Then, ever so gently, the specific autopsy of Theresa Hastings. After so many years prosecuting violent crimes, Brunelle had gotten used to photographs that most normal people would never, ever want to see. But there were twelve normal people directly to his right who would rather never, ever see the photos that Brunelle was about to introduce. But he had to admit them to make the conviction stick on appeal.

Usually he flashed his visual exhibits on the wall with the projector. Maps, charts, photos, those kinds of things. But close-ups of a neck sliced so deep you could see the windpipe inside--those weren't getting blown up on the screen. And if Brunelle had even considered it, Carrington's presence in the courtroom made sure he didn't do it. The jurors didn't want to see it, but they had to--it came with the job. But grieving family in the courtroom meant just a verbal description of the wound, admission of the photos, holding up an eight-by-ten image for the jurors to squint at--or look away from--and then move on to the payoff question.

"And following the autopsy, Dr. Anderson," Brunelle asked almost absently as he set the gruesome photos aside, "were you able to determine a manner of death?"

Brunelle awaited the standard 'homicide' response, then he'd sit down and let Edwards try to do something with it. But Kat squirmed a bit in her seat. Suddenly Brunelle regretted not having talked to Kat since flirting over the metal examining table.

"Uh," she paused. The jurors may not have noticed, but Edwards sure did. Her head shot up from her notepad. Brunelle could hear his heart pound in his ears.

"Non-natural," Kat answered.

Brunelle knew that was a bullshit answer. There were four manners of death: natural, accidental, suicide and homicide. The jury didn't know that, but Edwards did, and she'd make sure they understood when she'd finished her cross exam. Brunelle didn't know why Kat hadn't just said homicide, but he couldn't leave it at just that. Edwards would kill him on cross if it looked like he was hiding something.

"Let me phrase it a little differently." Brunelle handed Anderson the autopsy photograph of the slit throat. "Did Theresa Hastings die from having her throat slit?"

Kat paused again. She didn't bother to look at the photo. Even the jurors were starting to get it. "That would certainly be a possibility," she finally said.

Brunelle should have waited to think about his next question, but he was letting himself get flustered. Kat could always do that to him. "A possibility? Well, were there any other possibilities?"

Kat nodded. "When the blood toxicology report came back from the lab, she had potentially lethal levels of opiates in her system."

"Opiates?" Brunelle repeated. He hadn't bothered to review the toxicology. She'd had her fucking throat slit.

"Yes," Kat answered. "Heroin, most likely. I can't rule that out as a possible cause of death, given the level."

"Her throat was slit from ear to ear," Brunelle argued.

"I can't rule that out either," Kat answered. "Clearly that would be a fatal wound. If that hadn't killed her, the drugs would have."

Brunelle stared at his ex for a few seconds. He considered pressing her, but she wasn't going to change her testimony. She wasn't going to lie. He decided that last sentence would have to be good enough.

"No further questions."

Brunelle sat down and prayed Edwards didn't skewer his case too badly. He was afraid she'd spend an hour dragging Kat up and down that damn toxicology report and every last incision of the autopsy.

But it was a million times worse.

She only asked one question.

"So doctor," she stood up and posed the question from way back at counsel table, "you can't say with any degree of medical certainty that Ms. Hastings necessarily died from the injury to her throat, can you?"

Kat considered the question. She looked at Brunelle, then at the jury, then at Edwards again. "No."

"Thank you, doctor." Edwards sat down. "No further questions."

Brunelle just lost cause of death. And with it, maybe the entire case.

Kat stepped down and left the courtroom. Brunelle couldn't bring himself to look at her. He stood up and looked up to the judge.

"The State rests." He managed to sound confident, but he felt like throwing up.

***

"Non-natural?" Brunelle demanded as he leaned against Kat's office doorframe. It was late. Everyone else at the morgue had gone home for the night. "What the hell was that?"

"I thought," Kat shrugged without lifting her eyes from her microscope, "it sounded better than 'I don't know.'"

"Not much better," Brunelle countered. "I would have preferred 'homicide.'"

Kat finally looked up. "What's that lawyer rule?" she smirked. "'Never ask a question you don't the answer to'?"

Then she saw that he was wearing those ridiculous red leather stilettos. She laughed as she stood up and grabbed her coat from the back of the door. "Come on, sweet-cheeks. Let's go to your fundraiser."

But Brunelle didn't move out of the doorway. "You should have told me, Kat," he said. "I might lose the case now."

She crossed her arms. "You should have read my tox report. I sent it to you weeks ago. Now stop pouting and get out of my way."

She pushed Brunelle in the chest. He stumbled backward in the heels and grabbed her wrist. He regained his balance but kept his grip on Kat's arm.

"Let go of my wrist," she said after a moment.

"I think you kind of enjoyed screwing me today," Brunelle said.

Kat sneered. "It's been a long time since I enjoyed screwing you, David Brunelle."

She pushed him in the chest with her other hand in an effort to pull away her captive arm, but Brunelle grabbed that wrist too.

They looked at each other for a moment, Brunelle had a hold of both her wrists, their bodies inches apart. Then Brunelle pulled her against him and kissed her mouth. Hard. Almost as hard as she kissed back.

Without pulling his mouth from hers, Brunelle let go of Kat's wrists and started pulling up her skirt. Kat grabbed his tie with one hand and pulled him backwards as she fumbled at his belt. By the time she'd pulled him back to the examining table, her skirt was up over her hips and his pants were below his.

Brunelle picked her up and set her on the table. She spread her legs and pulled him against her.

She kissed him hard and pulled away with his lip in her teeth. She let it snap back and breathed, "Keep the shoes on."

Brunelle pulled her to the edge of the metal table. "Anything for you, Dr. Anderson."

***

"You know," Kat said as she fastened her seatbelt. "That's only the second time I've fucked somebody who was wearing high heels."

Brunelle looked at her sideways as he reached under the steering wheel to undo the stiletto straps. "If it was a guy, I don't want to hear about it."

He dropped the heels in the backseat. "If it was a girl," he said as he pulled his wingtips forward, "I hope you have pictures."

Kat laughed. "I never kiss and tell, Mr. Brunelle." Then she pointed at where he was tying his shoes. "Not gonna drive in heels, huh?"

"Not unless you want me to crash into a tree," Brunelle answered. "I don't know how you women drive in those."

"It's like that old saying," Kat smiled. "Ginger Rogers did everything Fred Astaire did, only backwards and in high heels."

"Whatever," Brunelle said. "I'm just glad I brought a second pair of shoes."

"Now you're even thinking like a woman," Kat laughed. "Always have a back-up pair."

Brunelle was about to start the engine. He stopped.

"What did you say?"

"Women always have extra shoes lying around," Kat repeated. "In the car, wherever. I've got three pair under my desk at work."

Brunelle thought for a moment. "You're right, Dr. Anderson. You're absolutely right."

He started the engine. "We're gonna be late for the fundraiser, Kat. We've got a little detour to make."

***

It wasn't the worst neighborhood in the city, but it was in the top two. Not broken-windows, bullet-ridden-car-hulks, bums-passed-out-in-the-gutters bad. It actually looked nice enough driving through it, as long as it was daylight and the doors were locked. No, it was bad, as in almost everyone who lived there was either a drug seller, a drug user, or both. Bad, as in sprawling apartment complexes used as department of corrections halfway houses for not officially 'released' felons. The types who aren't allowed to get jobs yet, and probably couldn't anyway given their records. So the only way to make money is selling drugs. Multiple drug dealers means competition, and competition between drug dealers means guns and violence. Most of the users just wanted to score their shit and find a place to light their pipe or jab that needle in their arm. A place out of harm's way. A place like Theresa Hastings' apartment.

"What are we doing here, David?" Kat asked as Brunelle pulled the car into the small parking lot behind Curly's building.

"I need to check something out," he looked right past her to the apartment door.

"You have to check it out *now*?" Kat pressed. "Here? At night?"

"You were here at night once before," Brunelle said as he stepped from the car.

"There were three hundred armed cops then," Kat pointed out. "Not just a lawyer in high heels."

It took Brunelle a moment to respond. He was scanning the area as best he could in the dark. The bare bulb over the apartment door was the only light in the back parking lot.

"What's that?" he mumbled. "No, I took off the shoes, remember?"

Kat rolled her eyes, then stepped out of the car too. She hesitated, then grabbed the shoes out of the back seat. "When the car gets stolen, at least you'll still have these."

She stuffed the oversized heels into her shoulder bag.

"What are we doing here, David? Can't this wait until daylight?"

Brunelle shook his head. "No. Edwards is gonna put Flowers on the stand first thing tomorrow morning. I need to pin this down tonight."

"Pin what down? It's been months since the murder. There's no way the scene is the same."

Brunelle smiled and grabbed Kat's elbow. "That's what I'm counting on. Let's go."

The apartment door was unlocked. Kat was surprised; Brunelle pleased. The lights were off inside, which was a good sign.

"Probably nobody here," Brunelle opined.

"Of course not," Kat answered. "Who'd want to rent an apartment where somebody was murdered?"

"Nobody." Brunelle clicked on the light. "But there's plenty of people who'd use it to shoot up and pass out."

The apartment was much like when they'd seen it that night, only worse. Plates, pipes, cups, needles, half eaten food, soda cans, condoms, even sanitary napkins strewn everywhere.

"Is somebody living here?" Kat asked.

"No," Brunelle answered, closing the door behind them. "It's being used as a crash pad."

Kat looked askance at him. "A what?"

"A place you can go to do your drugs," he explained. "Get your high and crash out. Maybe with friends, maybe by yourself, maybe with whoever's here when you walk in."

"I don't know, David, it looks the same as that night. And the victim was living here then."

Brunelle smiled. That cocky, lawyer smile Kat always hated. "Let's test your theory then," he smirked. "See if you can find any shoes."

Kat cocked her head at him, but then smiled. "Damn, David. That's tricky." She liked the puzzle of it. "Yes, let's see if there are any extra shoes anywhere."

She took off for the back bedroom before Brunelle could yell, "Watch out for the needles!" He stepped into the living room. "And the glass pipes. And the razor blades."

He shook his head. "How does anyone live like this?"

Brunelle searched the living room and front entry. No shoes.

Kat came out of the bedroom. "Wow, it stinks in there," she said. "But no shoes. I guess you're right. This is just a place where people crash and leave."

Then Kat put a hand on her hip. "You know, Mr. Brunelle, that's all very interesting, but I don't see why we had to do this on our big date night?"

Brunelle nodded, but didn't remember to smile. He was thinking. He took Kat's arm and they walked back to the small hallway that led to the bedroom and the apartment's only bathroom.

"Flowers' shoes were sitting in the pool of blood," he reminded her. "She left them behind and fled out the bathroom window."

Brunelle stepped into the small bathroom. There wasn't really room for Kat too, so she stayed in the hallway.

"But why does she leave out the window?" Brunelle asked, tapping his chin. "Why doesn't she go out the front door?"

"There's someone else in the apartment," Kat said.

"Yeah," Brunelle nodded, "that's what I was thinking too."

"No, David," Kat squeaked. "There's someone else in the apartment *right now*."

Brunelle pushed out into the hallway and past Kat.

"Evening, Mr. Brunelle," said Lawrence Carrington with a tip of his head. "Fancy meeting you here."

He had a knife in his hand.

Brunelle shoved Kat into the bathroom. "Do what Ginny did," he whispered. Then he turned back to Carrington.

"I could say the same to you, Mr. Carrington," Brunelle tried to sound cool. His heart was beating in his throat. "What brings you back here? Just paying respects?"

Carrington took a slow step toward Brunelle, then another. "No, sir. Not exactly. I've been keeping an eye on the place."

Brunelle tried not to stare at the knife. It was a fixed-blade hunting knife, the kind you'd buy at a sporting goods store.

"Kind of like a caretaker?" Brunelle asked. He could hear Kat slide the bathroom window open.

"More like a cop," Carrington replied. "Paying attention to who's doing what and why. So why you here, Mr. Brunelle? And who's your lady friend? She's fine. Ten years is a long time."

Whatever fake smile Brunelle had managed to keep plastered to his face drained away. "Cut the bullshit, Carrington. Why are you here?"

Carrington laughed. "Oh, now you tough, Brunelle? Now, when you ain't got no guards standing between us? Now, when you in my world?"

Brunelle wanted to say something, but his throat was clamping shut. Carrington was close, really close. And Brunelle suddenly remembered learning that cops are trained to stay twenty-one feet away from any bladed weapon. Carrington was no more than three feet away.

"I didn't forget what you did to me, Brunelle." Carrington's teeth were shining in the dim light, but he wasn't smiling. "And I meant what I told you when they dragged me out of that courtroom. I'm gonna kill you, Brunelle. I was gonna wait till you sent Ginny away for what I done, but now…"

"I know what you did to Curly," Brunelle tried to sound brave. "I know you slit her throat. And I know you didn't do it here. I just don't know why."

"Oh, I did it here, Brunelle. Done slit her throat on that mattress, right where your boys found her. But she was already dead."

"Drug overdose," Brunelle realized.

"Yep, back at my place. She was always trying to get higher. She used too much shit."

"That's an accident, Carrington," Brunelle stepped back into the hallway. He really hoped Kat was almost out that damn window. "You should've just called 911."

"You sent me to prison for ten years for a fucking accident, Brunelle!" Carrington shook the knife at Brunelle. "That dude started that fight! He deserved what he got! And I did ten fucking years for it! You think I don't know you gonna charge me with murder again?"

Brunelle considered. "Yeah, probably. It's called 'controlled substance homicide,' not murder. But yeah, we would've charged you."

"Fuck yeah, you would have," Carrington lowered his voice, but not the knife. "And then I never get out."

"So you drag her back here and make it look like a murder. She wasn't even living here anymore, was she?"

Carrington cocked his head. "How'd you know that?"

"The shoes?"

Carrington frowned. "The shoes? What the fuck about shoes?"

"Forensics didn't find any shoes here," Brunelle answered. "Not even on her feet. She didn't walk here barefoot, so that means she died someplace else. Somebody--you--brought her here. You slice her throat, blood pours out and it looks like she died from that, and here. Even better, Ginny's passed out here so you stick the knife in her hand and take off."

"Almost," Carrington answered. "That bitch Ginny woke up when I put the knife in her hand. She still high--totally out of it. She jump up and start all stepping in the blood and shit. Then she seen me by the door, screamed like I was a fucking ghost or something, and take off through the bathroom window."

Just as he said that, Kat finally got through the bathroom window. It was pretty high up, though, so when she landed outside, she made a big thump and let out a loud, "Oof!"

Carrington's eyes widened. "That bitch went through the window too!"

Brunelle stepped forward ready to chase Carrington out the door as he ran after Kat. Instead Carrington shoved the knife into Brunelle's gut.

"Don't go nowheres Brunelle," he said as Brunelle crumpled to the floor. "I'll be back to kill you after I show your bitch a little Rifle love."

Carrington ran out the door after Kat. Brunelle pulled his hands away from his gut; they were covered in blood. Then he heard Kat scream. He smeared bloody handprints down the wall as he forced himself to his feet and struggled to the door. He stopped in the doorframe. He turned and quickly scanned the kitchen counter. Then he snatched a steak knife and headed into the night after Carrington.

There was no sign of them at first. Kat must have taken off running with Carrington in pursuit. They didn't run by the door so the most likely direction was along the building and around the corner. As if to confirm this, Brunelle heard a scream come from that direction. He jogged as fast as his injury would let him around the corner. Any doubt he might have had that Kat went that way were dispelled by her broken heel laying in the pothole filled driveway.

Across the street was a small mini-park, the kind that cities put in when they have an empty lot they want to make look nice. Not room for much of anything except a couple of benches and some trees to block out the streetlights. Perfect place to assault someone.

Brunelle dragged himself across the street to the edge of the dark.

"Carrington!" he shouted, then spit out some blood. He tried not to think about all the reasons blood would be coming up into his mouth. "Let her go!"

There was no response at first, then Carrington's voice came laughing out of the darkness, "Come and get her!"

Brunelle nodded grimly. He tightened his grip on his small steak knife, then took a deep, painful breath, and stepped into the gloom.

It was going to take a few minutes for his eyes to adjust to the dark, and he didn't know if he had those few minutes, so Brunelle decided to combine stalling with a game of Marco Polo.

"Carrington!"

After a moment. "Come and get her, Brunelle."

Ahead and to the right.

"You haven't really done anything yet, Carrington," Brunelle tried. "The toxicology proves it was an overdose. I've got no evidence you gave the drugs to her. Without that, I can't charge it."

Silence.

"You panicked, man," Brunelle went on, yelling into the darkness. "But it's not too late. Just stop. Just don't do anything more and you walk."

Silence again, for a moment, then laughter. "You still don't get it, do you, Brunelle?"

Carrington stepped out from behind a tree a few feet ahead. Brunelle could make out that much. And he didn't have Kat with him after all. A bluff to coax him into the park. Brunelle couldn't see the knife but he knew it was there. The thought of it made his gut burn.

"I'm gonna kill you," Carrington marched toward Brunelle. "That's all this has ever been about. Killing you."

Brunelle stepped back and raised his small knife. He still couldn't see well, and his gut was on fire. He could feel the blood soaking his shirt and running down his pants. He was just glad Kat had gotten away.

"I don't give a fuck about Curly." Carrington stepped right up to Brunelle.

"I don't give a fuck about Ginny." Brunelle made a weak stab at Carrington but Carrington easily grabbed his wrist.

"And I don't give a fuck about that bitch of yours." Then he shoved his knife right through Brunelle's forearm.

Brunelle screamed as his steak knife fell from his hand and he dropped to his knees. He looked up at Carrington and suddenly wished he'd gotten to say goodbye to Kat.

"Well, his bitch cares about him!" Kat jumped out of the darkness and smashed her bag over Carrington's head. It sent him tumbling to the ground, his knife still in Brunelle's arm.

Carrington was down, but he wasn't hurt. And he was a lot bigger than Kat. He pushed himself onto one knee and smiled at her. She stood there, crouched like a batter at the plate, her bag ready for another swing.

"Get out of here, Kat," Brunelle managed to say through the pain in his arm and stomach.

Kat looked over at him but before she could say anything, Carrington jumped up and grabbed her by the throat. "You're pretty, bitch," he laughed. "We gonna dance once I kill your boyfriend."

He spun her around and wrapped his arm across her throat from behind.

"Hey Brunelle, you wanna watch me dance with your bitch before I kill you?"

Brunelle looked up from his knees. His eyes had adjusted enough to notice that the edges of his vision were starting to darken. Tunnel vision. He was losing a lot of blood and clearly going into shock.

So he wasn't sure if he was hallucinating when he thought he saw Kat wink at him.

She was still holding that big bag. Brunelle saw that she was starting to open it. He couldn't get up and help her, but maybe he could stall long enough for her.

"Listen, Ruffles...," he started, then spit out some blood.

"Rifle," Carrington snapped.

"Whatever, Ruffles," Brunelle said, fighting back a cough. "I'll make you a deal. You let her go and I let you live."

It took Carrington a moment before he started laughing. "I'll make you a deal, Brunelle. You shut up and I'll kill you quick."

Brunelle coughed out some more blood. "No, you shut up, Ruffles. You're just a coward. Always have been, always will be."

Carrington practically growled in response. "You think I'm gonna fall for that, Brunelle? You think I'm fucking stupid, Brunelle?!"

"Well, you left your knife in my arm. That was pretty stupid."

Brunelle didn't pull it out though. He knew enough about knife injuries to know the blade was actually slowing the bleeding. He pulled that out, his heart would be pumping blood right into the grass.

"I don't need no knife to kill you, Brunelle," Carrington said. "I'll snap your fucking neck."

Then there was a real snap. A loud crack that came from Kat's bag. Carrington craned his neck to see what she was doing, and that's when Kat jabbed the jagged wood of the broken of stiletto heel directly into Carrington's carotid artery.

Carrington let out a high pitched scream as Kat twisted the makeshift weapon, then pulled it out again. A spurt of arterial blood spilled onto her blouse before Carrington fell to the ground and started to bleed out.

Kat rushed to Brunelle. "Are you okay?"

"I love you," he replied.

"You're delirious," she said.

"You just saved my life."

"Not yet I didn't." She tore off a strip from her skirt and tied a tourniquet at Brunelle's elbow. "Can you stand up?"

"He got me in the gut," Brunelle answered. "But I think so."

"Good," Kat said pulling him to his feet. "I want to get out of here so the paramedics I call for you aren't tempted to save him before he bleeds out."

Carrington was trying to crawl away, but every heart beat sent a gush of blood out through the fingers of the hand that was trying to stanch the flow. He wouldn't get far, and no one in this neighborhood would help him.

"He'll be dead in about five more minutes," said the medical examiner as she dragged Brunelle's limping body out of the park.

When they reached the streetlights, Kat looked down at the splintered heel in her hand.

"Damn," she said. "Looks like you got blood on those pretty shoes after all."

***

It was a couple of weeks before Brunelle made it back to Curly's apartment. He made a point of always returning to the crime scene after each homicide case. There was something unsatisfactory in even a conviction when someone's life had been taken. A burglary, a robbery, even an assault--there was a victim who could be made whole. Usually. Mostly. But not with a murder. Even if you get the conviction, execute the killer even, the victim is still dead. It always left Brunelle needing a bit more closure.

So he went back to Curly's apartment. By himself. He always went by himself, and he didn't tell anybody at the office. That wasn't what it was about. It was personal. So it was after hours, but it wasn't dark yet. He wouldn't ever be going back to that neighborhood in the dark. The last thing he wanted to do was relive his run-in with Lawrence Carrington.

He let out an audible yelp when Ginny Flowers suddenly called, "Mr. Brunelle!" from the far side of the parking lot.

Brunelle turned and relaxed when he saw who it was.

"Mr. Brunelle!" Ginny practically ran to him and started shaking his hand profusely. Brunelle was pretty sure she was high. "Mr. Brunelle, I just want to thank you for dismissing the case against me."

Brunelle extracted his hand. "Of course, Ms. Flowers. I'm sorry for what you had to go through."

She waved away the suggestion. "Oh, no. No worries, Brunelle. No worries at all. It all worked out in the end."

Then she looked around, a wild-eyed scan of the area. "So why are you even here, Mr. Brunelle? The case is over."

"It sure is, Ms. Flowers." He tried to look her in the eye, but she couldn't stay still.

Brunelle sighed. "Can I give you a lift somewhere, Ms. Flowers? Maybe the mission? Or a recovery center?"

Ginny Flowers cocked her head as she processed the information. Then she got it. "Oh no, no, Mr. Brunelle. No. I'm good. Really. I'm real good. I'm gonna be all right."

She started to back away. "Well, goodbye, Mr. Brunelle," she said, then she turned and starting walking away in earnest. "Thanks again."

Brunelle grimaced. He wondered whether he'd be looking at Ginny Flowers' autopsy photos the next week. He looked down as his scuffed wingtips. Then he kicked a stone into Curly Hastings's apartment door, turned on his worn heel and walked away.

***

The inspiration for this story by author, Stephen Penner:

I've been meaning to write a legal thriller for some time now. My main character, Assistant D.A. Dave Brunelle, has been the star of several outlined stories, but there was always something missing that kept me from writing them out. Then I was inspired by my muse and imagined medical examiner Kat Anderson. She was the missing piece that took what would otherwise have been a dry prosecutor procedural and opened the story to its true thriller potential.

Dave and Kat will be starring in their own novel soon. After writing this story, I returned to a novel I'd outlined a few years ago but then stuck in a drawer. Armed with fresh inspiration and a fresh character (Kat), I reworked the outline and plunged into the writing. It tells the story of when Dave and Kat first met (over a corpse, of course) and is titled AGGRAVATING FACTORS. Look for it early 2012.

The Numbers Game

by Jonas Saul

I never thought I'd be up on first degree murder charges. The proof is in the numbers. I know this. But they don't.

I'm a vacuum cleaner salesman. I used to sell shoes, but now I sell Kirby's. I run door to door and try to sell my G8 Kirby upright vacuums. The killing has nothing to do with me, but one of the people I had just done a presentation for was murdered minutes after I left their house. I'm innocent.

This is my story. Call it a diary. I won't lock it. Besides, I don't have a lock or anything metal in my prison cell. They don't allow those things. So I will write my tale and let everyone know what I do and how I do it so they can see that I'm not a murderer. I can't afford a lawyer from the money I make selling vacuums, but I've got legal aid, although that's worth nothing. Maybe the Judge will read this.

It's lights out so I'll write in the dim glow I get from across the corridor. It's a short story so I'll be brief but there's two things you need to know up front.

I only got caught because I had Mrs. Gavin's shoes in my apartment, and someone saw my car in front of her home and wrote down my license plate number. That makes sense as I was there doing a demonstration.

I'm innocent. Remember that.

It's important.

***

Tuesday morning. The sun is shining high already and there's a slight breeze. I'm off to a great start today. I've hit twenty-two houses. Ten doors weren't answered, and twelve were rejections. The rule is, for every one hundred doors, you get into two. That means by the time I hit fifty, I should get in one door. Once I get in and show them how good the Kirby is, they'll want one for themselves. Although that's not always true, because for every four demonstrations, I only sell one. To break it down, I need to hit two hundred doors to sell one vacuum on average.

See what I mean about the proof being in the numbers? I live by that. It allows me to finance myself properly, as selling vacuum cleaners is one hundred percent commission. If I want a raise, all I have to do is hit another fifty houses per day for a week and I'll, on average, probably sell an extra vacuum per week. At four hundred dollars a hit in commission, selling three to five per week, I'd say I'm doing all right. I'm not rich, but these are just the numbers. I know the proof's there and that's how I get by, but in the end, they're just numbers.

I'm on Maple Street. It's still before lunch. Let's see how many rejections I can get. You see, that's the fun part. The more rejections I receive only means I'm closer to an open door. An open door is a potential sale. And, any open door is a chance for me to add a nice pair of shoes to my collection.

What people don't know is that I collect shoes. Mostly ladies shoes. I don't wear them. I'm not creepy. I just collect them. I have over two hundred pairs now from different cities in the States. Today I'm itching to add to that.

It's like a calling. I *need* them. I *have* to have them.

The next house coming up is a Victorian. Very nice white trimming and a manicured lawn. I'm sure the owners could use a new Kirby and I could use a new pair of shoes as I mentioned a moment ago.

I ran up the walkway and rang their bell.

No answer.

I rang it again.

I heard footsteps approaching slowly. The door opened.

"Hello?" A woman in her fifties stood in the doorway (It can be said, this is Mrs. Gavin).

"Hi! My name is Trevor Ashton and we're in the area today offering free carpet shampoos to you and your neighbors." I thrust out a bottle of Carpet Fresh and held it high in my hand. This always made me feel like those girls on The Price Is Right waving their hands in front of the items people were to bid on. "There's no obligation and for letting us clean your carpet you get a free bottle of Carpet Fresh. Doesn't that sound great?"

The woman seemed stunned. She looked at me a moment longer, evaluating my smile and then shook her head. She started to close the door.

"Excuse me ma'am," I said, reaching out and touching the door before it closed. "Is there a reason you wouldn't like a free carpet shampoo? There's nothing to buy and there's no obligation. It's completely free." I said this last part with a *I'm so excited I just can't hide it* flourish.

She looked at me and attempted a half smile. "I'm not feeling well. I've had hip surgery recently and I'm not up to company. But thank you anyway."

She started to shut the door again.

"But ma'am, you're the perfect candidate. Don't you see?"

The door almost closed. It stopped at the frame. I waited. It opened again, almost defiantly.

"I already get my carpets cleaned by a company that does a great job. I pay them often to come and do it. They were here about two weeks ago so the carpets are fine. Thank you."

"That's perfect. I love a challenge. Do you realize how much they miss? The Kirby, in under five minutes, would show you how bad they're doing."

She looked me up and down, her face showing her displeasure at my intrusion. In the end, I told myself, if I lost her I'd run to the next house and try again. Eventually I'd get in somewhere. That's a fact. It's in the numbers.

"The carpet cleaners that do my home are very good, and they're so cheap that I barely pay them a tip, and you want to know why?" She paused here like the drama queen I could tell she was. "Because my son owns the company."

Okay, here's a challenge. I just told her the company she uses sucks. It's her son's company. To her I've disrespected her family. I've got to talk fast and think faster.

"Let me ask you a question and then I'll leave. Is that fair?"

She held the door firm. It looked like she was getting ready to slam it in my face. I didn't wait for her to tell me to go ahead.

"Let's say you just went to the doctor and he told you that your cholesterol was off the charts. Arteries were clogging and he requires you to be hospitalized. He tells you to go home to pack your things and report back to the hospital by mid-afternoon. He also tells you to eat nothing until your return. Especially don't eat any fast food like greasy burgers because it could be what kills you." I use my hands a lot when I talk so I dropped the bottle of Carpet Fresh on her door step and emphasized my next point about hunger. "Now, you haven't eaten all morning. Your nerves were jangling because you were worried about what your doctor was going to tell you. As you walk out the front doors of his clinic—"

"Are you going anywhere with this? I have to get off my hip. Please hurry."

"Yes, ma'am, almost done. As you walk out the front doors of his clinic you see a beautiful diner across the street. You step a little forward and can smell whatever it is they're cooking. The sign out front says, *All you can eat bacon==> FREE!* You know the trick. Buy some eggs and get all the bacon you want. Your stomach turns and winces with the smell. You're going to be hospitalized that afternoon. This is your last chance to splurge, to dazzle yourself with the second love of your life: bacon."

"Is there a question in there somewhere?"

I continued as if she hadn't interrupted. "Even though it's free and you know it's not good for you, would you still go and eat that bacon? Even though it could kill you. The parallel is, even though they clean your carpet for basically free, after the damage I show you they're doing to your home, would you still have them over, son or not?"

I waited. Sometimes direct questions like this get a slammed door in the face. Other times you've intrigued them enough to take the bait and let you in to see what you're made of. This was that case.

The woman stepped back, a smug look on her face. It seemed she liked the fire in my pitch. "Okay, you win. Get your Kirby and let's see what happens, but I promise you, I won't be buying one. Just do the carpet and show me the results. We'll go from there. I'll leave the door open because I have to go sit down now."

She limped away from the open door. I turned and ran down Maple Street to my Pontiac, drove to the front of her house and retrieved the boxed vacuum from the trunk. After carrying it to her door I stepped in, closed the door behind me and quietly locked it. I always locked the doors for our protection. You never know what psychos might walk in while I'm doing a presentation.

I took my shoes off and placed them neatly beside a beautiful pair of red Jimmy Choos. They sat up so pretty, with a small heel and a lovely strap with little diamonds on it. Wow, the woman had class. These were also the shoes that got me charged with murder even though I didn't do it. Mrs. Gavin had less than two hours before she would be bludgeoned to death with a rolling pin and a meat tenderizer.

Although I couldn't know that at the time.

***

I entered her main living room and got the Kirby out of the box and then went about setting everything up. The display model, or as we call it, *our partner*, has an added piece that the customer's models don't have. It's a little circular window on the right by the air intake. It has small clasps to undo the top. I opened it and placed one of my hundred black cloths in it so we could see what was in her carpet.

"What are you doing? It was just vacuumed yesterday."

"I have to vacuum the carpet first to make sure there's no grit or sand in it otherwise when I'm shampooing I could cut the fibers of your carpet. My goal is to clean the carpet, not damage it." I said this with my best car salesmen smile. "After I've gone over it a little and nothing comes up then we can go right to shampooing. How does that sound?"

She nodded and used her right hand to say *carry on*.

What they don't understand is that I'm a Master Closer. Nobody gets it. No one understands me. I'm not a traditional salesman. I'm a Master Closer. Everything I do is to close the sale. Getting in the door is step one. Show the dirt is step two. Step three and four get convoluted, because in each house it's different, but eventually I get the shoes. Then I leave.

No one denies me the shoes. Ever.

I began vacuuming. Mrs. Gavin sat in the middle of her couch watching, her eyes brimming with suspicion.

The black cloth filled with dirt immediately. I stopped, unclipped the lid and laid it out flat in the corner of her carpet. I placed a new one in the glass, clipped it in place and started vacuuming again. I repeated this process ten times and then stopped and looked at her.

Mrs. Gavin's eyes were wide. "That's a lot of dirt," was all she could say.

I nodded. "Yeah, sorry about that. When did you say this carpet was vacuumed last?"

"Yesterday." She was in a daze, stunned.

"And when was it cleaned by your son's company?"

"A few weeks ago."

"Let me ask you one more question. What kind of a vacuum do you own?"

She looked at me. This is where the sale turns my way. Crucial moment. Time stopper. Egg popper. Head cracker, kill her and stack her. Here we go.

"Electrolux. I use an Electrolux, why?"

"That's why you have all this dirt."

I turned away and flipped the Kirby on. After a moment, I stopped to change the black cloth again.

"I don't understand," she said. "What's wrong with my vacuum?"

I turned to her. "You see this unit. It's an upright. No suction lost in hoses. The mouth where all the dirt comes in is right beside the powerful engine. The filter is in front of the engine. Not a single micro fiber gets near the Kirby's engine. In the Electrolux, the engine isn't filtered properly, so performance is jeopardized, and it's not an upright. You have a long hose. Think of it like this: a fire will destroy a home better than ten men outside trying to blow it down."

She frowned.

"The fire is the Kirby. Your Electrolux is just blowing wind. Which brings me to my next point." I turned and started vacuuming again. "Do you have fire insurance on your home?" I yelled over the sound of the Kirby.

I turned the unit off and unclipped the black cloth, placing it near the others.

"Of course I do. Why do you ask?"

I stopped and turned to her. "Really?" I sounded so surprised. "Well, have you ever collected? I mean, have you ever had a house burn down?"

She looked away obviously having no idea where I was going with this. They never do.

"So you pay a monthly or a yearly charge for insurance against a fire, and yet you've never had one. If you added up all the money you've spent insuring against fire, I'd be surprised if it wasn't in the thousands over the years."

Mrs. Gavin looked back up, biting on her index finger. Something was troubling her and it wasn't where I was going with this. Maybe it was my right eye twitching. It gets like that when I'm about to steal a pair of shoes. Or perhaps it was my voice. In the moments of closing, I can get like a preacher on a tirade.

"My point is this. You're spending so much money on something that has never happened, and probably never will happen, but yet dirt happens. It's right there."

I pointed at the fifteen square black cloths. "And yet you're not paying for the right equipment. You own an Electrolux and get deals on carpet shampooing."

I turned away to let her think about it and started my last bit of vacuuming.

"How much does a Kirby cost?" she asked.

And that was the last question out of Mrs. Gavin.

I turned back to her. "I have a question for you," I said, my finger raised for emphasis. "If you received a check in the mail for three dollars every day, would you be rich? Could you go out and buy a Benz or a new Porsche?"

She shook her head, biting away at her middle finger now. The sun shone through her living room window at an odd angle casting an ugly light on her wrinkles.

"Let's flip it. If you got a bill in the mail for three dollars a day, would you be poor? Would you have to declare bankruptcy? Would it all be over?"

She shook her head and started in on the other hand biting at her fingernails like they were enemies worthy of her teeth alone.

"That's what a Kirby costs. Three dollars a day. On our plan they're only $90 a month."

Really, they're $1899.00, but when you reduce it to the ridiculous, the numbers say that more people buy.

The proof is in the numbers.

She seemed stunned. Something was wrong. I could feel it. Now was the time to deal with the rest of my business.

"Ma'am, with all this dirt, could I go and wash my hands?"

She nodded and I stepped into the kitchen. She was quite the decorator. Everything in this room had colorful items placed on it. The fridge was a mirage of pictures and drawings from her grandchildren, no doubt. Knickknacks littered the top of the microwave and parts of the countertop. I pay close attention to kitchens. They say a lot about the people I vacuum for.

Beside the stove I saw what I was looking for. A pottery like container that held cooking utensils. I found a nice chopping blade, a whisk and two wooden spoons in it along with many other items. Who knew the meat tenderizer would be used in such a horrible manner in such a short time from then?

I turned on the kitchen sink to mask the sound of the drawers I was about to open.

I write this freely in the knowledge that any law enforcement officer reading it could only charge me with theft and snooping.

(*Drop the first degree murder charge, please. I'm innocent.*)

The second drawer down contained baking tools. The rolling pin lay there, innocent and not very threatening by itself.

I pulled it out. Then I touched other things along with the meat tenderizer. (That's why they have my fingerprints. Is there any law against touching things? Fuck!)

I washed my hands and stepped back into the living room. Mrs. Gavin was compliant. She didn't ask any more questions. She sat on the couch and stared at me. I finished masturbating and then cleaned up the carpet with the shampoo attachment on the vacuum.

After that I took the Kirby to the door and began packing things away.

"Mrs. Gavin, I wanted to thank you for allowing me to demonstrate the Kirby's power to you today. It's been a pleasure to show you its prowess."

I always talk to the client when I'm in their hallway, so as to judge how far they are from me as I'm slipping their shoes into my Kirby box. The nice pair of Jimmy Choos fit comfortably around the neck of the vacuum. The lid went on and I was ready to leave.

"You have a nice day now, Mrs. Gavin."

I could smell something was off. Something coming from the living room. Maybe she ate beans yesterday. How could I know?

I opened her front door slowly and peeked out at the street. No one was around. I took a moment to step back and look at Mrs. Gavin before leaving her home. She hadn't been too talkative during the last part of my demonstration.

She still sat on the couch although she was leaning to the right a lot more now. Must've been her bad hip. The sun was higher. It touched her below the knees, showing off her varicose veins nicely. They were so prominent that it almost looked like the blood was on the outside of her body.

I shook my head. Maybe I had a premonition of her death? Maybe I was looking at death?

I turned away not caring for the smell coming from her.

The street remained empty. I stepped out and shut the door behind me. I was clean as I'd washed my hands in the bathroom after masturbating on her carpet in front of her. No one could tell what went on in that house. There were no witnesses whatsoever.

I offered her a carpet shampoo for free. She took it. I gave her a bottle of Carpet Fresh. She allowed me in. I did everything right. I did steal her shoes, but is that a crime worthy of a death sentence?

I put the Kirby in the trunk of my car and drove home.

It was later that night, about 3:15am when someone knocked incessantly on my apartment door. I remember it was exactly 3:15am because that's when that guy kept waking up in the Amittyville Horror movie.

"What the fuck?" I yelled through the door. "Who the hell's out there?"

"Police. Open up."

My heart sank, my stomach dropped. How's that? Why would they be here? What could I have done?

Realizing I had no choice, I opened the door, even though I was still in my underwear.

Four police officers stood behind two men in business suits. One of the suits looked just like David Caruso on that television police show. The other cop looked like an asshole with his goatee perfectly trimmed and his earring dangling down like a faggot. I would later find out he was. An asshole and a faggot.

"Trevor Ashton?" asshole asked.

"Yeah, that's me. What's up?"

Asshole motioned with his hands to the four uniforms behind him and they rushed me, grabbing my arms and handcuffing me.

"Hey."

"You're under arrest for the murder of Eleanor Gavin. You have the right to remain silent. You have the right to an attorney…"

"I know my Miranda rights. Shut the fuck up and tell me why you're arresting me. What do I have to do with this woman?"

They pushed me against a wall so hard that I lost my balance and fell to the carpeted hallway of my apartment building. I could tell the superintendent wasn't using a Kirby.

Asshole leaned down to me and whispered his evidence in my ear like he was asking to fuck me.

"We found her body bludgeoned with a meat tenderizer and a rolling pin. She was torn apart on her living room couch. It was so bad that her abdomen was literally shredded, evacuating her bowels on the carpet. One of her neighbors spotted your car out front. It took us over a dozen hours to track you down through your license plate number, but we did. And guess what?"

He stopped and smiled at me. My heart was pounding so fast I thought he could hear its drum roll as well as I could.

"We found the killer's DNA all over the house. Hairs in the bathroom and kitchen sink. Fingerprints are still being lifted in her kitchen but you wanna know what the best part is? The killer's semen is still in her carpet, and some dripped on her corpse. We retrieved a fresh sample from her right breast an hour after she was killed. Well, what was left of her breast. My guess is, we'll find out that semen is yours."

I panicked. Of course I panicked. Some of the demonstrations I do can turn kinky. As I said previously, I stole her shoes. For me, it's all about the shoes. Sure I masturbate, but is that against the law? I asked her. She nodded her head yes. She even allowed me to finish anywhere I wanted. Now, tell me, with that kind of consent where does a courtroom get the right to question mature adults?

I waited until they got me to my feet and then I flipped out.

"You got the wrong guy!" I screamed. I turned to the wall and pulled the fire alarm with my front teeth.

"I didn't do anything—"

It was probably getting close to four in the morning. The cops were super pissed that I had caused so much of a raucous. They jumped on me and threw a couple punches in too. Then suddenly I felt their combined weight leave my back.

Something poked me in the ass cheek. I have never felt anything in my life quite as horrifying and exhilarating as being tased. I flopped and bounced on the floor like a dying cockroach. I pissed myself and begged for it to stop.

They hit me again.

My neighbor opened their door at the sound of the fire alarm and the cop turned his lightning rod off.

Within minutes they had me on my feet and were escorting me, carrying me to the waiting prisoner van.

I felt special. A whole van just for me.

Assholes.

I was booked and placed in a holding cell. The next morning they brought me in front of a judge who felt, based on what they had already found at the crime scene, that I was a flight risk. I was ordered held until trial.

That was eight months ago. Since then, I have festered in this rat hole. I can't sell anymore Kirby's and I can't collect anymore shoes.

I've often seen a prison guard with a great pair of Reebok's, but the bars hold me back. I still masturbate, but it's not as much fun.

In my eight months waiting for trial, I've written to shoe companies to receive their mail order catalogs, but my mail is inspected before it gets to me. I asked what harm there was in perusing picture catalogs. I went so far as to explain that they were my form of pornography. But still, the guards won't let me have them.

There's one more part that I have to cover before I leave this note for whoever finds it.

They gave me legal aid. I got a lawyer to talk to me two days after being incarcerated. His name was Delroy Conrad. He said he could get me off. I remember saying some half-assed comment like, "Oh *really*". He didn't like my attitude.

Another asshole.

Anyway, he's arriving here in ten minutes so I'm going to sum this up.

I didn't kill Mrs. Gavin. I touched her rolling pin and meat tenderizer. I touched her kitchen and bathroom. I even touched her, but that was because she offered consent. I stole her shoes. I have broken the law. But I didn't kill her.

Someone was either in the house with me at the time and murdered her moments after my departure, or someone entered the house as soon as I left.

It wasn't me.

I love shoes. They're my religion. They're what drive me. But not any shoes. They can't be store bought. They have to have been worn by a woman. I love men's shoes, but not in the same way.

That is what it's all about.

Shoes.

***

Trevor set the pen down and massaged his aching fingers. He had just over five minutes left until the lawyer showed.

Not enough time for a full read through, but I'll start anyway, he thought.

By page seven, he heard the guards coming. He piled the papers together and folded them in half, and then placed them under his mattress. At the same moment he stood, a guard stepped up to his bars.

"Open on eight," the guard shouted.

Trevor heard a click and the bars started rolling.

"You have a meeting. Let's go."

Another guard showed up, and both of them escorted Trevor along the corridor. They didn't handcuff him. They weren't rough. There was nowhere to go even if he decided to run.

The gray walls enhanced how he felt on the inside. He hated being here. He was in his late forties. It was time to think about the latter years of his life. Beating this murder charge was all that mattered, and Delroy said he could do it seven months ago.

Today would be the day Trevor found out how the investigation was going. He'd looked forward to this day with a sense of trepidation and elation. He may even be released that very day.

Wouldn't that be something, he thought. *The first thing I'd do when I walk out of here would be to buy a celebratory drink somewhere and then steal me some shoes.*

He entered the dank room where his lawyer sat waiting. Delroy's briefcase was sitting open on the long table. Papers were strewn about in front of him.

He gestured for Trevor to come and take a seat. Then he turned toward the guards and said, "It's okay, I've got it from here."

Trevor turned back and watched the two guards leave. He glanced down at their shoes and wondered if he'd ever get his hands on a good pair of Reebok's.

"Please, sit," Delroy said.

"You got good news for me?" Trevor asked without moving.

"I've got news, but I think you need to be sitting to deal with it."

Trevor's stomach flipped a little. That didn't sound like, *you're going home,* or, *I got the charges dropped.* That sounded more like, *you're fucked.*

He decided that sitting may be better for this. He'd wallowed eight months in prison, and they had no witnesses to the murder. All they had was him at the scene, and a valid explanation why. How could that be murder one?

He inched forward, pulled out the chair, and turned it around to straddle it, his arms on the back. This way, if things got shitty fast, he could find comfort looking under the table at his lawyer's leather shoes.

"We have a few problems with your defense," the lawyer started.

"Why? What problems? It's cut and dried. I didn't do it."

Delroy held up his hand. "Fair enough. But we do have problems. The prosecution has decided to profile this case and make a name for himself."

Trevor stood up, almost knocking the chair over. "Whoa, profile the case? Make a name out of it? What the fuck does that mean?"

The door behind him opened with a bang. Three guards stepped in. "Everything okay here?" the lead guard asked, a baton in his hand.

Delroy stood up and nodded. "Everything's fine. We're okay. You can leave us."

The guards filed out slowly and shut the door behind them.

"You have to remain calm. We need to talk. Remember, you're being held on first degree murder charges. Those guys out there," he motioned toward the door, "are on edge when you jump around like that.

Now sit down and stay seated. We have to get through this."

Trevor felt his hands shaking as he reclaimed his seat. This time he sat in the chair normally, pushing it up to the table.

Fuck him and his shoes. I don't want to see them anymore. If I'm really going down for murder, he'll be my next victim if he fucks up my case.

"The prosecution is saying you're the next James Lloyd or Jerome Brudos. That's going to be an easy sell with the jury after what they found in your apartment."

"What did they find in my apartment?" Trevor asked.

"Shoes. Women's shoes mostly. Some were defiled and covered in old semen. They're still looking for anyone who might've owned those shoes you have."

"Those two guys you mentioned. Who are they?" Trevor asked, completely ignoring the comment about shoes.

Delroy shuffled papers around. He opened a folder and then brought it in front of him.

"Here it is. James Lloyd was arrested in 2006. He was known as the Thurnscoe Shoe Rapist. Thurnscoe is a small village in England. He was arrested twenty years after his first rape. He was found to have over two hundred pairs of women's stiletto shoes that he kept at his workplace as trophies."

"That's not me," Trevor said as he shuffled in his seat. He was suddenly very uncomfortable with where this was going.

"Jerome Brudos was an American serial killer. They called him 'The Shoe Fetish Slayer'. After killing his female victims, he'd amputate their feet and dress them up in his vast collection of ladies shoes. I mean we're talking some pretty fucked up people here."

A rage built inside Trevor that he'd only ever felt when dealing with his mother. He wasn't like those idiots. He wasn't going to make it in a trial. He would never be able to sit still while some prosecutor inferred that he was the same as those other assholes. He'd rather be dead.

Delroy had stopped talking and sat staring at Trevor.

"You okay?"

Trevor nodded.

"You want me to go on?"

Trevor nodded again, struggling to control himself.

"Okay," Delroy said. "They're going to argue that a shoe fetish is an attraction to shoes, or other footwear, on a sexual level, and that when you steal the shoes, it's like a trophy. Certain serial killers will often take a trophy from their conquests. They're also going to say it's a psychosexual disorder and refer to it as *retifism*, because of what some French novelist did with shoes in the late 1700s."

"I can see we have a problem," Trevor said, his teeth clenching so hard he felt his jaw cracking.

"What do you see the problem is?" Delroy asked, raising his pen to his lips to chew on it.

"You say *because of some French novelist* blah, blah, blah. That tells me you haven't even researched it. You have no details on it. The problem is, how can you be my defense if you don't have a defense? You aren't working hard enough. I have a right to a fair trial, for fuck sakes."

Delroy set the pen on the table. "Trevor. Look me in the eye and tell me, did you murder Eleanor Gavin, or did you not murder her?"

Trevor couldn't believe it. His own lawyer was questioning his guilt. He wasn't on trial yet. This asshole was supposed to defend him. Innocent until proven guilty. What happened to The Pursuit of Happiness, the American Way, and white picket fences and shit?

"I'm innocent. I did nothing wrong. Yes, I'll admit, I love shoes. That's not creepy. What about people who tie each other up, or men dressed as babies in some submission role-playing bullshit? That's not me. I just like shoes. Come on, I'm the normal one here, and if you can't provide me with a good defense, then I'll have to retain another lawyer. I mean, seriously!"

Delroy gathered up the papers on the table. He piled them and tossed everything into his briefcase, and then slammed it shut.

"Tell me one more thing."

Trevor tapped his foot incessantly. It was all he could do to hold himself back from Delroy's throat.

"What does the key unlock?"

Warning bells triggered in Trevor's head. Pinging sounds resounded between his ears. He thought he heard a fire truck somewhere, but that was impossible. Too much concrete.

He collected himself and tried to drown out the noise going on in his head.

"What. Key. Are. You. Asking. About?" He stopped on each word. It was time for Delroy to learn that he wasn't dealing with a psycho. This legal aid bastard was dealing with a professional. An innocent one.

"Investigating officers found a key to a storage unit, or a warehouse of some kind, when they searched your apartment. After eight months, they're stumped as to what it opens. It would go a long way in your defense to cooperate. Tell me what that key opens."

"I have zero idea what you're talking about."

Trevor sat back and crossed his arms. They'd never figure out where the key goes. He used an alias when he rented the storage unit. The original key was thrown away after he had it remade so the storage unit name wouldn't be on it. If they found what was in that unit, things would get very interesting.

"Well, I guess that's it," Delroy said as he stood up.

"What's it?"

"I'll give everything I have to your new lawyer when he's appointed."

Trevor turned his head sideways and unclasped his arms.

"What?"

"I quit the case. I'll be asking the judge to release me as I can't properly defend you."

Trevor slowly stood up. He saw Delroy motion for the guards.

"Why can't you *properly* defend me?" *Properly* came out sounding like a little girl whining.

"Because, Trevor, I don't feel you're innocent. They found your semen on the woman's breast. From what we know of Eleanor Gavin, she wouldn't allow that while alive. There's no way she would've consented."

Trevor heard keys going into, and unlocking the doors. He couldn't believe what Delroy was saying. There were no witnesses. How could anyone suppose what Eleanor would like, and would not like?

"She was a regular church member. She fought for women's rights. She broke her hip when she tripped while helping an eighty-year-old woman move her furniture. Eleanor never married. As far as investigators could tell, she was a lesbian. So why would she give consent for a vacuum cleaner salesman to ejaculate on her person? The jury won't buy it. I'm done—"

Trevor dove, hands outstretched. He'd heard enough. Both his hands clamped onto Delroy's throat before his body hit the table between them. He tightened his grip with everything he had. Then he rolled sideways, causing the lawyer to bend at the waist, and roll with him.

Hands grabbed at his feet but were denied purchase. In under three-seconds, the lawyer had hit the ground with Trevor on top of him, digging deep into Delroy's trachea.

It felt like a wall had caved in when the guard body-checked him off the lawyer. Trevor took the impact on his right, throwing him four feet into the steel wall of the room. His head spun for a moment, eyes going blurry.

Then they hit him again. He didn't see it coming. After that hit, he saw nothing else as his vision faded to black.

***

Trevor woke in the infirmary. A doctor was dressing a wound near his eye.

The sharp pain of the doctor touching the injury made Trevor jump and try to knock the doctor's hand away. He came up short as his wrists were handcuffed to the gurney.

"Leave me the fuck alone!" he shouted at the doctor.

"Afraid I can't do that. Gotta fix you up."

"What'd they do to me?" Trevor asked, as he mentally did an inventory of his aches and pains.

"Nothing I can't fix."

"Anything broken?"

"Nope. Massive bruising in the face and arms but nothing broken. You got off easy."

"Hmmph."

Trevor eased back in the bed and let the doctor do his work. He spent his time plotting, evaluating.

After a while the doctor left and shut the lights out.

Trevor slept.

When he woke, he was back in his cell. The note was exactly where he left it. He held it up to the light from the corridor and read every single word. Nothing implicated him. He lay back on his mattress, although tenderly, and started to fall asleep with a smile on his face.

Things could be worse, he thought, *but they weren't. I'm going to beat this and then I'll add to my shoe collection. The proof is in the numbers. Trust the process. Follow and respect.*

I will walk.

* * *

It took three months for a new lawyer to be appointed and brought up to speed. They met in the same room as before. When Trevor entered the room this time, he had shackles on his wrists and ankles.

"Ah, guards, that won't be necessary," the lawyer said, pointing at the restraints.

"Sorry boss, but they stay on. Didn't you hear what happened the last time he met with his lawyer?"

"Okay fine. Leave us. Trevor, why don't you waddle over here and have a seat?"

Immediately, Trevor liked his new lawyer. Slicked back hair, wire-rimmed eye glasses that were pointed on each side like they held more purpose than just as corrective lenses, and a confident, *don't fuck with me* way about him. He stood until Trevor could *waddle* over and sit. Trevor didn't turn the chair around this time. He didn't want to look at the new lawyer's shoes. He was done with that for now. Prison had weakened his resolve over the last three months.

What more could another lawyer do for him anyway?

At least the table was clean. The attorney's briefcase sat on the floor, unopened.

"Good news," the lawyer said, as he pulled his chair in and sat down.

"Okay," Trevor nodded for him to go on.

"I'd offer to shake your hand, but well, you kinda can't right now, so we'll dispense with the formalities. My name is Vincenzo Marconi. I was assigned your case about two months ago. I read the previous lawyer's files, and almost got *my* gun to shoot him."

This made Trevor giggle a little. He tried to catch himself, but it was too late.

"It's okay. Laugh. If I was in your shoes I'd…oh, sorry, didn't mean that. Anyway, his files were all fucked.

Once I wrapped my head around everything, I started asking questions, and guess what I found out?"

"I have zero idea. I've kinda been busy lately with dinner parties and functions."

"Okay, I get it. Tough being locked up. No problem, because today is your lucky day."

"How's that?"

Suspicion peppered Trevor's thoughts. He'd spent almost a year waiting in prison for a trial that kept getting put off. A new lawyer sat in front of him saying there was good news. What could possibly be that good? What could make this lawyer smile like he was? Something was fishy and it stank.

"I re-questioned the witness."

Trevor shot forward. "There were no witnesses!"

"Calm down, calm down. Yes, there was. One witness. Eleanor Gavin's neighbor who called in your plate number."

"Oh, okay, sorry. What'd they say?"

"The neighbor couldn't be sure of the time of day. You see, they're placing the time of death somewhere between 12:30pm and 2:30pm. We have you entering the house before lunch. I can prove that your Kirby demonstration was less than an hour. You weren't present at the time of the murder."

Trevor leaned forward. "You know something?"

"What?"

"You sound like a lawyer. I like that. The other guy didn't. He sounded like a jackass."

"Great. And that's all the prosecution has. Check this out," the lawyer said, using his hands in the air like he was playing a saxophone.

What is it with the Italians and hands?

"I requested to see the original search warrant and I found a problem. It's something that happens a lot. Pretty common."

"What happens a lot? What are you talking about?"

"It's a technical problem that got the search warrant voided."

"Voided? How's that possible?" Trevor felt suspicious, but hopeful. Or was this lawyer a snake oil salesman?

What brand of shine is he trying on me?

The lawyer placed both elbows on the table and tented his fingers. "Pieces of the warrant were copied and pasted from a different case. *The suspect confessed to the crime* wasn't deleted from the warrant. You didn't confess. Therefore the warrant the judge signed was false. Ultimately, the judge was tricked, making the warrant null and void. This results in suppressing all the evidence from your apartment. The prosecution only has a neighbor with your license plate, but that's explained away. You were there doing a vacuum demonstration." Vincenzo leaned back and set his hands on his thighs. He shook his head a little. "Your previous defense attorney was a shit. This kind of thing can be easily overlooked when there are thousands of pages of police reports, but a good lawyer will find it. This means they have nothing on you. You're free to go as soon as we do the paperwork."

Trevor's eyes shot wide. "So the warrant thing. It's that important?"

"You bet your five dollar shoes it is. It's called a search violation."

Why all the jokes about shoes? What the fuck is up with this guy? Is he playing me?

"It's important enough to get you out of here."

"You serious?"

"Yup. They have to drop all the charges on the technicality and release you. This case is over. It's dropped. In two hours they're doing the paperwork. You'll be free to go. And you'll never see the inside of a courtroom. How's that for important enough?"

"Holy shit, fuck a goose and see if she's loose. That's great news. But what about my other lawyer?"

"What about him?"

"I attacked him in here. I assaulted him."

Vincenzo waved his hand. "Nothing to worry about. I showed the judge how bad his files were, and how you weren't being given a fair trial. Of course you'd be angry about that. Especially an innocent guy being wrongly accused. Delroy isn't pressing charges. He could if he wanted to, but he knows that I would embarrass his ass."

"Wow! Is this for real?"

"This is your first step forward in a brand new pair of shoes. How does it feel?"

Another reference to shoes. Okay, the noise in my head is telling me something, and I think I just figured out his game. I got you motherfucker. I know what you're doing. How could I have been so stupid?

"It feels great," Trevor said as sweat beaded on his forehead. He looked around to see who was watching. A camera sat in the corner near the roof, red light blinking.

I am being duped.

"Oh, don't worry about that thing. We get privacy in here. It's part of the rules."

Vincenzo set his briefcase on the metal table and opened it. He presented documents for Trevor to sign.

Two hours later, Trevor Ashton was released from prison. His lawyer had brought Trevor's car around for him.

They shook hands, and Trevor drove away as the sun dropped toward dusk.

He knew what they were doing. He could figure it out. You can't sell a salesman.

And he knew how he would get them for it.

He would make them all pay.

***

Trevor sat in his Pontiac and waited for the streetlights to come on. Real freedom was to be had tonight. He knew their plan. He'd figured it out. But his plan was better, and it had taken all of the four days since his release to set it up.

Nobody pulls the wool over my eyes. Nobody.

He checked his mirrors. A few vehicles drove past his car, but nothing looked untoward. As far as Trevor could tell, no one was watching him.

He looked down at the passenger seat. The Louisville Slugger sat smiling at him. For a minute he could almost hear it talking to him, caressing his ear with words of duty and honor. It would do what it was made for. It would serve him. It would be loyal. But most of all, it wouldn't judge him.

He looked in the rearview mirror again and saw someone sitting in his backseat.

"Hello Mrs. Gavin." Trevor didn't even jump. It was a common event when the owners of the shoes he had recently stolen would pay him a visit. They often hung around for days on end. Usually until he stole another pair. Then he'd get a new visitor. They always watched when he would masturbate on their shoes, until he got a new pair.

"Trevor."

"Lovely evening," he said.

She nodded at him. Then said, "Why are you going to do it? You don't have to."

"Because. I do have to. I need my freedom."

"But those women are innocent."

"Isn't everyone?" he asked.

"Trevor, walk away. The lawyer wasn't playing you. You're too smart for that. Let it go."

Trevor shook his head and looked across the street at the shoe store. It was 9:21pm. They would be closing in nine minutes. He had to leave in seven.

"They played me. I know their kind. But tonight they pay for it."

"You used to work at a shoe store. Over ten years, until you got fired. All those women you sold shoes to, and then looked their names up off their credit cards. Following them home and taking the shoes they'd bought." Mrs. Gavin looked down at her lap. "Trevor, how many women have you killed?"

"I'm smart. They will never catch me."

"Trevor, how many?"

"I lost count after I'd collected 120 pairs of shoes. Sometimes I'd killed them, but didn't get the shoes in time. Only two had been unconscious and walked away, but they didn't report it to the police. I got them both, days later. Don't worry Mrs. Gavin, I clean up my mistakes."

"Is that why you started selling vacuums? To clean up after and have a plausible reason to be in the victim's house?"

"What is this? Why are you so curious? You're dead. Fuck off!"

He looked at the clock. 9:26pm.

Time to go.

Trevor eased out of the driver's seat and walked around to his trunk. He opened it and retrieved two red cans filled with gasoline. After slamming the trunk, he opened the passenger side door and grabbed his partner, Louisville.

A distant pair of headlights were coming toward him. They were too far to see him yet. He hustled across the street to the small strip mall, and opened the shoe store door.

The young female clerk walked toward him, key in hand.

"Oh, sorry sir, but we're closing right now. Could you come back tomorrow?"

He set the gas cans down and looked to the right. Another clerk was helping a woman in her forties try on a pair of black heels. He counted three women in total.

"I'm sorry. I was on my way home from the baseball game," he said, and then pointed at the gas cans. "I ran out of gas. My car is a block away, and then I remembered my wife said she needed a pair of red pumps. I cannot go home without a red pair of pumps, size eight."

He smiled in his best car salesmen role.

The clerk with the key couldn't be over twenty-five years old. She looked at the other clerk with a question on her face. The other clerk nodded.

"Let me lock the door so no one else comes in, and then we'll set you up."

"Oh, thank you, thank you."

Trevor glanced at the walls looking for the pumps. They were right behind the older clerk who was still helping their last customer. He saw Mrs. Gavin standing in the corner shaking her head. He almost shouted for her to leave. These women were his. He was even getting an erection, and Mrs. Gavin could ruin it all for him.

The lock clicked behind him. The young clerk pulled down the blinds on the two large front windows, and yanked the chain on the *open* neon sign to turn it off.

He stood leaning on Louisville and waited.

She turned to him, pocketed the store key and said, "What you're looking for is right over there."

She didn't see it coming. He leaned down as if to set the bat on the floor, but in fact he was winding up. The Louisville came around on a smooth curveball responding arc and connected with the side of the clerk's head in the temple area. It hit her so hard that he heard the audible crack of her skull.

He couldn't believe his luck. A home run with one hit.

He turned to the other women. Both their faces were masks of shock. They were paralyzed with fear. Neither one moved.

He jumped around a square floor display of sandals. His wooden partner hit the back of the customer's head as she tried to duck, knocking her to the floor.

"Now if that isn't a sack of potatoes, I don't know what is. I should've tried out for the majors," he yelled.

The older clerk was screaming now. She bolted for the back room. Trevor gave chase.

Damn is she fast, he thought.

Behind the counter, around a corner, into the small doorway and into the back room, he chased her. She started tossing piles of shoe boxes down behind her. He tripped over a couple and lost ground as she ran for the back door.

"Fuck!"

How could he have known the back door would've been open?

He righted himself and continued to run, this time hopping over boxes and dodging the others.

She was five feet from the back door. She would disappear in seconds.

He stopped, wound up and threw the baseball bat with everything he could muster.

The bat raced across the open air, pinwheeling as it went.

It was a perfect throw. At the moment it would have hit her head, she made the door and dropped from view as she turned the corner.

The bat hit the outside stairwell railing and clanged down the stairs behind the fleeing clerk.

"Fuck, fuck, fuuucckkk!"

"She's going to call the police," Mrs. Gavin whispered in his ear.

"I know."

He ran to the back door and looked outside. She was gone. Nothing moved at all. He grabbed his partner, locked the door and bolted the three locks along its frame.

Then he ran back to the front and retrieved one gas can. He opened it and soaked the front of the store in gasoline. He grabbed the other can, coughed a few times at the fumes, and ran for the stockroom. He started near the back door and began soaking everything around it. With all the shoes and cardboard boxes, he knew the shoe store would go fast.

He'd done it before. When they almost caught him five years ago at his previous job selling shoes, he had to burn the store down. Almost didn't get out that time, but he had a better plan tonight.

After emptying both cans of their burden, he tossed them aside and made his way back to the two women lying dead or unconscious on the carpeted floor.

The fumes were becoming overwhelming.

"You should've done this first and then poured out the gas," Mrs. Gavin said.

"Fuck off Mrs. Gavin."

The young clerk wore running shoes. Nothing much sexy about that. He turned to the customer. Her feet were bare because she had been about to try a pair on. He glanced around and found the boots she had come to the store in. They were worn, ugly, brown boots with a small zipper on the side.

"Motherfucker. I hate when they aren't sexy shoes. Now I can't even finish on these women. Ugly fucking whores."

Time to leave.

He grabbed the bat and started pounding on the wall two feet in front of the counter. He knew exactly where to make contact. Yesterday, he had played the role of a comic book store owner from Los Angeles. He was in the area scouting locations for the next big store. The landlord of the strip mall had given him a tour of the empty unit beside the shoe store.

There was no alarm system currently monitoring the empty unit. Yesterday he saw that the lock was a thumb latch on the inside. It would work perfectly.

After ten hits with his loyal partner, he had broken through the drywall. The hole was big enough to crawl through.

He brought out a pack of matches, lit one, and tossed it toward the back room. Instantly, the gas caught, flames rising like a witch burning. A second match produced the same result at the front of the small shoe store.

He waited and watched. It was good to burn. He loved the heat.

Mrs. Gavin watched him from the far corner. She was shaking her head in disgust.

He flipped her the bird.

The young clerk's hair caught. He waited a moment more to watch her skin start to melt near her neck.

Trevor smiled. He was free. This is what freedom meant. Freewill. To do as he pleased. At all times.

He slid his one leg all the way through and bent to pass into the empty unit. Then someone started screaming.

He looked back into the store. The customer had woken up. The hit must've not been as hard as he figured. She stood up off the carpeted floor and scurried around, her hair and face aflame.

The wail that came out of those melting lips caused Trevor to almost tear up in pleasure. A light popped from the heat, making him jump.

He laughed.

"My job is only half done tonight. Gotta go. Bye."

He slipped the rest of the way through the hole and ran to the back of the empty unit. It was an "L" shaped unit with the back door on the side of the complex; which meant that, if someone was watching the front of the shoe store, or the back, they couldn't see him exit.

He opened the side door slowly. No one in sight.

Trevor slipped out, closed the door, and ran along the building toward the side street where, two blocks up, he'd parked the rented van.

He walked slow, so as not to attract unnecessary attention. He heard a siren in the distance. A woman was screaming. It had to be the older clerk that got away out the back door. She'd called the authorities and now she watched the flames burn her co-worker.

All in a day's work.

Also, Mrs. Gavin was gone.

Maybe that young clerk will come talk to me now. Or maybe not. I didn't steal her shoes, after all.

He got to the van, started it, and raced away from the burning shoe store intent on finishing the evening properly.

***

When they'd released him from prison, they were obligated to give him back his key. The one that nobody could figure out what it opened.

He thought about that, and how close they came to finding his storage unit. He pulled up in front of it. No one had followed him, and he was sure the storage unit facility was empty.

He was completely alone with a vehicle that wasn't traceable to him.

He opened the unit and stood staring at all the boxes of shoes and mementoes from the whores he'd killed. He was amazed at what he had amassed over the last fifteen years.

A cool evening breeze picked up and brushed across his face as he felt emotions rising in him. It brought him back to when his mother would dress him up in high heels at the age of five. She'd always wanted a girl. She even called him girl's names until he was ten years old and demanded he be called Trevor, as that was his real name.

She'd beat him and humiliate him for being male, but he got used to it. He wanted to be a girl too, just so he could please his mother. But nothing pleased her. Nothing ever could.

He remembered the day he killed her. He was nineteen. She was sitting alone in the living room, knitting another pair of pink winter gloves for him because he always lost his.

Of course I lost them, you fucking whore. I could never wear that shit.

The thought brought his smile to a solid line. Whenever he recalled memories of his mother, he brooded. She got off too easy. He should have hacked her to pieces instead of using the pillow on her face to suffocate her. He should have torn her vagina out to make her a man.

Just to see how it feels, bitch.

After all the times she kicked or punched him in the groin, she'd explain that it wouldn't hurt that much if he didn't have that fucking stuff. He couldn't remember a week where she didn't kick him in the balls or try to tear them off. He was surprised when he grew up that everything still worked.

"Yeah, well, fuck you, mom. You're dead, and I'm sending as many whores as I can with you to hell."

He started unloading the storage unit, filling the back of the van.

Halfway through, he thought he heard someone walking. He stopped and listened.

Nothing.

No way. No one could be out here.

He started loading the van again.

A firecracker went off somewhere. He felt pain in his left leg. The boxes in his hands fell from his grip.

"What the…?"

Trevor lost his balance and dropped to the concrete. He looked down and saw blood coming out of his jeans below the knee.

I've been shot? he asked himself, not believing it.

"Good evening, Mr. Ashton."

That asshole faggot with the dangling earring stepped out of the shadows. It was the same asshole who arrested him at his apartment almost a year ago.

"You know, I knew that key was for a storage unit. All the guys back at the station kept trying to figure out where the secret compartment was at your place. But, I thought for sure that you'd store everything off site. Wait until they hear I was right."

"How did…how did you find me?" Trevor asked, the pain reaching intolerable levels.

The cop stepped closer, a gun extended in his right hand. "Prior to your release, I canvassed every single storage facility in the greater metro area. Do you realize just how many there are? Man, it took me almost two months to get to this one. The owner, a nice German fellow, said you come and go at night, but he sees you here and there. He recognized your photo, but without a warrant, I couldn't get the exact unit number. No judge was going to give me a warrant with you being released and the charges dropped. No way this side of Sunday."

"Released? Charges dropped?" Trevor said as he sidled up against the brick wall. "My lawyer, Vincenzo. What he said was true? You guys weren't playing me? I was released for real?"

The cop laughed.

What an asshole.

"Of course. He's your lawyer. We don't play games. People could be killed if we released potential murderers without proper documentation. There really was a technicality problem. You were free to go. But not now. Look at this warehouse. You could open a shoe store with all these, and my guess is that I will find fingerprints on dozens of these shoes that'll point to persons deceased. Am I right?"

"Fuck you. I can't believe Mrs. Gavin was right."

"What? Mrs. Gavin? What the hell are you talking about?"

"Nothing."

The cop raised his weapon and fired from four feet away. The bullet tore into Trevor's right knee.

"Holy shit! What are you doing?"

"Killing you, because you don't deserve to live."

"You're a cop. You can't do that. You have to read me my rights."

The cop was shaking his head. "Nope. Tried that once. Didn't work. The justice system sucks for guys like you. This is the only way to cure you. Think of it like I'm doing you a favor."

"*This* is a favor?"

"Yeah, watch."

The cop closed one eye and aimed slowly in circles.

"No. Wait." Trevor begged.

The gun went off. He felt a punch in his groin. Trevor looked down. The bullet ripped a hole in his crotch, severing his penis, and ripping the skin off the edge of his scrotum.

"There, all cured. See ya around."

Trevor screamed. The cop walked away.

"You can't leave me here. I'll bleed to death. I can't walk!"

"That's the idea."

"They'll catch you. You can't kill people and get away with it."

"You did."

After a moment, Trevor heard him say from the darkness on the other side of the van, "The gun I used is untraceable. This will go down like a simple robbery. I'll write the report myself and make sure the judge hears about what's inside your little storage unit. I'll be back in an hour in my cruiser after I receive the call that there's gunfire in the area…"

The pain rose to excruciating. He couldn't hear the cop anymore.

His life source slowly ebbed from the three new holes in his body.

He looked up at the stars, but couldn't find God.

Mrs. Gavin sat beside him, smiling. He looked away, his strength diminishing.

His mother stood in front of the van now.

He forced his eyes open to stare at his mother.

"Fuck you, mom. Fuck you. It's all your fault. Every woman I killed was for you."

His eyes shut. The pain ceased.

Then nothing.

***

The inspiration for this story by author, Jonas Saul:

Back when I was twenty-three years old, I walked door-to-door selling Kirby vacuum cleaners for $1899.00 each. I sold a considerable amount and made good money. It wasn't about sales as much as it was about being a Master-Closer: always closing the sale with everything you say. I came up with the idea of a shoe-collector/murderer working as a vacuum cleaner salesman because the cover was great. He had every excuse to be in multiple rooms of the house where investigators would locate his DNA. He could be at the scene of the crime and unless someone actually saw him doing the act, he couldn't be prosecuted. Of course, my character actually does murder women, but that's besides the point.

If It Wasn't For Sylvia

by Christi Craig

Sylvia Drake had a knack for killing things, which seemed loosely related to a line running from the base of her palm. "Straight to the middle finger," a psychic pointed out a year ago. "Your luck. Very bad."

"That doesn't even begin to explain it," Sylvia had said, as she broke down. With that, the psychic pulled Sylvia's hand to her chest, leaned over the table, and promised Sylvia a cure.

Sylvia paid the extra money and, since then, began her days exactly the same way. She turned her head towards the East before she opened her eyes in the morning. Carefully, she rose out of bed, stepped into her slippers and threw on her robe, tying the belt right over left and then left over right. She made her way straight to the kitchen, taking twelve steps in a row and then hopping once to avoid "unlucky thirteen." Once at the kitchen counter, she shook a dash of salt into her right palm, let the grains slide down to the tips of her fingers, and tossed them over her left shoulder. From the pocket of her robe, she pulled out a tiny bell and rang it in a continuous movement from her feet to her head and back down again.

"There," she always said out loud when she finished. She had to admit, she was feeling better. But, she still couldn't keep a vase of fresh flowers alive for more than a day. That would be the real sign – the burning bush – that proved her luck had turned.

Bad luck hadn't always plagued Sylvia. She won the cake raffle at the school fair three years in a row in middle school. She was her mother's good luck charm that time her mother dragged Sylvia and her little sister out to Las Vegas while her father was there for business. Her father spent two whole days in meetings, and Sylvia's mother got tired of sitting by the pool and watching Disney movies on the hotel room TV with Sylvia and her little sister. So, her mother sneaked the two of them into the hotel casino to play some slot machines. Sylvia was supposed to be reading a book to her sister. Her mother only wanted half an hour, she said. But, on accident, Sylvia punched the play button. Her mother pinched her, but then the machine lit up and started playing music. Twenty dollars, scrolled up on the digital screen. Then, her mother slapped Sylvia's shoulder and told her to push it again, and again when the casino concierge wasn't looking. Her mother hauled in two hundred dollars that night, and she took them to dinner. Sylvia got to sip a virgin Strawberry Daiquiri out of a giant plastic wine goblet to celebrate.

Everything changed when Sylvia got to high school and turned arrogant. "What happened to my sweet little girl?" Her mother liked to hiss when they fought about curfews and Sylvia let her swear words fly. Sylvia dragged her best friend Betsy into her mother's bathroom one afternoon to show her the antique hand mirror her mother kept on her dresser. She knew better. Her mother warned her not to touch it, not to break it, for more reasons than just bad luck, but her mother's words were like a dare. She held up the mirror and started making fun of her mother, who had begun to look like the wicked stepmother in the Snow White movie her little sister watched in repetition. Betsy laughed when Sylvia twirled around chanting "mirror, mirror" in a sing-song way, so she twirled faster and faster and then she lost her grip. The mirror fell and broke into three pieces. Sylvia picked them up and begged Betsy to help her glue them back together. But the pieces wouldn't stick, and Sylvia cut her hand trying to press them into the frame. Her mother was livid. She frightened Sylvia with a raised fist and a curse of "seven years."

It didn't take long for the bad luck to kick in. Sylvia broke the handle on the front door of the church when she tried to open it on her way to confession that next Sunday. She managed to kill every plant in the house the weekend that her mother went away with her girlfriends. All Sylvia had to do was water them once – which she did, she told her mother – but they all turned yellow and limp. Then, Betsy called her one night and told her out of the blue not to come over for a while. It had something to do with Betsy's little brother and his hamster that died the last time he let Sylvia hold it.

"He thinks you held it too tight," Betsy said, "and that's why the hamster died." Sylvia laughed off the idea but rubbed the soft flesh between her thumb and index finger where the hamster had bit her. "He's such a brat," Betsy agreed. "But my mother can't stand to see him cry. I'll see you at school."

Later that summer, Sylvia caused a car accident when she rode her bike across the street. She wasn't hurt, but the driver in one car screamed for an ambulance and walked away with a neck brace.

"Seven years," her mother taunted her.

When Sylvia's sister started collecting injuries while Sylvia was babysitting, her mother's taunting turned to concern. It was her own fault, Sylvia whined. Her sister rode too fast on her bike down the hill of the driveway and cut her leg on a rock when she fell. She climbed the tree near the wood pile, fell, and broke her arm. She pulled away from Sylvia's grip when she was yelling at her, for being a total dimwit and not listening, and she ran out into the street. Sylvia couldn't catch her in time.

"I should never have put you in charge," her mother whispered at the hospital. She didn't speak to Sylvia at the funeral. And she barely glanced in the direction of the front door when Sylvia finally moved out. "You're almost eighteen anyway," her mother said, as she stared at a vase of dead flowers on the coffee table.

Sylvia jumped around from job to job for a while after that, quitting each one after some mysterious accident or another. Her time at the Bridgetown Mall pet store maxed out after six months, when the whole flock of canaries keeled over the first night she closed alone. She lasted a little longer at Maxine's Flower Shop on Main, until Maxine invited her to help with some flower arrangements. A fresh delivery of roses for a wedding wilted within hours of opening the box. But it was the near-death experience at the Harwood public library that really freaked her out. Sylvia was shelving books in the back. She worked in the back on purpose, turning down a promotion for a front desk position, so that she stayed out of everyone's way. She couldn't be completely to blame when Mrs. Cornelius tripped over Sylvia's foot and hit her head against a shelf. She could be blamed, however, for taking too long to call 911. It was just that Sylvia panicked at the sight of all that blood, some of it on her own hand after she reached down to help Mrs. Cornelius. Most of all, she feared the truth: that she really was a catalyst for death. Sylvia resigned from the library the next day, to save the others, she told herself.

That's how she ended up at Peterson's Funeral Home, a one-stop shop when it came to bereavement services. Dick Peterson needed someone who was willing to work the front *and* back of the funeral home. After she begged him, saying she'd answer phones, file papers, work the grounds, whatever, he hired her. The grounds, she said, wouldn't be a problem. She'd been in charge of the yard at her house when she was in high school. And, while she wasn't exactly sure what "preparations" meant, she'd do whatever it took.

He scribbled some notes and mentioned make-up. "On clients," he said, as he raised an eyebrow.

She answered, Yes! A little too enthusiastic. She wasn't afraid, she told him, to touch a corpse. Surrounded by death, she figured, she couldn't possibly do any more harm.

Peterson's Funeral Home sat right off the main highway that ran through the city of Harwood. It was a simple building, but it sat on the prettiest lot around. Sylvia often took walks around the cemetery during lunch and made up stories about the people who were laid to rest there. Inside, decorations were kept at a minimum and any greenery was made of plastic. With fake plants and clients coming in on a stretcher, Sylvia had little to worry about in the way of killing. Mr. Peterson, himself, looked to be on a path of destruction that would have nothing to do with Sylvia. He weighed more than Mrs. Peterson was comfortable with, as evidenced by the lunches she packed for Mr. Peterson: salads, raw vegetables, "rabbit food," as he called it. He was diabetic, he told Sylvia once, but he wasn't dead.

Yet, she thought.

She kept her distance, because she wanted to keep her job.

Sylvia moved to an apartment closer to the funeral home, she coaxed her mother out for coffee once every few months, and she tracked down that psychic, the best in the county, she'd heard. Wake up to the East, never walk more than twelve steps at a time, throw the salt and ring the bell. Bad luck couldn't last forever, she told herself.

The atmosphere at Peterson's was quiet and meditative, and Sylvia grew accustomed to working and living alone. She spent her time in the office or in the preparation room and considered herself an artist of sorts when it came to dressing the dead. She was in charge of "setting the scene," as Mr. Peterson called it, and she painted faces, sculpted hair, and shaped hands in an effort to recreate what was once living. And, like many artists, her work elicited tears, anger, sometimes disbelief.

Speaking of work, a Mr. Clive Barrows would be waiting for her this morning, his wake set for the evening.

Clive Barrows, age 62, loving husband of Virginia, father of Sharon Miller (nee Barrows) and Justin Barrows. Five grandchildren. Worked 20 years at the Harwood Post Office. Member of the "Oldies but Goodies" bowling team (Tournament champions in 2000 and 2001), fixture at Jimmy's Bar on the corner of Highway 10 and Meadow Ridge Drive.

Sylvia guessed, after typing out the obituary, that Clive Barrows was overweight. Jimmy's Tavern was famous for Deep Fried Onions, Jalapeño Poppers, and Dollar Taps during happy hour. As Sylvia put on her coat, she predicted a face with smooth transitions from cheek to chin and a bulbous nose that would require an extra layer of foundation, to cover broken capillaries. And perhaps some bruising. Mrs. Barrows had mentioned an "accident." A bar fight, or a car accident. Either way.

When Sylvia opened the door to the funeral home, she ran straight into someone other than Mr. Peterson. This man was thin and tall. He wore a white shirt and tie and smelled of cigarette smoke masked by cologne. And, when she stepped back and looked up, she saw a smooth, young face and with a head full of chestnut brown hair.

"Sorry about that," he said. He put both hands on Sylvia's shoulders and directed her out of his way. Then, he bounded past and ran to little gray coupe parked right outside. It took Sylvia a few seconds to recover. He'd touched her. He didn't know. She watched him through the glass of the front door, as he searched for something in his car, until she heard Mr. Peterson call her name.

Mr. Peterson sat in his office chair, his hands behind his head.

"I'm interviewing that young man today, Sylvia." She'd forgotten he'd put out a want ad. Mr. Peterson was hinting at retirement, or at least reducing his work hours, and he planned on taking Mrs. Peterson on a month-long cruise soon. "I want you to meet him," he told Sylvia. "He's a good fit, I think." Mr. Peterson looked past Sylvia and nodded. She turned around.

"Max Cooper," said Mr. Peterson, "meet Sylvia Drake."

Max walked up to Sylvia with his outstretched hand. She studied his hand for a second: clean, strong. His hair slipped across his forehead and hung just above his eyes. Very blue eyes. Sylvia's whole core warmed up by ten degrees, and she felt dizzy. She pulled at her shirt and folded her hands together.

"Sylvia doesn't shake hands," Mr. Peterson explained. "Nothing personal, Max."

Max shrugged. "That's too bad." He winked at her. "Here are my references, Mr. Peterson," he said, as he handed him a paper and leaned on the desk. He pointed at something and nodded, sending his hair forward again. He brushed it back, stood up straight, and turned to face Sylvia again.

"How old are you?" she blurted out.

Both Max and Mr. Peterson cocked their heads.

"You look—" too good, she thought "—so young," she said, "to want to work at a funeral home," she said. Mr. Peterson cleared his throat.

"I'm twenty-eight," Max said, confident, "I was top of my class at Northwestern. I did an internship at Roth and Brown, which isn't in bereavement services but is sales just the same. And what about you, Ms. Sylvia Drake?"

He was arrogant. All the good-looking ones are, she thought. She tucked her hair behind her ear. Her jaw tightened.

Max waved his hand. "No, no, I'm just teasing. But —" he paused. "I'm pretty good at guessing." He walked a circle around her, which sent goose bumps up her back. He rubbed his chin. Sylvia looked away. "I'd say…you're twenty-five?" He held the last syllable when Sylvia squinted at him. "Twenty-two."

He was good.

"And what do you do around here, Sylvia?"

Mr. Peterson spoke up, saying Sylvia was his right-hand gal. He explained how she worked every inch of this place and then some. "Except she doesn't get her hands dirty, if you know what I mean." Max said he didn't know. "Embalming. That's up to my son Stewart." He went on to call Sylvia valuable, irreplaceable, said he was lucky to have her.

Lucky.

Max took a step towards her and reached down to the floor.

"Looks like you dropped this." He handed her a newspaper clipping: Mr. Barrows' obituary. When she took it from him, his fingers brushed hers. She swallowed hard.

"Mr. Barrows?" she asked, without saying thank you to Max. "He's in the back I presume?"

"See? Always working," Mr. Peterson said. Max nodded and ran his fingers through his hair again. Sylvia looked at her watch and told herself she didn't have time for all this. For Max. She hoped he would stay out front.

Mr. Peterson was the one who wanted an assistant. She would keep to herself in the back, on the grounds, buried in paperwork.

She pushed through the swinging doors that led from the lobby to the back of the funeral home, to the long hallway that took her to the preparation room. To her relief, the temperature shifted. A hint of formaldehyde filled the air. Stewart must have left fairly recently. Stewart usually worked during the night hours and slipped out just before dawn. Sylvia had only seen him once, when a fire at the nursing home had left three dead from smoke inhalation and he was caught working later than usual. When she walked in on him, her blood ran cold. Stewart was pale, wax-like, and the only reason she knew he wasn't an apparition was because he had jumped, screamed like a girl, and then turned beet red. She thought he might be shy and soft-spoken, but once he opened his mouth, he surprised her with his foul language.

"Can't you fucking knock?" and "I've been up all God-damned night," followed by "Jesus Christ, you scared the living shit out of me." Then, he stared her down until she backed out of the room. Now, when the air smelled too strong of chemicals, she made a point to peek in the window of the door before she burst in.

In the preparation room, Sylvia put on a white jacket, for warmth as much as for cleanliness. She ran her hands under hot water, dried them, and slipped on her gloves. Then, she pulled back the sheet that covered Clive Barrows.

He was exactly as she predicted, which meant moving him from the gurney to the coffin would be cumbersome. Mr. Peterson wasn't always the best helper when it came to lifting. He had a bad back, among other issues. She debated if she should get Mr. Peterson right away, when she realized she might need his help in getting Mr. Barrows dressed.

His family had sent along a pair of overalls and cowboy boots. The button-down shirt would be easy enough to maneuver, but the overalls.... She held them up and considered the size and stiffness of the denim. Then, she reached into the bag and retrieved a photo of Mr. Barrows. And, a beer stein. She shook her head; the things people wanted to bury with the dead, she never understood.

She spread the clothes out on a table and set up the photo. Then, she reached into the cabinet below and pulled out her box of make-up. In the year that Sylvia had been working for Mr. Peterson, she had acquired a full palette of colors for the face, eyes, eyebrows and lips. She studied the photo of Mr. Barrows and decided warm beige would suit him. Sandstone lipstick matched the color of his lips in the photo. Looking at Mr. Barrows now, she saw that his eyebrows, full and a bit unruly, wouldn't need any color but might require a touch of hairspray. As she turned back to the table, she heard the squeak of the swinging door. She turned around, expecting Mr. Peterson. Instead, she saw Max.

He stood in the doorway, grinning, until Sylvia addressed him with her own Stewart-like stare.

"Mr. Peterson sent me," he said. "He thought you might need a hand."

"He just interviewed you." Sylvia balled up the overalls and then shook them out again.

Max walked over to the gurney. "He said I should start right away. Mentioned something about Barrows being a two-man job. I can see why. You do the make-up?" he asked.

Sylvia unbuttoned the shirt for Barrows. "I get them ready. Make-up, hair, clothes. I don't really need your help." She looked back at Mr. Barrows. "Well. I might need help moving him around."

He pulled the sheet back a little more. "Does it ever get to you?"

Sylvia started to speak, stopped, and then looked right at Max. "I work alone, Mr. Cooper. If you'll just help me get him into these overalls, and the coffin...." She handed him a pair of gloves.

They dressed Mr. Barrows in silence. It took the two of them together to get the boots on, and Sylvia was grateful for the gloves; her hand bumped into Max's twice. Then, Max stepped back towards the door.

"Now what?" he asked.

Sylvia held up her make-up box. She laid out foundation, blush, the lipstick. She smoothed back Mr. Barrows' hair with a comb, then parted it on the side and made a nice crescent-shape curve with his bangs. The sides of his hair were a bit long, so she tucked them behind his ears. He looked distinguished, she thought. Then, she unbuttoned the collar of his shirt so she could put on his face without smearing make-up on the shirt.

With her thumbs, she massaged the foundation onto his skin – as a last rites, of sort. For Mr. Barrows, she took care to spread the foundation into the base of his hairline and covered the bruising around his nose. Maybe he left the tavern in a drunken stupor, fell, and hit his head and face on the curb. Maybe he died in a car accident that wasn't his fault. Either way, he deserved a gentle touch. She put on a new set of gloves and shaped his eyebrows with hairspray. After she dabbed at his mouth with the lipstick, she let out a long sigh. She looked back at Max, who was still standing in the corner, and said Mr. Barrows was ready to move.

When it came to lifting, Mr. Barrows proved to be heavier than they expected, and they dropped him into the coffin, hard. Max apologized, to Sylvia or to Mr. Barrows, she wasn't sure. She buttoned the collar of Mr. Barrows' shirt all the way to the top, smoothed out the straps of the overalls. Then, she placed his beer stein into his perfectly folded hands.

"You're good," Max said. "But there's just one thing." He picked up the photo of Barrows. "This is him?" He asked. He looked from the photo to Mr. Barrows and back again. "He's too...stiff."

Sylvia rolled her eyes. "You're trying to be funny."

"No, I mean, stiff as in straight. Look at this picture," he said. He showed it to Sylvia again. "Here, he's jolly. He would never wear his collar buttoned up so tight. His hair is all roughed up in this photo. You've made it too, well, done. And, can't you make him smile a little?"

Sylvia pursed her lips and a surge of anger forced the air out of her nose. She started to explain to Max about the science of the dead, about the fact that the expression they wear in their last breath is the expression they wear to the grave, but Mr. Peterson burst in through the doors.

"Family," he said, winded. "They're early. Mr. Barrows—" he waved his arm in a frantic circle, "—to the viewing room."

Mr. Peterson left to settle in the family, and Sylvia threw her make-up back into her box. When she looked up, Max stood over Mr. Barrows with his hands in the coffin.

"What are you doing?"

He held up the photo again. "I don't see why the family gives you a picture if you ignore it. I'm just adding a few final touches." Then, he closed the lid and nodded to Sylvia. "All set." Sylvia stormed towards the coffin and reached out her hand to raise the lid.

"Sylvia!" Mr. Peterson stuck his head in the doorway again. "The viewing!"

Sylvia shot Max a look and together they pushed Mr. Barrows through the open doors.

The family stood, sat, stood again. No one approached Mr. Barrows at first. But after Max opened the lid and stepped back, a woman that Sylvia could only assume was Virginia made her way to the coffin and stood there. The woman grabbed hold of the edge of the coffin and wavered a bit. Then she turned to Max, to Sylvia, to Mr. Peterson. Her eyes welled up.

Disbelief, Sylvia thought. She'd seen it before. But Virginia began to speak, and she said something Sylvia had not expected.

"He's perfect. Thank you."

Max nodded, in respect, and Sylvia stood up on her toes to see Mr. Barrows with his hair askew, his collar undone, his beer stein in one hand and his other hand turned palm up so that he appeared to be flipping off anyone who viewed him.

"Just like the photo," Max whispered to Sylvia. He winked and bumped her with his elbow. "I think they like our work."

"Dammit. Don't touch me," she sneered.

"You're mad?"

Sylvia wouldn't look at him.

"Come on, Sylvia." He gestured to the family, now gathered around Mr. Barrows, crying, laughing, and hugging. "Look at them. They're more relieved to see him like they remember him than in some stiff presentation."

"Stop saying that. Stiff. That's not funny. This is a funeral. He's dead. They might like what you did, but I don't." Sylvia turned to go. She stopped short though and looked back in his direction. "And, neither will Mr. Peterson." She shook her head and squinted, hoping to put the fear in Max.

Instead, he smiled.

Always, he smiled.

She didn't know what got to her more, the curl of his lips or his hand in her work. She left the room and spent the rest of the afternoon in the office, filing paperwork and fuming over the mix of emotion Max stirred up in her.

She ignored Max, too, for the whole next week, which wasn't too difficult. Mr. Peterson kept him busy, showing him around the grounds, teaching him about the art of coffin sales, schooling him on the various funeral packages Peterson's offered. Max picked up lunch for the three of them on Friday, but Sylvia declined his invitation to join them in the break room. She ate alone, she said, and claimed she had to organize supplies and clean the plants. Later that afternoon, she made a fresh pot of coffee and took two cups to Mr. Peterson's office, under the guise of checking in with Mr. Peterson. Max had taken over the space that was the sitting area in Mr. Peterson's office, and he had his feet up on the coffee table. He sat up when Sylvia walked in and offered to take the coffee. She walked around him and set the cups on Mr. Peterson's desk.

For several weeks, Sylvia spoke to Max only when necessary and never said more than she needed to say. He tried to engage her, though. He brought her a brochure of the flower arrangements and asked her about the details on the mums. She directed him to Mr. Peterson. He came to her with the price list for coffins and wondered out loud if she thought they should run a discount for older models. She gestured to Mr. Peterson's office. Finally, Max showed up in her office and set a coupon for lunch at the Winslow Inn on her desk.

"What?" she said, as she glanced at the coupon. "Winslows is nice. I'm sure Mr. Peterson would like lunch out."

"It's not for Mr. Peterson."

Sylvia's face felt hot.

"It's for you and me."

She pushed the coupon back towards Max and shook her head.

"Come on, Sylvia. Mr. Peterson leaves next week for his month-long cruise. It'll be you and me, and we can't go on not talking. I thought we could go to lunch, get to know each other better. I could make it up to you, that whole Barrows bit." He pushed the coupon back to her.

She looked at it. "It says 'one free lunch buffet.'" She raised her eyebrows.

"I figure you don't eat much. We'll share a plate."

She rolled her eyes.

"I'm kidding. I'll buy my own. Yours is free. You pay with the coupon. It'll be lunch between colleagues. I'll tell you everything you want to know and you can tell me what you love about this place."

He leaned on her desk. His hair bobbed above his forehead again. He wouldn't break his gaze. So blue.

Dammit, she thought.

"Fine," she said. "On Friday. Fridays always seem to be quiet."

He slapped the desk. "Okay then. Friday. Me and you and Winslows."

Thursday night, Sylvia stared into her closet. She never had trouble deciding what to wear for work. This is ridiculous, she thought. But there she sat, studying her wardrobe, or lack of one. She pulled out a skirt and a pair of khakis and dug through shirts. In the back of her closet, she reached for the pair of shoes she wore last year – when she took herself to the Linden Hotel for a New Year's Eve cocktail. The shoes weren't fancy, but they were more than her usual black flats. She decided on a simple V-neck shirt with a loose, black skirt that hit just above her knees. She chided herself the whole time she ironed the skirt and dug through her jewelry box for a pair of hoop earrings.

The next morning, she woke up early and forgot to open her eyes to the East. She panicked, then forced herself to stay in bed another fifteen minutes, hoping to fool the Fates into thinking that she was still asleep. She tried again.

Turn to the east.

Left over right, right over left.

Step. Hop. Don't lose count.

Salt over the shoulder, twice for good measure.

Ring the bell.

Her stomach fluttered all the way to work, and when she pulled into the parking lot, she was disappointed that Max's car wasn't there. She sighed and parked herself at the front desk. Mr. Peterson came in and said good morning, but he didn't ask about Max.

By ten o'clock, when Max still didn't show, she walked into Mr. Peterson's office.

"Did Max quit?" she asked him.

Mr. Peterson scrunched his eyebrows. "Of course not. We got a call last night. I thought I left you a note on your desk. Adriana Quinn went down during the Women's Luncheon at the Presbyterian Church yesterday. Massive heart attack. Her viewing is set for tomorrow, the funeral on Sunday, so he's off meeting with the family. You know Mrs. Quinn, not to mention her daughter, always a bit of an eccentric. They're trying to keep the funeral low-key, so her sister asked that we come to them. Max will be in tomorrow. Which reminds me...." He pulled open his desk drawer and pulled out an envelope.

"Here's some petty cash. I fly out tonight with the Mrs. We're off for our cruise, God help me. She's packed three suitcases, and none of those clothes have anything to do with me." He shook his head. "Anyway, I'm giving you $500 cash in case something comes up and I'm not here to sign checks. You shouldn't need it."

Sylvia took the envelope. "Have a good time," she said, cut short by an unexplained feeling inside.

"I'll meet with Max this afternoon to finalize the details, but you'll have to keep him on track tomorrow. I trust you. I'd stay, but my wife would kill me. Hell, the cruise might kill me!" He let out grunting sort of laugh and closed his desk drawer. "Better start the paperwork." His look ushered her out of his office.

The next morning, Sylvia found Max sitting at Mr. Peterson's desk with his feet up.

"Peterson's out," he said. "I'm in charge."

"We'd better get to Mrs. Quinn," she said.

"Right." He winked. "You're in charge."

He didn't say a word about Winslow's, and neither did she. Walking down the hall to the preparation room, she told herself it was better this way. Safer, for him and for her. And really, she shouldn't care.

She wouldn't care.

She'd focus. On Mrs. Quinn.

Adriana Quinn went to meet her Lord and her beloved husband at the young age of fifty-six. Philanthropist and President of the Women's Society, Adriana Quinn directed hundreds of thousands of funds to needy organizations across the county. She is survived by one daughter, Mona, and a house full of designer shoes and clothing. Estate Sale will follow her funeral.

"Kind of a funny obit, don't you think?" Max handed her the paper, and she acted like she hadn't read it.

"I guess."

"Her daughter's a nut-case," Max said. "She paced the kitchen and smoked non-stop. Then, she insisted we bury her mother in her best 'mother fucking shoes.'" He paused to see if Sylvia would react, she was sure. "I'm quoting, just so you know."

"I'm not a prude," she said.

"Never said you were." She saw the edge of his lip curl again.

Sylvia said that she didn't know Mona personally, but she'd heard rumors about how Mona would crash her mother's Society events. The Women's Society was a lot of prestige and a little bit of volunteer work. Mona had been seen wearing combat boots with short skirts and sporting a rock star boyfriend to formal events. "Once she even got arrested, the short clip about the upset printed right next to an article on the money Mrs. Quinn helped raise at the fashion show."

"I believe it. She didn't have one nice thing to say about her mother. Mrs. Quinn's sister ended up asking her to leave, which really pissed her off."

Sylvia pulled back the sheet and uncovered Mrs. Quinn. Max stepped up behind her.

"Damn," he said.

Mrs. Quinn's face was contorted and bruised from the heart attack and fall.

"They said she hit a table pretty hard," he whispered. "Can you fix it?"

Sylvia moved to the side, giving herself some breathing room. "Probably. Looks like I'd better get started."

"Question is," he said, "can you fix her up by lunchtime? I still owe you a free buffet." His hand brushed down Sylvia's back. She jumped and ended up hunched over Mrs. Quinn. "There was a piece of lint," he said.

"You can't touch me," she told him.

"What's with that, by the way?"

She could feel her face turning red, so she fished around in the bag that held Mrs. Quinn's clothes. "I just…it's for your own good," she said. Then, she picked up the bag and moved over to the table. Max followed her.

"I don't get it."

"You won't get it. You'll think it's ridiculous, but just trust me."

He brought Sylvia her white coat and gave her a pair of gloves. "You're going to have to tell me. 'Just trust me' doesn't cut it."

Sylvia shook her head and handed him Mrs. Quinn's suit. Taking the clothes, he stepped closer.

"So. I can't shake your hand. I shouldn't brush off the lint. I can't even tap you on the shoulder. Like this?"

Sylvia dipped away from his finger.

"No." She squinted. "Not even a tap."

"What if you trip and fall, I shouldn't try to catch you?" He slipped his arm around her waist before she could move, and she lost her balance trying to pull away, and then she really was falling. He really did have his arm around her. Tight. He pulled her up, and close, and she froze.

Her knees went weak under his spell of cigarette smoke and strong cologne, and his hair tickled her nose. She was that close. And even though she hated smokers, and Max's blue eyes frightened her, or something, she wanted him. The word "love" popped into her head and ricocheted down to her stomach, up to her throat, and throbbed at her temples.

She closed her eyes. "Please."

Max loosened his arm and let her step back.

"I'm bad luck. Terrible luck." She turned back to Mrs. Quinn's things and set them along the table: the suit - "Everything I touch goes sour" - the jewelry – "to say the least" - a pair of red high-heeled shoes – "most of whatever I touch ends up dead."

"Shit," he said.

"Exactly," Sylvia said, relieved and disappointed that he finally heard her.

"Those shoes," he said.

"What?"

"Do you know what kind of shoes these are?" he asked.

She stared at him. "Are you even listening to me? I said 'dead.'"

"Valentino." He took them and turned them over, and she saw the name on the sole. "Worth a car payment, and a half," he said. "I only know that because my ex-girlfriend begged me…and I mean begged…." He paused. "Then, she threatened me…to buy her a pair. Think she ever wore them?"

"Your girlfriend? How would I know?"

He smiled. "Mrs. Quinn. I dumped the girl. I couldn't afford her." He handed the shoes back to Sylvia.

She studied them, the heel of one pressing into her palm. A glossy red peep-toe topped with a stiff red bow and dressed on the inside with smooth leather, there wasn't a mark on them. "I don't see any scuffs, not on the toes, not on the bottoms. No. They must be brand new."

"I bet they're your size. What are you, an eight?"

"Seven and a half," she said. She set them on the table and laid out the jewelry: a diamond ring with blue stones along the sides of the setting. Probably sapphire. And a necklace. Huge. If she didn't know it was Mrs. Quinn, she'd think it was costume jewelry.

Max was closer to her now. He handed her the shoes. "You should try them on." Sylvia moved to her right. He took her hand, and she jerked it away.

"God, you just don't get it. I told you…," she whispered. She was losing her grip. The more his actions repulsed her, the more they drew her to him.

"Right. Sorry. But, here. Try these on. Really."

She thought he might be nuts, based on that look in his eyes, that smile. "It's just you and me here," he said as he leaned into her. "She's never worn them. You have to."

The smells in the room were confusing her; they were intoxicating. A hint of chemicals, a waft of cologne, the smell of new leather. Sylvia's stomach flipped, her toes wiggled and her calf muscles twitched. She looked over at Mrs. Quinn. Then at Max.

"Fine, but I'm not doing it in here."

Sylvia marched out into the hallway and placed the Valentinos on the floor. Then, she slipped her feet out of her flats and rolled up her jeans. Max leaned back against the wall with arms crossed and his eyes on fire. Sylvia couldn't stand it; she turned her back to him. She stepped into the right. The left. She stood up straight.

She turned around. "Oh my," she said. She was eye to eye with Max now. "These are like a dream." She looked down at the toes, each bow teasing her with its sexy curves and shiny patent leather. "They're so comfortable. How can that be? They're so high."

"A car payment and a half," he said. "Walk the runway, Sylvia Drake."

Her heels struck the hallway floor, solid. Confident. Her whole body was electric, a far cry from the Sylvia who'd stared back at her in the mirror that morning. With her hands on her hips, she turned in one smooth action and threw her best runway pose – indifferent and entitled.

"Beautiful," Max said.

Another wave of heat rose up from her back and engulfed her.

"Don't be ridiculous." She tried to sound irritated, but in her voice she heard something else, something giddy. Heels clicking, she breezed past Max and bent over to pick up her flats. Then, she sauntered back into the doorway of the preparation room. The sight of Mrs. Quinn's body, partially uncovered, jarred her just as she walked into the room and Sylvia choked. She stumbled, then kicked off the shoes and stepped back into her own. She should have stayed out in the hallway, if only to linger a minute longer in those shoes, those feelings.

After Max helped Sylvia dress Mrs. Quinn and lift her body into the coffin, she told him to go. She brought her own lunch, plus Mrs. Quinn's family would arrive soon enough. "You're in charge now," of escorting them to the visitation room, she said, of getting the flowers arranged and set. Sylvia would finish with Mrs. Quinn.

Sylvia worked her ritual with the make-up as usual, the massage, the lipstick, an apology as she slipped the shoes onto Mrs. Quinn's feet. Before she pulled the lid closed, she hesitated. No one would notice, she thought, if Mrs. Quinn wasn't wearing shoes. She looked over her shoulder. She looked down at Mrs. Quinn.

Philanthropy was her passion. Sylvia took off the shoes and held them in her hands.

"Where is she? Goddammit!"

A young woman with cropped hair, torn jeans and a t-shirt stormed into the room and pushed Sylvia aside: Mona. Sylvia tried to wave her away – "You're not supposed to be in here –" but she was still holding the shoes, and that seemed to piss off Mona even more.

Mona grabbed the shoes from Sylvia and poked at Mrs. Quinn with the toes of them. "She looks so fucking pitiful in that coffin." Her shoulders heaved once. Then, she turned to Sylvia with a strained expression.

"I swore, this woman would never make me cry again."

"I'm sorry," Sylvia said. "I was just putting on the finishing touches." She looked at the shoes.

"And these," Mona growled. "She was such a philanthropist. My ass. She was selfish. Do you know how much time she spent at those fucking parties? How many families she could really feed if she'd skipped the shoes? She didn't need these. Look at them. She never even wore them."

Sylvia was relieved her walk down the hallway didn't leave a mark.

"They were her prized possession. Shoes, can you believe it?" She threw one shoe on the floor and gripped the other with both hands. She turned it upside down on her knee and started pushing, hard, bending the shoe, pulling at the heel.

"What are you doing?" Sylvia asked.

"Breaking it. Piece of shit." Mona pulled harder, but the shoe wouldn't give. She threw it across the room. "Get rid of those shoes," she said. "Don't you dare bury her with them. Do you hear me?" She shoved her finger into Sylvia's face. "You leave her feet bare and cold and raw, just like the people she left behind." Then, Mona turned back to her mother. "Do you hear me?" she whispered.

Sylvia said yes. She didn't move until Mona left the room. Then, she picked up the shoes and put them on the table next to her make-up box. After Mrs. Quinn's hair was brushed and her hands crossed, Sylvia slipped the shoes into a bag. She would take them. Mona was very demanding, and Mrs. Quinn was dead.

"All set," she told Max, and she helped him move Mrs. Quinn to the viewing room.

Visitors came and went for the next two hours, and all Sylvia could think of was the hallway, standing eye to eye with Max, the shoes. She felt guilty, dangerous. "A little exhausted," she told Max, even though he said, twice, that he'd pay for dinner and still not call it a date.

She'd end up taking the shoes to Goodwill, sooner or later, but for that night she kept them. She wore them while she heated up a frozen dinner, crossed her legs and swung her foot while she ate by candlelight. She sat in her chair in front of the TV and admired her toes that peeked out just beyond the patent leather, red-ribbon swirls. She sure felt pretty watching the evening news and was entranced by the new shape of her foot when she heard a knock at her door.

"Hey."

"Max!" She slammed the door, kicked off the heels and shoved them in the hall closet.

"Hey," he said again when she opened the front door wide enough for him to come in.

Pulling at her old tank top and tightening the ponytail in her hair, she considered keeping the lights turned down. Then, she brushed off her nervousness by marching right over to her couch and twisting the lamp switch. Max sat down in her chair.

He stared at her for a second and then said he was worried. "You took off, so quiet. Besides," He leaned forward. "I still owe you dinner."

"You keep saying that, though we talked about lunch, and it's too late for dinner anyway. And you don't owe me." Sylvia said she wasn't dressed for going out. She didn't have any cash, tomorrow was the funeral, and there was one more excuse she would have rattled off if Max hadn't interrupted.

"I'll wait for you to change. Appetizers and drinks on me. The funeral doesn't start until noon." Then, he blinked those damn blue eyes and brushed his hair back with his hand.

He wouldn't take no for an answer.

Sylvia relented. She stepped into her best pair of jeans but threw on a t-shirt; she put on frosted lipstick but ignored the urge to do more. She would keep Max at arm's distance, for more reasons than the fact that she was nervous as hell. She opened her own doors and leaned against the passenger side of the car as they drove and sat near the window at Hob's Tavern.

After a beer and a half, she realized that she was hungry after all. Two more beers later, she forgot all about keeping her distance. The waitress set down her beer bottle dangerously close to Max's, and Sylvia didn't bother to move it. When Max reached over Sylvia's hand to grab a sweet potato French fry from the other side of the plate, he brushed against her fingers, and she didn't flinch. Not on the outside anyway. The beer kept her calm and her eyes stayed glued to Max's eyes, and she giggled about the fact that his hair danced when he spoke.

She asked him question after question.

He was an only child, and no he didn't mind it. Really, his mom spoiled him but his dad, on the other hand, was a crusty old man with a resentment towards college. He worked as a carpenter, Max said, and never got a college degree. Max mimicked his father, who grunted and complained about these young people who thought hard work was learning how to tie your tie and press enter to send an email. "A racket! A drain of your time and money!" Max boomed, his hair bobbing in agreement.

So, Max set out to prove his dad wrong. Sure, he hadn't gotten too far; it was bad luck that he got let go from Roth and Brown, but good luck that he ended up at Peterson's.

Luck, Sylvia whispered, more to herself than to Max, and she closed her eyes.

"What about you?" he asked, his hand warming the top of hers now.

She pulled away.

"About that," he said. "The no touching. I've been thinking." Sylvia closed her eyes again. "Now hear me out," he said.

Max pointed out that Sylvia said everything she touched was ruined, or broken, or whatever.

Dead, she said to herself.

He put both hands up now. "Let's just say…what if…." He pushed his hair back and Sylvia could hardly stand it. "I initiate? Then, it isn't the same. Whatever bad luck streak you think you have doesn't count. You're not touching me, I'm touching you." He picked up her hands. "Don't move. Just watch."

He curled his fingers around her hands and held them for several minutes.

They sat in silence.

Sylvia's heart pounded.

Max kept his eyes on hers.

The waitress stopped by once and asked if they wanted another drink. "It's on the house," she said. "Some guy at the end of the bar just won the jackpot on the bar-top slot machine."

Still watching Sylvia, Max said yes and squeezed her hands. "See? It works," he said. "Let's dance."

"What?" But Sylvia went unheard. Max wouldn't let go. He pulled her to the dance floor just as Van Morrison rang out from the DJ's speakers, and Max swung her around to the tune of Moondance. Max put his hands all over Sylvia, and she let her body fall into his.

He cupped her shoulders, and she leaned back. His hands rode the curve of her spine, and she melted into a dip. Pulling her up, he spun her around and then traced the shape of her arms, sliding his hands all the way down to her palms. He laced his fingers in hers and put her arms around his waist. Sylvia forgot, for a moment, all the reasons she was bad luck.

"I didn't know dancing could be like this," she said.

Her hands found their way up his back, and she buried them in his hair. Oh, that hair. A deep breath, she took a very deep breath, taking it all in: the fog machine, the smell of spilled beer, cologne up close, a hint of sweat, happy.

After the dance, they didn't stay long at the bar. Max took her home, and she asked if he'd like to come in. *Would he like to come in!* She didn't know what she would offer him, but she definitely wanted him to stay.

This is crazy, she thought as they stood at her door. But, under the light of the moon, in the brisk, cool air, everything had changed. As Max stood behind her, his hand slid around to her stomach and he leaned down, she thought to kiss her neck. Then, he reached just past her feet.

"You have a cat?"

The neighbor's cat, usually a nuisance and mean any time he escaped outside, twisted around Sylvia's leg.

"That's Murphy. He lives upstairs. I'm not sure how he got out." She bent down too and let the cat come to her hand. Murphy rolled his head in her palm and Sylvia's hand scratched down his back. He purred.

"I know exactly how you feel," she whispered, as she scratched her way back to his neck and ears.

She shooed him over by her neighbor's door and pulled Max inside. There was kissing - oh, the kissing – and several minutes on the couch. Flushed, Sylvia stood up and said she needed a drink. Max headed off for the bathroom. While he was gone, Sylvia remembered the shoes.

She giggled as she scurried to the hall closet, grabbed the shoes, and ran to her bedroom. Max might think her a little strange, that she had the shoes, but then again, he was the one who convinced her to put them on in the first place. Standing four inches higher, Sylvia posed in front of her mirror. She let down her ponytail, put it up again, pinched her cheeks. Then, she headed towards the bedroom door.

She must have snagged a heel in the carpet, or had one too many beers, because all of a sudden she was flat on her face. She sat up, looked around, went to stand and lost her balance again. The right shoe, the one that Mona had been working on at the funeral home, bending and pulling and twisting, had given way. The heel was broken, and the shoe looked hideous on Sylvia's foot now. It was a sign, she thought. For sure, a curse from Mrs. Quinn. She should never have taken the shoes. She should never.

"You have to go," she told Max. She pushed him away and said she couldn't explain but that he really had to leave.

"Sylvia."

She stood there, unable to speak.

"It's okay," he said. "We were moving a little fast. I get it." He moved to kiss her, put his hand on her shoulder, but she winced.

"Come on."

She stood against the wall and, without touching her, he pinned her there. Then, he whispered into her ear.

"Sylvia Drake, you drive me wild. Did that first time I saw you." She closed her eyes until she heard him sigh and leave out the front door.

That night, she was restless, tossing and turning. She got up once, at four in the morning, to throw the shoes in the garbage outside. Then, she threw a pinch of salt over her shoulder for good measure. When she woke up at six, she followed the psychic's instructions to the tee.

Wake to the East.

Twelve steps and a hop.

Salt.

Ring the bell.

She looked in the mirror. Something was different, of that she was sure, but she couldn't tell if it was good or bad.

As she left for the funeral home, Sylvia ran into her neighbor on the front steps. Her neighbor sat crying, with the cat in his arms. When Sylvia asked what was wrong, the neighbor said, "Dead. Can you believe it? I found him this morning, dead on the porch."

"Was he sick?" Sylvia hoped.

"No. Healthy as a horse. A big bully, tough as nails. You know how he was a bully. He growled at you more than he meowed." The neighbor's laugh became a sob, and Sylvia's stomach tightened. She apologized and then ran to her car. Gripping the steering wheel, Sylvia drove, as slow as possible, to work, hoping to be late enough that Max would already be there. Hoping her gut instinct was wrong. But when she pulled into the parking lot, it was empty.

She walked into the funeral home just in time to hear the phone ringing.

"Sylvia?" Mr. Peterson's voice echoed over the line. "I've been calling all morning. You're late."

"Yes."

"How'd it go with Mrs. Quinn?"

"The funeral is today," she said.

"Right, right. I'm all mixed up out here, don't know a Sunday from a Monday. Jesus. Is Max around?"

"No." Sylvia swallowed hard.

"Well, track him down. Tell him to call me. We're on some island in the Bahamas for the day, and they've actually got decent service here. Tell him to call by noon your time."

"Of course." She hung up the phone and ignored the pit in her stomach. She tried Max at home.

No answer.

She called his cell and got his voicemail.

She paced the lobby and stuck her head out the front door and paced again. Then, she realized she would have to call the one person she dreaded calling: Stewart. She hated the thought of talking to Stewart, but he would know. He kept the police scanner on all night. He always knew.

"There was an accident," he said. "A grey coupe. I heard mention of St. Augustine's Hospital. Flight for life, that kind of shit. Nobody died, though."

"He's not dead?"

"Who?" Stewart asked.

"It's my fault," she said, as she hung up the phone. Then, she called him back. "Mrs. Quinn is happening today. You have to be here."

"The hell I do."

"Stewart!"

"I don't do fucking funerals. Peterson knows that."

"It's an emergency. Mr. Peterson - your *father* - I can't...I'll explain later."

Sylvia didn't wait for his answer. She hung up, grabbed the petty cash, and headed straight for her apartment. She would throw together one bag. That was all she would need. It had only been a year; she'd barely grown attached to her apartment. She scratched out a sympathy card for the neighbor, the least she could do, and tossed her bag in the trunk of the car.

Before she left, when she cleared her things out of the bathroom, she had refused to look at her reflection in the mirror. But, pulling out of her driveway, she caught her own eye as she checked the rear view mirror. She'd seen that look before, that fear and disgust. Just when she thought she was on the brink of something new, maybe even something good, she discovered that nothing had changed. Nothing would ever change. Maybe Max didn't die this time, but it wouldn't be long. Of that, she was sure.

At the information desk in St. Augustine's, she found out that Max was on the fifth floor. She had to lie and say she was family. She could have gotten in trouble, but lying was the least of her problems. When she walked into his room, she pulled back the curtain and saw him. His head was wrapped in gauze. A cast ran around his waist, crossed over his chest, and covered his left shoulder, arm, and hand. His left leg was in traction.

There was an accident, Stewart had said.

"It's my fault," she whispered again.

Max opened his eyes and turned his head slightly. "Sylvia." He tapped his right hand gently on the mattress in a gesture for her to come closer. She shook her head, unable to speak.

"Sylvia, stop." He patted the sheet again, but she still refused. "Listen. After I left your house," he explained, "I was crazy. Thinking about you. Hell, I was still a little drunk. I pulled onto the main road, and an oncoming car slammed into me. I didn't feel a thing." He had the nerve to smile. Sylvia, however, began to cry.

"Put your hand here next to mine," he said again. She reached for him and then stopped. "Dammit, Sylvia." He tried to scoot his body closer to the edge of the bed, grimacing with each millimeter. Afraid he might fall off or hurt himself again, Sylvia moved in towards him. She put her hand on the bed if only to settle him. His pinky grabbed onto hers and pulled her hand in, one finger at a time, until he could grasp the whole of it.

"Sylvia Drake," he said, "you're not so powerful. Look at me." Her eyes locked onto his and he held her there. "I'm not dead. In fact, you may have saved me."

After the accident, he said, they did a CT. They found an aneurism in his heart. "Just in time," he told her. "Surgery's tomorrow." They were confident, he said. "Caught it just in time," he told her again.

"You hear that? You think all your bad luck put me here, but your luck is what will keep me here." He tugged at her hand, so she leaned in and put her face next to his.

"Oh, Max. I was so sure...."

His hand squeezed hers harder. Then, his body wrenched a little.

"Max?" She sat up and saw his face was turning blue.

"Max!"

She would have run for the nurses, but Max's hand, she couldn't let go. She stood up and leaned across the bed to reach the call button. She punched it over and over until one, then two, nurses arrived. They tried to push Sylvia away so they could get to Max, but she refused to let go of his hand.

"I can't," Sylvia told them, hoping they would understand.

As they wheeled in the crash cart, Sylvia shoved herself against the head of his bed and pulled his arm up and away, making room for them to crack the cast and get to his chest.

"Ma'am you'll have to let go," one nurse said, but Sylvia locked her hands around Max's arm. The nurse tried to peel her off, and still she refused.

"Do it anyway!" the doctor yelled.

Bodies scurried, wires were set, someone counted, 1-2-3, and then a high-pitched squeal preceded the shock that jolted through Max and shot through Sylvia. She held his arm tighter, this time she really couldn't let go, and she took the pain.

Again.

Again.

She deserved it, she told herself.

Each time the electricity cut like knives from her toes to the top of her head, and each time she saw a different image.

The mirror. How she let go during that last swing around, on purpose, because it meant more to her mother than anything else.

The hamster. How she did squeeze it hard after it bit her, until it stopped moving.

Her sister. How she pulled her out of that tree, and then lost her grip.

And then, too close to the curb and never listening, how Sylvia shoved her too hard and pushed her sister out into the street.

Mrs. Cornelius. That really was an accident.

And Max.

The shock.

The pain.

She should have known better.

She was selfish. Irresponsible, her mother would say. "Sylvia," she heard.

The doctor had settled; the crash cart shoved back towards the door.

"Sylvia."

She glanced at the nurse standing next to her, who stepped back and nodded her head in Max's direction. His fingers twitched under her hand and he repeated her name.

This time, Sylvia didn't hesitate. This time, she didn't think. She touched his hair, his face, his mouth.

"My god, Max, you're alive."

"Sylvia," he said.

She held his hand and looked into his eyes, anticipating so much, but what she saw threw her stomach in a lurch.

Slowly, he pulled his hand from hers. "Don't touch me," he whispered.

"Please."

***

The inspiration for this story by author, Christi Craig:

I've been known to stroll through a cemetery on a sunny day, but not because I was paying respects to anyone in particular. I've also been caught staring at the shoes of others, though I'm not a connoisseur of footwear. Every headstone tells a story, and every pair of shoes reveals a secret. So, writing a story that incorporated death and shoes (in one way or another), I assumed, would come together naturally. What amazes me about writing, though, is that nothing ever unfolds in the way we anticipate.

I began the first draft of my story with Max Cooper in the spotlight as the one who dressed and prepared Clive Barrows and Adriana Quinn. But soon after I got him to the funeral home and in front of the clients, the energy in the story dropped, with quite a ways left to go in the draft. Then, Sylvia Drake stepped out from the sidelines. She was always a part of each funeral scene, always harboring a bit of animosity towards Max, and something about her stubborn silence demanded more of my attention. Once I turned my sights on her, the rest of the story took off. Even so, it wasn't until I neared the end of that first draft that I realized how large a part Sylvia played in the story as a whole, as well as in the lives of every character she met along the way.

The Deadest One

by E. Victoria Flynn

If I can just lay it out like the bones of a canvas frame, prime it and give it a good, clean going over, I'm sure as anything, it will all come clear. It's like when I was a kid and I sat at the kitchen table drawing pictures, all purple and blue and black, and sang that song I made up: *Hey ho/ Ho hum/ Big ol' train weighs a ton/ and here comes Daddy, the deadest one.* Mama, she liked to tune me out at times like that. The therapist told her I needed to work through the loss in my own way, and I know that's what tore her apart the most. She loved Daddy, I know she did, despite the names she called him behind his back.

After Daddy was gone, Mama started in to worrying about everything I did, like she expected me to be swallowed up by the deep, dark night in my sleep. So she bought one of those video monitors, like the kind you put in a baby's room to keep it safe. Well, I was pretty much still a baby anyway and it didn't phase me none.

Then I started playing like I was on TV and I put together songs and dances. I listened for Mama from the other room, sometimes laughing, sometimes not. When I got bigger and was in school, Mama said she had to start working because the money was running low, and she went about putting cameras up in every room. She thought I didn't know nothing about them, but I did. I watched her too.

I was lucky to find Eden, my muse. She was big and beautiful like the sun, and the things she showed me poured through me like rain. Eden spoke in color—all hot smoke and swirling light. She watched the tick-ticking from inside my mind, and turned it like a clock. Every time she did, my pictures changed.

"Morgan, baby, you have got to put the pencils away. It's time for school," Mama said while she ran through the house click-clacking a new pair of lime colored pumps across the linoleum.

"But, *Mama*," I said, pleading for more time.

"I swear, child, you are just like your Daddy when you get to drawing. A train could come barreling through and you'd be none the wiser..." She stopped short and turned to the coffee pot. "Just get dressed, Morgan Marie. Now!"

I rose from the table on shaky legs and slipper-skated to my room. There was never enough time in the mornings or enough crayons in the box.

Eden waited for me in my room inside a cardboard dollhouse with magazine picture wallpaper and bottle cap chairs. I sat on the floor—eyes closed, back straight, quiet hum to my breath—a tiny Buddha awaiting enlightenment, and spilled.

"Jenny Hart drew a picture of a horse yesterday. It had fire eyes and stamping feet and it could fly, but it didn't have wings. And she said it was better than all my pictures and Katie said it was too. And then William and Lance laughed at it, and said drawing was stupid, and Jenny and me were both stupid."

A wash of warmth and light spread through me from my toes. I felt a rush along my spine as a pastiche of overlapping textures tripping along variant strings of hues and tints shot up like fireworks exploding across my inner landscape.

"I pulled Jenny's hair and told her *she* was stupid. I said she was bad. I told her she had a whole head full of bad and she was going to hell."

Swirls of color pulsed in me, erupting from deep, down in my belly all hot and sweet: pinks tumbled with blues and greens, shadow and light. Shapes emerged and danced. Places unfolded—some I'd seen in picture books; some, brand new. Eden turned the clock.

**

It was some time later that I got to school and found Jenny Hart, miss high and mighty, caught half-way up a cottonwood tree. Mrs. Bragg stood at the bottom, her hair done up in little curls twisting about her head like tiny snakes just hatched from a nest. "Jenny Hart, you come down from there right now!"

"I can't," Jenny said, and started in to cry. She was bent over hugging a huge, old branch. Her feet dangled from either side, her dress hitched up in the back and from below you could make out a line of pink panties. A group of boys stood around laughing and pointing.

"Then for God's sake, Jenny, hold on. Mr. Thatcher's coming with a ladder."

"I can't, Mrs. Bragg. I'm *scared*." Jenny took to bawling then. Her long, stick legs trembled below the branch and you could tell she was hanging on as hard as she could. I thought about the marks I get on my face when I fall asleep on top of my chenille bed spread, little round vines and flowers budding up my chin and across my cheeks. One time I colored them in with one of Mama's blue pens and played a game of Jungle Girl. I imagined Jenny would have some pretty good marks up and down her arms to show for it.

"It will be okay, Jenny," Mrs. Bragg said, trying what she could to soothe the girl. "I can see Mr. Thatcher coming now. Just you hold on." Jenny's legs trembled more and more and her arms clinched tighter to the tree. Her shiny, black ballet flats had come loose. They hung precariously from her toes until one slipped down, and landed between a set of marbled hostas. That's when Jenny peed.

"Awe, gross!" said Adam Hanson. Sprinkles of pee caught on the wind splattering our faces and hair. Mrs. Bragg turned away to wipe her face with her sleeve. Jenny wailed. Her other shoe came down on Mable Fischer's head. Then Jenny fell.

***

It was a game of Truth or Dare. It had nothing to do with me.

Still I thought about Jenny Hart for some time, about her fire-eyed horse and her trip to hell. I thought about Daddy and his train. I thought and I drew and I painted what I thought. I got so good I won some awards.

I got to visit around the state for competitions and Mama came with me. In high school I even won a trip to Washington D.C., but I ended up so sick I couldn't go. It was just as well, Mama said, because she couldn't get the time off work. I was down right mad, but my paintings went without me and I won a blue ribbon and a college scholarship. I couldn't have done none of it without Eden.

***

I saw Mama do it, turn on the cameras. *Flick. Click. Whir.* The sound of home buzzed through my bones like a cavity being drilled. I knew what she was doing. I was home for the summer and she was trying to keep me safe. But I'd spent a whole year away from her, a whole year at school in a dorm room with a roommate, and I'd come through just fine. I wasn't scared to leave her house. I was relieved. Then I was back home, back to the watching.

"Morgan, I'd like it if you could go visit your Grandmother. She hasn't seen you in the longest time. It would mean a lot to her."

"Grandma Mary? Mama, she freaks me out."

"Don't talk like that, Morgan Marie. She's an old lady by herself. Besides, are you going to stop coming to see me when I get rusty?"

"Mama," I said like I was five years old again. In that house I was always five years old.

It was strange to me to feel the change of the familiar when I came home. Everything looked so much the same, but there were little differences I almost couldn't see—new pillows on the couch, an afghan stretched across the back, different cups hanging from kitchen hooks. My room was kept, but missed the things I'd taken with me to school. Still Eden's cardboard house waited under the window with its torn, sweater rugs and tissue paper shades. I looked for Eden between the clutter.

"Mama keeps it like a prison in here," I said. "I know she says she's just looking out for me, but I don't need her watching me every damn minute. It's like I can never be anything but a kid to her. No matter what I paint, she looks at it like I'm still drawing little dolls and horses."

Colors turned and spun, a vibrato of light. Tick. Tick.

***

Blank, white, sparse—Grandma Mary's apartment felt like a sanitarium.

When I pulled in she had been stationed behind the patio doors in her house coat and slippers, her head covered in pin curls waiting to set.

"Grandma Mary!" I said through a glowing bouquet of summer flowers I held like a shield.

"Put those in the kitchen. I have no place out here," she said. Her voice likened to corn flakes in waxed paper.

"Grandma, where's that picture I painted of you and Mama when she was a baby? You looked so beautiful. It should be out here so people can see it."

She looked around at the walls and the floor like she'd never seen them before. "Oh, I don't know. I must have thrown it out."

"Thrown it out? That painting practically got me into school. You can't have thrown it out."

"Oh?" she said. "Are you in school?"

I don't think she even knew who I was. An alarm sounded in the stale, white kitchen scaring me so bad I was ready to stop, drop and roll. "What's that sound?" I said.

"Must be time for me to take my pills," she said and scooted into the other room.

The apartment looked like it hadn't changed in thirty years, but she'd only been in assisted living for the last few. There was not one spec of color in the whole place save for the red call cords hanging down every now and then in case she needed help. There were plastic slip covers over white sheets over hard furniture that would have had broken springs had anyone ever used them for anything but being polite. There weren't even pictures on the walls.

"Grandma, Mama says you've been spending time with the other ladies around here."

Grandma Mary scooted back to the living room carrying a water glass and a small stuffed animal. "Well, yes. Sometimes one of them will get to talking about something that's going on. The woman next door loves to gossip. She knows everything about everybody."

As she talked, Grandma Mary stared out the patio doors while her hands smoothed over the animal in her lap as if she were petting a favorite cat. "Last week she told me the woman down to the far end—she's still young, you know, but she was in an accident sometime back and needs help doing things—her daughter is going to have another baby and each one of those kids has a different father. Can you imagine?"

"No, I guess not," I said, eager to be done with it. How could a person look like she was always waiting for something to happen and at the same time look like she was done waiting for anything at all? I counted tiles in the cheap drop ceiling. One near the kitchen had an ugly brown water stain. A few tiles over was a ventilation grid. I swear I could see a tiny red light shining through there, just barely, like a video camera.

**

I sat at the park, sketching in my book, mad as hell. The pictures were frantic and fast. Eden was pouring me full to the brim—saplings sprouted from the ground, two leaves at a time growing exponentially into thick cottonwoods, each with a heavy, outstretched branch, each exactly the same. Row after row, trees sprouted, grew, stretched. They became a cadre. A battalion. An army.

Around the trees pockets formed like hungry, talking mouths in the ground and inside the mouths were eyes pointing in all directions. The watching was like being eaten alive. Like burning from the inside out.

Joggers and bikers passed, scouring me with their eyes. A middle-aged couple walked by holding hands. They were being led by an anxious dog sniffing for squirrels. I ripped the pages from the book, stuffed them in my bag, and started again.

"Morgan."

I was startled. My arm slipped and scraped a thick, black line across the page.

"Oh, I'm so sorry." It was Katie, keeper of the fire-eyed horse, on a bike. I could feel my face, hot and flush, my own eyes aching. "I'm surprised to see you here," she said. She almost looked genuine.

"Yeah, well, I was out," I said. Small talk was never small enough for me and seeing Katie didn't do much to broaden my outlook.

"Are you home for the summer? I heard you got a great scholarship."

"Yeah, I'll be around for a while."

"We should do something, you know, go see a chick flick or something."

"Sure," I said. "We could do that."

"Cool. It's a date," she said. When she rode away she looked back and waved.

***

I couldn't look at Mama. Every morning she clacked around the house before work, always in brightly colored pumps, always talking. I tried to steer clear, but my room was never big enough to paint in, and even if it was, the carpet would be splattered in ruin. Instead I worked out on the three season porch in full earshot of Mama's click and yack.

"I'm so glad you made it over to see Grandma Mary yesterday. That just means the world to her. She hasn't been doing well. You never know if it's going to be a good day or a bad day. We're lucky we have such a well loved facility near by."

I sketched out a horizon line and a stand of trees in the distance. A storm was coming from the east.

"I'm going to be a little late tonight, honey. We have a meeting about a new system the hospital is putting in. I swear they just love change for the sake of it. Did I tell you that last winter they moved our offices to the other side of the hall and then two months later moved us back again? I don't know what good they got out of it, but it took me almost that long to get all the paperwork straightened out."

There was an old car out in a field along the highway. It was red and rusted and curvy. Wild blue chicory and Queen Anne's lace grew up all around it. Next to the car was a barnboard sign that said *Strawberries Stop Now* in messy white paint. An old man sat on a folding chair under a canopy, his feet rested on a wooden crate. I sketched the car, the man, the sign.

"If you get hungry just pull something out of the freezer. I haven't had time to get any real cooking done."

The phone rang. Mama clacked over and picked it up. She put her hand over the mouth piece, "Honey, it's for you, a girl named Katie."

***

Friday night Katie picked me up. We went to a movie about a college party that led to a stolen car and a bank robbery. One of the frat guys fell in love with his girlfriend's mom and they flew off with the money to Tahiti. Katie laughed most of the way through it. I slouched down in my chair, thinking about mothers and how crazy they all are.

"Do you want to go get some food? I'm craving ice cream and grilled cheese," Katie said after the show.

"Yeah, okay," I said. Spending the night out with Katie beat spending it at home with Mama, and the diner down the road would be open late.

Katie ordered a chocolate malt and a sandwich with fries. "You know, I always felt a little weird around you after Jenny died," she said. "It's like, you knew or something. I used to imagine you made it happen by thinking about it."

"We were eight," I said. "I wasn't even there when she climbed the tree."

"I know, but it was spooky. One day you're telling her she's going to hell and the next she's dead."

I stared her down. "It wasn't the next day. It was at least a month later. The two things aren't even related."

"No, I know," she said. "I get it, but when I was a kid it was spooky. I thought you had special powers and you were going to come after me next."

"What? That's just stupid."

"I know. And then growing up I was always kind of jealous of you. It was like, first I was scared of you, then I wanted to be you."

I didn't get where she was going with all this. I wondered if she wanted to hang out so she could unload some weird baggage she'd been carrying around.

She stirred her malt, watching it twirl in the tall glass. "I mean, you have so much talent. You're so good. I wish I could do what you do. I couldn't even draw a stick figure. Turns out I have a pretty good eye for photography though."

"It's all I do," I said. I felt sick. Into the canvas was the only place I could go. They all thought I was crazy growing up, but they couldn't do what I could, they couldn't build worlds. And they didn't know Eden.

Katie looked at me, her face flushed. "But you're incredible," she said.

The whole night was weird like this, Katie telling me her secrets like she hadn't a friend in the world and there I was suddenly hearing them like they mattered. What was stranger yet was that she wanted to hear mine, what I'd been doing in school, what I was painting, like it was some big mystery in her mind unwinding. It wasn't until about one o'clock in the morning that she took me home in her mom's old station wagon, the radio playing late night rock. I had a headache pounding away at the back of my skull, but I felt a little lighter too, like a big red balloon itching just to float on up into the sky.

"I'm so glad you came out with me tonight. I've been wanting to talk to you for a long time," she said.

"Thanks. It was good. And weird."

"We could do it again, you know. There's this old house up on High Hill that looks like it's glowing at sunset. You should see it. You could paint it."

"Yeah, maybe. I could take some pictures if the light is right."

"Okay," she said. "I'll give you a call." Then she leaned over and kissed me.

***

The night sky turned opal with cool air settling near the ground in patches of fog. The heat was still in the pavement, but the grass was wet with dew. Mama's moon flowers were big-faced trumpets watching me pass.

Still up and sitting at the kitchen table, Mama fixed me in a heavy stare as soon as I opened the door. "Nice you could make it home, Morgan. I don't suppose it occurred to you to give me a call and let me know you're still alive."

"Geez, Mama, it's not that late."

"Not that late? It's nearly two o'clock in the morning. What have you been doing?"

I didn't want this, to talk to her, to see her. "What's it your business anyway?" I said. "I'm not a kid. I can do what I want."

She looked like I'd hit her. Her eyes narrowed, her cheek bones cracked. "So that's it, is it? You're feeling all grown up now that you've been away. You think you can take care of yourself? Well, by all means, go ahead and take care of yourself."

I was going to my room, fighting back the way I always did, alone with Eden talking me through, but this time I stopped. This time I turned around and looked Mama straight in the eye. "Don't you get enough of me watching me through your cameras, Mama? Don't you get enough *Morgan Marie* everyday? You've been watching since I was a little girl. Give it up. It's sick. You're sick, Mama, and I'm *not* your little girl."

She looked dumb and old. There was nothing left to come tripping from her endless mouth. I went back to my room, slammed the door and tore the cameras from their sockets.

***

It felt good to sleep in with the light slipping through the blinds at a late morning slant. Mama didn't come knocking at my door like she usually did. The quiet filled me, made me feel expansive and free. I hardly sat up before Eden got to work.

Spin. Tick.

Late in the afternoon the phone rang. Mama was nowhere in the house and I'd been painting with the music turned up, still in my pajamas. By the time I reached the phone the line had gone dead. Then it took to ringing again. "Morgan? It's Katie." An hour later I was sitting in that old station wagon on the way up to High Hill.

"You look cute today," she said and reached over and took my hand. It wasn't a choice I'd made, only that I liked this feeling of not being alone. There was something Katie and I shared the night before that maybe had been building up through the years, an understanding about what we really were in the world. She got my art like a pulse in her, and I realized all that time she'd been trying to make contact.

"Are you okay?" she asked when we got to the top of the hill and parked the car. We walked to the stone overlook cresting the city. There was a heat in the air that started at my feet and crawled up the back of my legs. I felt it hold me like a quick-growing vine. A panic set in across my chest.

"I'm fine," I said, but when I did my hands went in a wild sweat. She watched my face lose its color.

"Morgan," she said. "Morgan, hey." She held me, but we had sunk to the ground. I was dizzy and thirsty and my hands were shaking. "Morgan, oh my god, I'm so glad you're okay. You scared the shit out of me."

My eyes burned. Colors, images, words flashed through my mind. Eden hadn't stopped messing with the clock and it was overwhelming. The hill rose up to me and retreated. A rush of wind shoved past my face taking the shape of a woman. Katie spoke, but it was music churning in my ears.

"I just need a drink," I said and I hoped that she could hear me out there with all the music and light.

She pressed a bottle to my lips. "Take it slow. We have time."

It was Mama then come swimming from a lake of cold, fresh water. Her face was my favorite, what it was when she still wore her hair in long braids and skirts that swept her ankles. She had a pair of leather sandals with straps up to her knees, the kind that made her look ethereal. It all broke in me then. Tears spattered my shirt. Ugly sobs rolled out like thunderstorms. Katie kept me close, but I knew I was too much for her. *Hey ho/ Ho hum/ Big ol' train weighs a ton/ And here comes Daddy, the deadest one.* I was too much for Mama, there's no way Katie could hold me down.

We sat like that until my hands slowed and the music quieted. We moved to a shade tree behind the boarded up house. Katie brought out food and my sketch pad though I told her I couldn't draw. I felt drained away, an empty cloud after a storm. I'd be disappearing soon.

"I had a fight with Mama," I said. "Ever since Daddy died she's been keeping me like a precious little stone. I just want to break out and run."

"So let's," she said. "Let's just put all our stuff in the car and take off down the road. We'll be like 'Thelma and Louise'. Without the killing."

"She'd find me no matter where we went. One day we'd be in Mexico sitting by a pool and we'd hear *click click click* and we'd look up and there she'd be in those perfect little shoes and that perfect little dress. She'd say, 'Morgan Marie, what are you trying to do to me? I've been looking everywhere for you.' And she'd sweep me up and carry me home."

"Then we'll move in to this little house. She'd never look here, it's too close. She could fly across the world looking for you and you'd be right here all the time."

I wanted to be a part of Katie then, to have her thoughts mix with mine, two colors blended so thoroughly we'd glow. When I kissed her she smelled so clean and spiced with cinnamon. There was such a comfort in her softness I could hardly hold on.

The sun set behind the house lighting a fire to the trees and the bandy old place. I sketched tentatively. A red-bellied woodpecker worked at the roof line tapping out a beat while Katie took pictures with an old point-and-shoot camera. She liked the surprise of film, she said, and photographed my hands. I drew halos around her head, around the bird, around the house.

***

Mama was waiting up again, but without the hardness of the night before. "I've been thinking, I haven't been fair to you. You're right, you're not a little girl and I have to get used to it. You have to make your own way. I'm sorry for being so hard on you."

"I know, Mama. I know you miss Daddy too."

"I do, sweetie. I wish he could see you now. He'd be so proud of the work you do. You have his talent, that's for sure."

Daddy used to sit with me at the table, crayons and paper all spread out, and draw intricate scenes for me to color in. I'd scribble them up as fast as I could and ask for more, but he was patient and taught me how to slow down.

"I got you a present," she said. She took a box from the counter and slid it across the table. "I thought that if you agree to let me know when you're going to be out late, I would agree to give you your space."

It was a cell phone, a nice one, with a touch screen and a key pad and camera. "You can put your music on there too. I got you the whole package. Is it a deal?"

"Sure, Mama," I said. "I'll call from now on. Thanks."

"And, Morgan," she said. "How about you give Grandma Mary a call tomorrow?"

"Okay. Good night."

***

I was trying something new, mixing golds and coppers, creating deep shadows and bright light in a kind of flat, Byzantine contrast. The bandy little house became a bandy little cathedral in a field of clover and milkweed.

Eden came out to check on me. I always knew when she was watching behind the shades of my eyes. She made a certain vibration run through my whole body.

I swept a band of Pacific blue across the canvas. "Look at this. These colors are jumping from the frame. It feels like I could just walk right in." I outlined Katie, a haloed Madonna clutching the red-crested bird to her breast.

Something plunged inside me: a jolt of static, an aftershock.

I dropped my brush. "Eden, what are you doing?"

Blue-black night, sound like rushing trains.

I stepped back, watching the brush strokes and hues play off one another. "Stop, it's too much," I said, shaking my head to release the clanging, expecting the last coins to drop from the slot.

She let up, easing on the blackness, then firing two last rounds of spastic dark into my periphery. They felt like warning shots.

I wanted to throw something, to run from the room, from Eden, but there she was inside me, she'd always been. There she was, just like Mama, always watching, always influencing everything I ever done.

***

I drove to Grandma Mary's for the distraction. She sat outside her neighbor's apartment in a plastic chair drinking a glass of iced tea. "Well, what a surprise," she said. "Dory, this here is Morgan, Camille's girl. Come and sit down, honey. Meet Mrs. Walker."

I planted myself and my bag alongside Grandma Mary and accepted a glass of tea. It was a hot day, but in the shade there was a nice breeze coming off the pond. I watched the center fountain spray its cool cascade across the flat surface and barely kept myself from jumping in.

"Morgan, what a lovely name. Tell me what it is you do," said Mrs. Walker.

"I'm in school," I said. "I'm a painter."

"Oh," Mrs. Walker said. She had a slight tremor when she spoke. "Didn't you tell me that Camille's late husband was an artist, Mary? Why, you must take after your father."

Grandma Mary was very eager to please her friend. She grew a wide smile and spoke right away. "Yes, he was. He worked for some big outfit. Advertising, I believe, but it's been some time. Camille has been carrying on with that other fellow for years now. I think it's high time they do something about it."

"What *other fellow*?" I asked. Grandma Mary was going off the deep end, Mama didn't date.

"Oh, Darlin'," Mrs. Walker said. "You look white as a ghost."

Grandma Mary said, "You know, honey, that fellow who puts in those cameras. Tom, a nice man. He put one in my apartment when I moved in, just in case. I feel much better having it there too. You never know when something is going to happen."

The tightness started pulling at my chest, and my breath stole me away. It was the music that pulled me under.

***

"Morgan." It was Mama calling me in from outside. I had been poking a stick in the messy soup at the foot of the old hickory tree where a mass of slugs had come out in the wet to crawl across each other's backs. One by one I picked them up with my stick and put them on the hickory board swing. I was planning on giving them a ride. "Morgan," she called again, but I was too content and the mud was too fresh to leave behind. "Morgan, honey, it's Mama. You're in the hospital, baby. You need to wake up."

***

I'd had a panic attack they said. Was it my first time? Yes, Mama said. No, I said. I needed to eat, Mama said. No, I said. I needed my rest, Mama said. No, I said. Why was I being so hard to put up with, Mama said. Who's Tom? I said.

***

Tom was a private investigator, a very nice man, a widower. He lived out in the country on a quiet road with three horses, an alpaca, and a brood of hens. We've been eating his eggs since I was seven years old and Mama never introduced me because it was always too soon.

"You've been carrying on with this guy for eleven years and you never told me? I'm your daughter for Christ's sake. What else? Do you have kids somewhere I don't know about? A house on an island?"

"Sweetie, this isn't the time or the place. Let's just get you home and we can talk about it."

"I don't want to go home with you. I don't trust you."

She put her hand on my arm. "Morgan, please. Just come home with me and I'll tell you everything."

"No, Mama."

***

I felt hollowed out. I wondered if there was any me left inside or if I was exactly like those thin chocolate bunnies that looked so good on the outside but just fall apart in my hand. I didn't know what to do, so I went out to the cemetery to visit Daddy.

The old gate stood open to a field of trees and stones. I followed the foot path to the right and up a narrow stairway. His headstone still shined in red granite.

Robert Ulysses Quinn
Beloved Son, Husband and Father
September 13, 1971-May 21, 1997.

The boxwoods Mama and I planted were trimmed to neat round tufts. I sat at the graveside and traced the letters in his name. I didn't talk to Daddy like people in movies do, pretending he could hear me from under the ground or up in some magical paradise littered with virgins and molted angel feathers. I knew anything I had to say to Daddy would travel to him on the thin wire that connected him and me from the start. Instead I laid in the grass, six feet above his moldy remains, and fell asleep.

***

The phone buzzed in my bag, vibrating against the headstone, waking me up as evening was setting in. It was Katie. "Are you okay? I just called your house. Your mom sounded upset."

"Where are you? Can I see you?"

Katie met me at the park with a stack of photographs and a candy bar. "Your mom has had a secret lover all this time and you didn't know?"

"Yeah."

"That's incredible. Are you going to meet him?"

"I don't know. I'm sure he knows all about me though. He's probably the one who convinced her to put all those cameras up in the house."

"Wait. What?"

"Video cameras. Mama's been recording my life since I was seven. Every day of it. Until last week when I ripped them all out."

"Whoa. That's hardcore."

"Yeah, well."

"Your mama has issues."

"Yeah. I'll probably end up psycho too. You might want to take off before I go all bat-shit on you."

Katie put her arm around me and laid her head on my shoulder. "I like your crazy."

"I still have Jenny's shoe."

Katie sat up then. "What?"

"Jenny's shoes fell off. I found one in the plants at the bottom of the tree."

Katie kept quiet for a long time. A family of geese waddled up, honking and nudging at the ground. I thought about the day I found that shoe beneath the leaves, how I wrapped it in a brown, paper napkin and tucked it in my bag under my books, hoping Mama wouldn't find it. It felt like something I shouldn't have, something forbidden and alive—soft black leather scuffed at the toe. Jenny Hart, the second death of my life.

"I don't know a lot about you," Katie said. "I mean, I've known you for a long time, but not really. You've always been different, kind of off limits. I think that's what I've always liked about you."

The geese waddled off to another bench in a long, jabbering line. A little girl tossed popcorn onto the grass.

"So I've decided," Katie said. "You're not going to scare me away, not yet. It's kind of an adventure being with you. I want to know what happens next."

It was getting dark. The sky took on a deep, summer sapphire. As the park thinned out I felt restless and cocky. I was sick of it all, everything happening around me like I was in the middle of some weird social experiment, Mama's little mouse in a box. I wanted to move my legs, to scream, to pull out my hair. I wanted to grab the earth around the middle and squeeze it until it burst. I was a hyena laughing and wicked and wild.

"Let's go," I said and we ran into the trees.

***

I infused myself with Katie and she with me. The ground slid off, leaving us to navigate an atmosphere of gritty want on a plane neither of us had touched before. I grew like a cracked cicada crawling from its crisp shell, my wings wet and veined, my colors dawning in the night. Katie broke from her intrepid form, head drawn back, hair spliced with leaves and lichen, arching into a feral thing caught in my grasp. Her feet buckled. Her arms twisted out, my American Kali in blue.

***

"We've changed."

"We have."

"I want to paint you like this."

"I want to take pictures of you."

"I want to sleep under this tree. Let birds make nests in my belly and pick at my eyes."

"It smells like rain."

"Nighttime is never long enough."

***

I didn't go home that night or the next. I didn't eat Mama's food. I didn't drink Mama's water. Still she found me. I knew she always would.

"High Hill, I haven't been here since you were a baby. The city's grown so much. Over where that shopping mall is used to be a farm and a big field. There were always pheasants running all over the place. It used to drive the hunters crazy they couldn't go out there with their guns and shoot them so close to town."

I had been alone on the hill drawing the house in the morning light. Chickadees rushed in, lit on the stone wall, rushed out. Two squirrels in the heat of argument tutted and scuttled from tree to tree knocking at loose twigs and pine bows. I captured one on the page, a tiny king with a tuft-up tail.

Mama sat beside me. "Morgan," she said. "I am truly sorry. I've made so many mistakes."

I ran my fingers along the page, the tips blackened with charcoal. "I want to come home," I said. "But I want you to let me be for once and for all."

Mama sighed. There were grass stains on her shoes.

***

I lay naked and prostrate on my bed, eyes on the ceiling, unfocused. The windows were open, the house, dead silent. A storm rode in, whipping the wind horse.

"I need something to paint, Eden. I need it like a fever."

Tick.

She turned the clock, thrashing me awake— *pumpkins in October; a baby wet and white drawn fresh from the womb; fire seizing between a maze of copulating bodies boozed and boiled in sweat under the Harvest moon.*

Acrylic paint pots lined the floor. I chose a sable brush, number 4, with a soft round point and dipped it in cerulean blue. Sliding the cold, damp bristles over my nose, I arched up curving around my eyes, losing it at the temples. Lines outstretched in leaves and whorls—deep magenta, mars black, prism violet, phthalo green—down my neck, my shoulders, my breasts. I was canvas and paint, dark and light, shadow and sun. I smelled of sweat and desperation.

***

When Katie found me hours later, I had covered canvases in all manner of condition scattered from my room to the porch. Torn sketches were pinned to walls and stacked on the floors. A careful collection of shells and stones lay on a baking tin beside the door. There was music too, and dynamite in her kiss. I stained her body with mine, then washed her clean.

"Let's find this Tom guy," Katie said.

"What do you mean, like hunt him down?"

"Yeah, find out what he's about. Don't you think it's weird he's been okay with not meeting you all this time? What's his deal anyway?"

"Mama makes it sound like everything's on her terms. She's planning a dinner for the three of us. I'd rather gouge out my eyes."

"Then let's do it. Let's hunt."

Katie hadn't been inside our house since the birthday party Mama had for me when I turned nine years old. It was my golden birthday and she invited every one of my classmates. Most of them had shown up, probably due to their parents' good graces rather than their own sense of social obligation. We played the normal party games, ate the normal party food and drank three gallons of fruit punch. Later, when we were taking turns spinning each other on Mama's sewing chair, Adam Hanson threw up spraying red goo across everyone's front end and the white wall behind Mama's sewing table. The whole room smelled of hot strawberries and bile.

There was a sense of celebration in Katie's arrival. It felt like an unveiling to me as I uncovered the cardboard wreck of a child's dollhouse. "This is where Eden lives," I said. "My muse."

Katie's eyes focused and tipped up, squinting at the crooked walls. "This is so cute. You even have a tiny toilet. You made this?"

"Yeah, well, with Eden's help."

"I can't believe you still have it. I made dollhouses out of tissue boxes, but my mom always threw them out."

"Mama wanted to get rid of it a long time ago, but Eden wouldn't hear of it. She likes it here, she says."

"What? You mean you actually talk to her?"

"Yeah, she's Eden, of course I talk to her. How do you think I made those?" I said, pointing to the canvassed mess surrounding us.

Katie watched me for a minute with a sort of half-thought question resting in her brow before turning to look at the room. When she did it was as if she had just noticed it, her head moving so slowly it looked as though she were cataloging everything around her. Finally her eyes paused on a painting away from the clutter, flanked by bird nests and second hand rosaries. It was the painting I'd done of her nursing the bird in front of the bandy little house. I meant to have it framed.

"Wow," she said. I couldn't read her face. She walked to it, looked hard into the eyes, reached up, pulled back. She studied the lines of the face, the bird, the breast. She took in the cathedral glow. She held her breath.

I jabbed the end of a brush into my thigh, waiting.

"This...is intense."

I bit my lip.

"Morgan, this is intense," she said again. I studied the back of her neck. Eden vibrated below my skin as Katie melted into the painting. I tried to shut Eden out, to kiss Katie and bring her back. Eden shifted, spinning the clock. I reached for Katie, but she flinched, and pulled away. My chest tightened. I fought it, focused on my surroundings, held to the images before me, let my body sink to the floor. Katie's back was still to me. The painting. Her hair. Her neck. I grabbed a handful of sheet, the edge of the night stand, breathing, breathing. Eden pushed her way through tick-ticking the next thing, a new thing—*cattle in the streets of Pamplona, a birch forest, a farm with a warm glowing light.* The music rose from the bottom up. I would not slide under.

When she turned to me, Katie's eyes were changed, hard. "I have to go," she said. She took her bag from beside the bed and walked from the room. I still held the sheet quaking in my fist.

She did not call or answer her phone. I would not press her. I blamed Eden. "Why are you doing this? Why are you pushing me so hard?"

A prairie fire recently doused, smoldering under a late afternoon sun.

"You're trying to keep me to yourself. You shove your way in whenever you want. You spin me in whatever direction you chose, and I get dizzy. I can't focus."

The call of crows behind a forest curtain, the ice blue sky of late November.

"I'm done. With you and Mama, I am done."

Wet summer pavement steaming after a shower, damp kindling and ash expecting a fire ring flame.

I reached out, half way to tender, and smashed the cardboard house.

***

Mama said his name was Tom Cote. She'd made dinner plans for us on Friday night at the supper club on the lake. I was to dress like a lady, she said. I was to do my hair and look presentable. She said I was spending too much time alone and needed to lighten up. I had no intention of waiting until Friday night to get the goods on Mr. Tom Cote.

The advent of the internet had largely bypassed Mama. If it weren't for the evolving face of her job, I am quite certain technology would have passed her by all together. She had no idea of the ease to which one could get information on any person they so chose in a short manner of time.

I did a search for "Tom Cote, Private Investigator" and found him in a wink. His office was downtown behind a flat-front facade done up in modern face. I didn't enter, but wandered past, window shopping the summer displays. I was more interested in his private life. I wanted to see his house.

Certain he'd be working in the middle of the day, I found my way out to Weary Road and down a long drive lined with lodgepole pines. There was a large wooden sign that read *Red Pine Ranch* and a closed gate barring my way. I pulled the car down the road, parked near a scrub-brush ditch and doubled back. The gate was a deterrent, but it was easy to navigate through the hulking trees guarding the enclave and reach the yard. The house was more of a log cabin, the kind you see in resort vacation magazines with sweeping vistas, fish cleaning tables and cars loaded up with dead deer. I could hear a dog barking from somewhere behind the house.

My feet crunched pine needles and gravel as I traversed the yard. A woodpecker knocked out a code from high up in the trees. My phone rang. It was Mama. I sent it to voice mail and crossed the front walk. The phone rang again. I turned it off.

The place was kept trim and rustic—split rail wrap-around porch, wagon wheels and flower barrels, a sun dial set out with red geraniums growing from below. Around back there were out buildings and pens. The dog slowed his barking, a St. Bernard behind a tall chain-link fence. The alpaca lugged along its enclosure flanked by pecking chickens and a fat, white goose. It wasn't the kind of place I could see Mama feeling too comfortable.

I peaked in windows. The kitchen was big and stainless steal. Everything looked tucked in its place, ordered and arranged. I tried the back screen door. It was locked. A pair of dark green mud boots waited by a bench.

I didn't hear a car pull in or see one out front, but there was a sound from inside. I followed the wrap-around porch checking through the windows on the first floor, a stocked pantry and laundry, a dining room, the living room in hunter green and mauve, overstuffed leather couch, braided rug.

There was a flick of shadow across the room near a doorway. I jumped to my right and came to another room with curtains drawn closed. Voices. I cupped my hand to the window, straining to hear. "Don't you think it's weird he's been okay with not meeting you all this time? What's his deal anyway?"

"Mama makes it sound like everything's on her terms. She's planning a dinner for the three of us. I'd rather gouge out my eyes."

"Then let's do it. Let's hunt."

A bolt of panic shot through my heart. For one moment I couldn't move. The cameras were still in my room. They were probably littering the house. I ran across the porch to the back steps imagining cameras in the beams and trees, at each window and door. A wooden plank creaked as my foot hit. My breath was spastic, slowing me down. I reached the back steps, no dog in the pen, no boots at the door.

"Morgan."

I jumped.

"Mama?"

"What are you doing here, couldn't wait til Friday?" She looked lopsided. It was the boots. They were on the wrong feet. She held the dog on a short leash.

"Why aren't you at work?"

"Oh, I sneak away sometimes. It's just so peaceful out here, don't you think?" I thought she looked deranged.

"Where's your car?"

"I think I'm the one that should be asking questions, don't you? What are you looking for? And where's your little girlfriend?"

The cameras. She'd seen everything. "You know, don't you, Mama? You know where Katie's been."

"Oh, baby, I know more than you can imagine."

The look smeared across Mama's face was more of an unrecognizable mask, something she'd picked up at a Halloween sale and saved over for a special occasion. A spider's web of lines reached out from the corners of her eyes spreading in a geometric shambles across her cheeks and down to the hard ridges of her chin. There was a coldness in her of damning spite and ridicule. What was once motherly was gone, and in her place stood a hornet, greedy and greasy at the mouth, slobbering for some unnamed satisfaction owed.

"Then what do you want?" I said. "What the hell am I supposed to do for you?"

She stood there with the dog poised as if she were summoning up his feral instincts readying for an attack. "I gave you my life, and you just spit it away." Her voice was even, the center of cold control. "I gave up everything to take care of you, and you just walked all over it. You just take whatever you want, do whatever you want, and don't even concern yourself with me. You're a spoiled little brat."

"What? Is this about Katie now?"

"Katie? You think I care about that little slut? She's nothing. You're just like your father, you can't see outside your own precious little world."

"What then? What do you want from me?"

"You don't know, do you, Morgan? You don't know a damn thing about me. All this time I gave you my life and you didn't bother to learn one damn thing about me. I was great too, do you know that? I had talent. I was to be a fashion designer. I even won a few awards of my own. Then you were born and it gave me an excuse to stay home. I had a chance to do it, but it was always all about your father—his talent, his time, his work—but it was okay because he took care of us. Then he died and all I could do was work and take care of you."

"You blame me?"

"I'm trapped, don't you get it? Tom takes care of me, but he doesn't do any better than you. Nobody's noticed me in a long while. I even had to force you to need me."

"What do you mean 'force' me?"

She sighed and walked the dog over to his pen. He stopped at the door refusing to go in. She gave him a short kick in the hind quarter, and closed and locked the gate. She slumped on a stump, dropped her head into her hands, covered her eyes.

When she looked up she said, "I needed to keep you safe. If I couldn't have my dreams, I could at least keep you safe. When I went back to work, I wanted to keep an eye on you at home. You had baby sitters, but I couldn't trust them, they were just high school kids. That's when I went looking for the cameras, and I found Tom, a surveillance specialist. You were so little, and it was just me. I just tried to keep you safe. But you grew up and I couldn't let you go. Don't you get it? You're all there is to me."

I couldn't tell if this was Mama or just another act. Since Daddy died, she'd become a powerhouse of control and focus. She didn't shed tears. She built a fortress with me at the center.

"What else?"

Her eyes were red and marbled, her resistance gone. "I kept you home from DC," she said, and her body rattled with sobs.

**

Eden came pushing her way in. I shoved her down, though I felt her vibrating, my hands agitated and cold. There was no sense to Mama, she was like a whimpering heap in a pinewood jail. I thought of the time just before the DC trip, how sick I'd been, nearly incoherent, slashing pains behind my eyes. Mama couldn't take off work. She'd had Grandma Mary come stay with me. There was a lot of daytime TV and soup from cans, but I couldn't stomach it. Grandma wanted Mama to take me to the doctor. They'd fought about it one night while I lay in my room with a cold washcloth on my head. Mama swore I'd be better soon if Grandma Mary would just keep on. Eden was nowhere then. She always disappeared when the internal weather turned bad.

"Mama," I said not knowing where to start, not getting the picture puzzle in front of me. It wasn't just her face that was a shambles, it was the whole woman, a broken down wreck. I crouched in the mire at her feet like I did as a girl—her at the kitchen table fitting money to paper, me begging for attention. "Mama, do you want some water?"

Her sobs droned on for a minute more. Snot and tears colored her dress. "Baby," she said. "Go get my bag. It's next to the refrigerator."

I pulled myself up, the dog watching my every move. Eden tempted me as I walked, pulling my attention to contrast and detail. I turned back to Mama cajoling the dog through the wire fence, her green mud boots still on the wrong feet, her hair wet and flat—a perfect frame for the Devil.

The house smelled of potpourri and beeswax, cinnamon and orange. The scent reminded me of Katie up on High Hill. I wanted her then like nothing else, the reprieve of her touch, the wildness in her heart. I swore to myself I would give her space, but I turned on my phone all the same. The messages were both from Mama. "Morgan, honey, I need you to do me a favor. I have to work late tonight and I won't be able to get over to Grandma Mary's in time to pick up her medication. Would you please be a dear and stop by the pharmacy for me? I worry about her running out."

"Morgan, it's Mama. I really do need you to call me, honey. I am just swamped here at work and I need you to run a few errands." But Mama hadn't been at work, she'd been at Tom's. I walked through the house, listening for voices.

Everything about the place was perfect, clean and shiny. I expected to look down and see a bald man looking up at me from the hardwood floors. *Wink.*

Down the hallway, past the living room, I found the master bedroom with its four poster bed and flat screen TV. The decor was masculine and dark. I looked for pictures of Mama and Tom on the walls and bedside table, but there were only ducks and loons and fishing poles. The next door was closed, but unlocked.

Opposite the door, a desk was clogged with electronic gadgets, cords, lenses, batteries. Monitors were mounted on the wall above, and to the right of them were shelves stacked with initialed and dated boxes. I bumped the mouse and a monitor came alive with a crooked still shot in black and white—junk piled across a carpeted floor—the left over debris of Eden's cardboard home.

I opened the closet. It was heaped near to the top with surveillance equipment. In the corner were Mama's lime green pumps, one tipped over on its side, the other with its toe pressed under the weight of a box labeled *School* with no date. I opened it to find rows of tiny tapes neatly arranged, all dated, beginning with 8/10. I took the first tape out and put it in the player on the desk. On the monitor was my dorm room, empty, just days before moving in.

Mama was waiting for me at the kitchen table. She held an unlit cigarette in her hand, not that I ever saw her smoke. Behind her was a wall of rough stone decorated with the head of an eight point buck. Her posture reminded me of that first night out with Katie.

"Hard to resist looking around, isn't it? I guess you found the tapes," she said.

"Yeah."

She pushed her feet up under her and I could see, for just a minute, what she must have looked like as a girl. "The oldest ones are in the attic, I can't bring myself to throw them out. You used to sit in front of that dollhouse singing that horrible song for hours and talking to your imaginary friend. I prayed you'd grow out of it."

Mama leaned back in the chair and closed her eyes. She started singing, "Hey ho/ Ho hum/ Big ol' train weighs a ton/ and here comes Daddy, the deadest one."

"I got your messages. You said you had to work late."

She didn't open her eyes, just laughed. "This is it, Kiddo. This is where I work." Then she sat up. "I guess you didn't know your Mama is a common, domestic wage slave."

This knocked me back. "You work at the hospital," I said. I couldn't take my eyes off her, she was losing it.

More laughing. "I was fired a couple years ago. A fat nurse in support hose caught me stealing drug samples off a patient cart. Tom took pity on me, been washing his underwear ever since. I'm full service."

Who was this woman? I had nothing left to say, her story was impossible.

"I clean the house, cook his food, wash his clothes, stay the night...I do everything a wife does except I take home cash instead of a ring. I told you, Tom takes care of me."

"What drugs were you stealing?"

She groaned. "Thorazine and sleeping pills, to finally get rid of your precious Eden."

***

Eden seized me as if she were right there in the room—her grip was death tight, a punch in the gut and a hand at the throat. I heaved for breath, but she shoved me out of the way. Floods of pictures, this time of my life, rushed through me like a child's flip book spun reel to reel. *Click. Spin. Whir.* My limbs moved of their own volition in spastic teeterings and jerks. I felt my body meet the wall nearest me and somehow didn't fall. My arms swiped at shelves knocking things over, battering the floor. A carnival of images and sounds, one on top of another, crossed and garbled, chucked and reformed. My hand found purchase on a rack of deer antlers hanging on the wall, grabbed hold, and held on. Eden pushed, my arm swung still holding the rack, and I fell to the ground.

***

"How did you get here, Morgan?"

"I don't know."

"Tom found you and your mother."

"Oh."

"Do you know where your mother is?"

"No."

"Do you know where Eden is?"

"No."

"Listen to me, Morgan, this is important. Are you listening?"

"Yes."

"Your mother is dead."

"No."

"Morgan, your mother is dead. You had a fight, and now she is dead."

"No!"

"Morgan, it is important that you try to remember. There is no Eden. You had a fight with your mother, now she is dead."

"Where's Katie?"

"Katie won't be coming, Morgan. I need you to do something for me. I need you to look at your painting and tell me what you see. Can you do that for me?"

"Yes."

"Right here. Tell me what you see."

"It's my painting. It's Katie holding that little bird. It's Katie."

"Look again, Morgan. Tell me what you see."

"I told you, it's Katie up on the hill by that glowing house, our little house."

"Look again, Morgan. Look at the picture. Morgan, look at the picture. Tell me what you see. It's not Katie in that picture, Morgan."

"It's...a little girl."

"What's that little girl's name, Morgan? Tell me who is in the picture?"

"Jenny Hart holding her little black shoe."

***

The inspiration for this story by author, E. Victoria Flynn:

I am continually interested in the idea of the muse and the role it plays with individual artists. When I first set out to write this story, I wondered what would happen if an artist blamed her muse for destroying her career and plotted to kill it. As I learned Morgan's back story, however, I discovered that it wasn't only Eden who maintained control over the contours of Morgan's life, but Mama's deceit as well.

Taken

by Lori Gordon

Ethan Wilde turned up the collar of his thin leather jacket. There was a hell of a nip in the air. He rubbed his hands together and wished it wasn't so bloody cold. It was only October, for Christ's sake. A man should be able to take a walk this time of year without freezing to death. He guessed what they said about Chicago was true, it ran hot and cold.

Just like him.

He stood on the edge of Oak Street beach, admiring the magnificent skyline that framed the lake and the way the city lights shimmered on the water. For a city that had risen from the ashes he had to admit the architecture was brilliant. He'd visited a slew of cities in the states and abroad in his former life, but none of the places he'd visited had a skyline that rivaled this one. He liked the edginess of cold steel and weathered brick towering over the water, and the contradictions they posed. Lakefront tranquility and a thriving metropolis, it didn't get much better than this.

The truth was he hadn't taken time to appreciate the city the last time he was here. He'd been hell bent on killing Sierra Montgomery and exacting revenge on the bastards who had stolen his life and turned him into a monster. The whole fiasco had ended in quite a blood bath. He hoped the dead were rotting in hell, although by now, they were probably plotting along with Lucifer, scheming to bring about the earth's demise.

He wouldn't put it past them.

The wind kicked up, turning the night even colder. It was insanity to be standing on a beach this late at night with no shelter. He shoved his hands in his pockets and decided to keep walking. Ethan wasn't in any hurry to go home. Too many issues waited there. The old man and his newfound family were expecting a changed man.

What if deep inside he was still rotten to the core?

There was no point in thinking about it. Time would tell. He picked up his pace, falling into step with a group of tourists. With any luck they would lead him somewhere interesting. He needed a drink and to kill some time. He felt a twinge of longing for the pubs back in London. Pints of Guinness and no bullshit, other than the tall tales drunken blokes spun until the wee hours.

It didn't take long to realize he was out of luck. He found himself on Oak Street, smack dab in the middle of the Gold Coast's shopping district. High-end boutiques and trendy eateries gobbled up the pavement setting his teeth on edge. Fate was against him. He didn't know the city well enough to navigate his way to the type of establishment he was looking for. He supposed he could window shop. It wouldn't be the worst idea to pick-up a gift for Sierra. She had saved his life, after all, even though he'd been inches away from killing her. If that didn't deserve a token of appreciation, he was nothing more than a two-bit shitter and should be ashamed of himself.

Ethan shook his head and glanced inside a shoe shop, thinking of all the birds he'd known who'd thought a pair of killer heels and a scantily clad ass would tame him. The twits had been lucky to escape with their lives. A few of them hadn't, like that bitch cooking in hell.

He rubbed his hand over the two-day old beard he sported. His thoughts were taking him down a dangerous road. He had to put the past behind him, to carry on, keep a stiff upper lip and all. He grunted, "Sure mate, easier said than done."

There was no point in loitering. Might as well go home and get the reunion over with. Ethan turned towards the street and shivered as the first drops of rain began to fall. Within seconds, a torrential downpour let loose, made worse by the driving wind. Hail pelted him from all directions.

"Jesus Christ!" He ducked under the awning of the shoe store and cast a longing look inside. His eyes narrowed. The windows steamed up, distorting his view, but his adrenaline kicked into high gear. It was a good God damned thing he hadn't had a drink or he'd have thought he was imagining things. A figure emerged from the back room but it was impossible to see much more than shadows and shapes. The person — he couldn't be certain if it was a man or woman — squatted down and appeared to study something on the floor. Ethan realized his curiosity was obvious so he turned sideways and assumed a casual stance. No need to advertise that he was watching.

The figure rose. Ethan tensed as he watched the figure lift a pair of naked legs from the floor, its feet dangled lifelessly in a pair of killer stilettos. Whoever the person was wrapped the naked legs around their neck, keeping a firm hold on the ankles. At least Ethan assumed they had a firm grip because the figure began to back up dragging the body towards the back room. Moments later, they vanished into the darkness.

"Bloody hell." Ethan scowled, jerked off at what he'd seen. He couldn't ignore it but the last thing he needed was to get embroiled in a red-hot mess within hours of landing in Chicago. Something very wrong was going on inside the shoe store. Whether it was drug-induced rape or far worse, he didn't have a notion, but something bad had just gone down.

The glare of headlights from passing cars hit the rain-splattered window of the shop and illuminated the inside. Ethan rubbed his eyes at the distorted images reflected in the glass. The top of a half-naked mannequin stared back at him, red lips parted in a sultry pot. Another sat with legs crossed, wearing platform strappy heels. *Bugger. That rather complicated things now, didn't it.* The chap inside could have been fiddling with a mannequin.

He took stock of his surroundings. The streets had suddenly emptied. No doubt all the late night crawlers had found shelter in the trendy restaurants and bars. He was utterly alone. He cast a wary glance at the rain, pulled his jacket over his head, and ran out into the storm.

***

Sierra Montgomery glanced at Luke. He poured himself a shot of vodka and tossed it back without so much as a blink. Skinbone Harris swore under his breath, "If that sonofabitch lets Luke down, I swear I'll kill him myself."

"Give him time," Sierra urged. "He's not that late."

He treated her to a steely glare. "I don't know how you can be so damn forgiving."

She didn't have an easy answer. Ethan Wilde had almost succeeded in killing her and everyone she'd grown to love during the Foxtrot ordeal but the truth was they'd all been pawns in a hideous game. Ethan had been torn from the father who loved him and raised by a mother who'd considered him the devil incarnate. It was little wonder Ethan was so screwed up.

Shark scrambled up from his seat on the sofa where he'd been nursing a soft drink. "I propose a toast. To letting the past remain dead and buried, and to new beginnings."

Luke Preston refilled his glass and raised it. "And to Shark — a damned good kid if ever there was one."

Shark blushed and pushed the hair from his eyes. "To Luke, Sierra, and Skinbone who have welcomed me into their hearts and into their family, much love to you all."

Skinbone snarled and shot up from his seat. "What the hell is the matter with all of you? We can sit here and drink and try and make ourselves feel better or we can cut the crap. Ethan Wilde has conned all of you. He's no more reformed than a hog chewing on human remains. The sooner we acknowledge that and move on the better."

Sierra watched the color drain from Luke's face as a result of Skinbone's words. She grabbed Skinbone's arm, squeezing it hard. "What the hell is the matter with you?" she whispered in an angry tone. "Do you really want to ruin this night for Luke?"

"I'm not the one who's ruining it," Skinbone snapped.

Luke finished his drink, grimaced, and wiped his lips. "Will the lot of you stop treating me like I'm some doddering old fool that needs to be pacified? Ethan will be here." He turned to Skinbone. "If you're not ready to accept him as your brother yet, I understand. You're free to leave, though I'd prefer you to stay."

Sierra folded her arms across her chest. "You heard the man, go if you want to."

"Ah hell." Skinbone raked his hands through his hair and shook his head. "I just don't want to see any of you hurt. The man is trouble. I feel it in my bones."

The front door burst open, letting in a chill. Ethan Wilde stood framed in the doorway. "Don't stop chatting on my account, brother," he challenged a cocky grin on his face. When Skinbone didn't respond, Ethan shrugged. "It's all right, mate, I wouldn't trust me either, especially if my bones told me otherwise."

Sierra watched Luke's face light up. His eyes danced in appreciation at the sight of his offspring. Ethan shrugged off his jacket, tossed it on a nearby chair and crossed the room in a few quick strides, embracing Luke in his arms. "The prodigal son has returned home at long last, if you'll still have me that is." The bantering tone left his voice, "I won't blame you if you've had second thoughts."

Luke's arms tightened around the younger man, the son he'd spent half his life searching for. There were tears in his eyes as he patted Ethan's back. "You are always welcome in my home."

"I'm afraid you're stuck with me for now, at least until I land on my feet." Ethan broke the embrace and turned to Sierra. "I don't know quite what to say to you. You saved my life and gave me hope. That's more than anyone's ever done for me. Thank you. The words seem small in comparison, but they do come from the heart."

Sierra wasn't prepared for the onslaught of emotions she felt at confronting her would-be killer face-to-face. She knew he'd been damaged and his actions were a result of a lifetime of brainwashing and torture but it was hard to reconcile the smiling stranger with the cold-eyed killer who had murdered her ex-fiancée and her best friend.

Skinbone sat down beside her and wrapped a comforting arm around her. She felt petty for being angry with him earlier and squeezed his hand. She wiped a tear from her eye and nodded at Ethan, throat suddenly dry. "You're welcome."

Ethan stood in the center of the room. His gaze turned to Skinbone. "I owe you an apology, mate, for shooting you and leaving you for dead. I don't blame you a bit for having reservations about me, but I will do my best to prove to you that the drugs and therapy worked and that I've become a right good chap. I know it will take time and that Luke has been more of a father to you than he ever had the chance to be to me, but I don't plan on letting him or Sierra down, I can assure you of that."

"If you can do that, we won't have a problem," Skinbone allowed, but Sierra could feel the tension in his arm. She moved closer to him, knowing how much those words cost him.

"Fair enough." Ethan glanced at Shark. "You may be the one bloke in this whole mess I didn't intentionally hurt."

Shark lowered his eyes and studied the floor. "But you did hurt dear Damsel and that is hard to forgive. Please, do not disappoint us."

Sierra watched Ethan's reaction. He drew himself up and extended his hand to Shark. "Understood."

Shark refrained from accepting the handshake, but with his customary good grace, he walked over to the bar. "May I offer you a libation after your tedious flight?"

Ethan ignored the snub and wiped his palms on his jeans. "Sure. Do you have Makers Mark?"

"I believe we do." Shark busied himself, setting a glass on the bar, and searching for the right bottle. An awkward silence fell across the room and Sierra searched her mind for something to say. The truth was, seeing Ethan again was much harder than she anticipated.

A sharp rap on the door startled all of them. Sierra glanced at her watch. Almost midnight. Who would be coming by at this hour? No one moved. She sighed. A roomful of men and not one of them willing to answer a damn door.

She slid out from under Skinbone's arm. "I'll get it." Her eyes narrowed in frustration at the testosterone around her turning into useless lumps of clay. She reached behind and checked for the gun she now carried at the small of her back. Keeping one hand on it, Sierra swung open the front door.

A wide-eyed teenager stared back at her, hair limp from the rain, shifting from foot-to-foot and biting a fingernail.

"Oh. Oh my God. You're Sierra Montgomery, aren't you?"

Sierra still wasn't used to being famous. After the death of her ex-fiancée, she'd gone from being a wanted fugitive to playing an instrumental role in bringing down a rogue FBI agent and a multi-billion dollar corporation in cahoots to overthrow the government, although the extent of the horrific plot had been kept under wraps. She gave the girl an uncertain smile. "Can I help you?"

The girl couldn't contain her anxiety. "I'm looking for Shark. Is he here?"

Sierra glanced over her shoulder, raising a brow. The girl was attractive, but far too young for Shark. She opened the door wider, enough to allow the bedraggled girl entry.

Shark finished pouring Ethan's drink and blinked in surprise. "Melissa? What are you doing here?"

The girl was wringing her hands in a comic bookesque dismay. "I'm so sorry to bother you, but I didn't know where else to turn."

His brow creased in concern. "What's happened?"

The girl gulped down a sob. "My best friend, Cherie, she's missing."

Shark cast a wary glance at Sierra. "I met Melissa while I was out walking Cupcake. Her family owns the brownstone next door. She's a very level-headed girl for her age."

Sierra understood. There was no romantic entanglement and the girl's concern was real and not just a flight of teenage fantasy. She inserted herself between the two. "Why do you think your friend is missing?"

Melissa burst into full-out tears. "I never should have covered for her," she wailed miserably. "Now I don't know what to do."

"It's okay," Sierra comforted, "we all make mistakes from time to time."

The girl's sobs grew louder. Sierra glanced at Shark, who demurred, shaking his head. Shark was one of the sweetest human beings on the planet — so his response was uncharacteristic, tweaking Sierra's curiosity. She wrapped her arm around the girl's shoulder and led her to the couch, motioning for Skinbone to move aside. "Tell me what happened and why you think Shark can help."

Melissa shrugged off her jacket, looked around, and wiped her nose on the sleeve of her cashmere sweater. The only sound in the room came from the ice cubes clinking in Ethan's glass as he raised it to his lips and took a healthy swallow. The girl hiccuped and spoke in a halting voice, trembling over each word.

"Cherie's parents are very strict — a lot stricter than mine. She met this boy, a man really, he's in college, and he invited her to a fall formal. It's all she's been talking about for the last month, all she could think about even, she was so excited. She knew her parents would never let her go, so she told them she was spending the night at my house."

Sierra pursed her lips, sure she knew where the conversation was headed. College boys and date-rape drugs were far too common.

Melissa worried the collar of her sweater, pulling it up over her chin and biting it with her lips. "Anyways, Cherie came over straight after school. She bought a dress for the dance a couple weeks ago and was keeping it at my house. There was a pair of shoes she was dying to get at a little boutique just off State Street called Own My Sole…"

The sound of glass shattering on the hardwood floor caused Sierra to jump. Ethan was already grabbing a hand towel to mop up the mess he'd made by dropping his drink. He treated Sierra to a crooked smile. "My apologies for the commotion. Must be jet lag. Don't mind me, I'll just be cleaning things up."

The girl flushed. "Maybe I've come at a bad time."

"No," Sierra reassured her, "go on."

"Cherie never came back. At first, I thought maybe she decided to buy another dress, or that she met her boyfriend somewhere else, but he's been calling me all night, frantic that Cherie never made it to the dance…no one has seen or heard from her. I know I should have called the police but I don't want to get Cherie in trouble with her parents, and she hasn't been missing for forty-eight hours." She sent Shark a shy glance. "I don't know exactly what it is you people do, but I do watch the news and I know you and Shark solved the mystery of who killed your fiancée and that other scientist, so I was hoping you could help me find out what happened to my friend."

"Listen, luv," Ethan poured himself another drink and waved it at Melissa. "You may be a wee bit in over your head, and this isn't a merry band of private investigators. My best advice? Go to the cops with your suspicions. Tell them the last known place your friend was spotted was at that shoe store. The police will be better equipped to serve you."

Sierra sent Ethan a blistering glare. "You haven't even been here an hour and you're making judgment calls?"

He leveled his gaze at her. "I'm just saying this may not be something you want to get involved in."

"That's not your choice to make," Sierra responded through gritted teeth. She had an aversion to people telling her what to do.

Shark perked up out of his apathy. "Indeed, if fair Melissa is in need of our services we are happy to oblige."

"Not a good idea, mate." Ethan's tone held an ominous edge. "Leave it to the coppers."

"Do you have a problem, Ethan? If you do, please enlighten us." Skinbone walked over to the bar, a dangerous glint in his eyes.

"Not at all. Can I pour you a drink, *brother?* You look like you could use one?"

Sierra watched the exchange with interest. Ethan Wilde was hiding something, but for the life of her, she couldn't imagine what it could be. She also knew Skinbone wouldn't rest until he shook the truth out of his adopted brother, but for now, they had a desperate and terrified teenager on their hands. Sierra turned her attention back towards Melissa.

"Are you sure Cherie didn't change her mind about the dance and go home?"

"I'm positive," she sighed. "Cherie's father is a prominent Minister, which is why he is so strict with her. He and Mrs. Monroe — Cherie's mother — are hosting some event tonight. Mrs. Monroe called my house to remind Cherie of something. I covered by saying she was taking a shower and that I would give her the message."

"Do you have a recent picture of your friend?"

"I do." Melissa dug in her bag. When she looked up again her eyes filled with hope. "This is Cherie. *Please, please find her.*"

Sierra stared down at a picture of a gorgeous light-skinned African American young woman with a complexion the color of caramel, and curly shoulder-length brown hair. The girl's smile was bright and infectious and her deep brown eyes crinkled at the corners with the hint of laughter.

"So you'll help me?" Melissa asked.

Sierra wasn't sure what to say. Her heart went out to the girl, but they weren't in the business of finding missing kids. She didn't want to make a promise she couldn't keep.

Shark spared her from answering. He reached for the picture, turning it over in his hands. "I'll see if I can turn up any information, but I'm not certain how much help we can be. Locating a missing person takes time, and if your friend is in trouble, time might be the one thing she doesn't have."

***

Ethan Wilde settled into his room with a heavy conscience. He'd come to Chicago prepared to make a new life, to start out clean, and then this bloody teenager shows up out of nowhere, landing him in the thick of things. The turn of events certainly placed him in an awkward situation. What the hell was he going to say? That he was strolling about town, apprehensive of showing up at his father's home and by the way, during that stroll he might have seen a woman being dragged by her ankles in the very same shoe store the girl had mentioned. Even to his jaded ears, the story sounded highly implausible.

He stripped off his clothes, only to put them back on a moment later. Sleep would elude him so he might as well make good use of his time. A little investigating was in order. He cracked open his bedroom door, hoping his housemates were either fast asleep or at least tucked into their rooms for the night. Granted, his father, Luke Preston had purchased a mansion on Astor Street, but it did him no good if the occupants were milling about. Luck was on his side. He crept down the staircase and let himself out, grimacing at the cold and rain waiting to greet him.

He wasn't quite certain Chicago was his kind of town.

Sierra paced the suite of rooms Luke had provided for them. Until now, she'd been content with their current arrangement. She still wasn't ready to go back to the house she had inhabited before her life was upended a year ago, but she was suddenly regretting her decision due to the lack of privacy living with Luke and Shark provided.

Skinbone came out of the shower, wearing only a towel. His long, damp, jet-black hair skimmed his shoulders. A beat of desire rushed through her. Never in her wildest dreams would she have imagined herself intimately involved with a paid assassin — but real life seldom resembled fantasies or dreams. He came up behind her and began massaging the tension in her neck and shoulders. He kissed the tender spot just below her ear.

"Tell me what you're thinking, little one."

She turned and wrapped her arms around his waist. "I think Shark's friend has a valid concern. No teenager involved with an older boy is going to go out for shoes on the day of a big dance and not come back."

His fingers probed her skin, seeking out the tightest knots and kneading them with a warm, firm touch. She sighed and nuzzled against his broad chest. "What I don't understand is Ethan's reaction, or why he, of all people, would advise going to the police. It's odd, isn't it?"

He ran his hands through her hair, pulling her closer. "Ethan is odd." His breath tickled her ear. "Why should that surprise you?"

"It bothers me more than it surprises me. You know how I hate things that don't make sense."

"That curiosity of yours is going to get you in trouble one day." He pulled her hair to the side and kissed the sensitive curve of her shoulder.

Sierra shivered with pleasure, backing out of Skinbone's embrace. She grinned up at him. "But that's what I keep you around for — to keep me safe."

He raised a brow, folded his arms across his chest, and peered down at her, a look of mock consternation on his face. "Oh, so you think that's all I'm good for, do you?"

She shrugged and answered in a flippant tone, careful to keep her expression neutral. "Well, that *is* on the top of the list."

"Hmmm, top of the list, huh?" He sighed and wrapped his arms around her. "I think you may need a refresher course in a few other things I'm good at."

She tried to squiggle away, but he tightened his grip. "You ought to know by now you can't escape me that easily."

"I seem to recall I was actually quite good at eluding you once upon a time," she challenged.

"Ah, but you see, sweetheart, we've moved passed once upon a time and into happily ever after." With one swift move, they tumbled onto the bed. Sierra dissolved into a fit a giggles as Skinbone set out to prove a few of the many other reasons she kept him around.

***

Unlike New York, Chicago, apparently was a city that slept. Perhaps that explained why Chicagoans were a tad less surly than their East Coast counterparts, they knew when to call it a night. A few drunken college students tumbled out of bars here and there but for the most part, the streets were cold and empty. The irony that the same expression could have once described him wasn't lost on Ethan. For the first time in his life, he was realizing he did have a soul, and it was all thanks to Sierra Montgomery.

Life was a hell of a lot simpler when one didn't have a conscience. He could have been home, tucked into a warm bed with nary a thought to disrupt his sleep. Instead, he was skirting raindrops fast turning to snow and freezing his goddamn ass off all because some bloody teenaged girl hadn't heeded her parents warning not to get all hot and bothered over an older boy.

His footsteps slowed and he shook himself, thinking of how ridiculous he was being, risking frozen limbs because some bird had her knickers in a knot. He almost turned back, and he would have too, if the curious images he'd seen earlier at the shoe store hadn't kept nagging at him.

Bloody hell, he was turning into a bleeding-hearted fool.

Ethan dashed across the street, paying no heed to the traffic lights. A cab came barreling out of nowhere and almost clipped him. He gave the driver the finger and did a piss poor impression of a menacing S.O.B. Back in the day, he would have caused the cab to crash and burst into flames. Ah, for the good old days. He shoved his hands into his coat pockets and frowned. Reformed evil wasn't all it was cracked up to be, there was something to be said about possessing the ability to destroy things at will.

Ah well, that was the price to be paid for months of therapy, drugs and treatment to turn him into a regular, far less dangerous bloke. He had to suppose there was a reason and purpose he would come to appreciate one day. At least, he hoped so. The goody two-shoe act he was pulling tonight was quite an adjustment for him, and one he wasn't quite comfortable with yet.

All in good time, mate, he cautioned himself, all in good time. He cupped his hands over his eyes and pressed his face against the glass windows of the shoe store. Nothing seemed amiss. Mannequins in various stages of nudity leered at him from inside the lush, tony boutique.

He snarled back at the plastic, taunting faces. "So you think you can toy with me, do you? Don't even try it, my vapid little beauties. I'll bet you my left kidney something isn't quite right here. That's right; I dare you synthetic lovelies to prove me wrong."

He'd let his hair grow out while he was in treatment. It whipped across his face as a gust of wind kicked up from the east, courtesy of Lake Michigan. Ethan pulled his black hair back into a makeshift bun and strutted down the obnoxiously long block until he reached an alleyway. He rounded the corner and swore under his breath. A semi idled in the alley, the large mouth of its back door yawning wide to accommodate corrugated containers from the shoe store being hand loaded into its belly.

Wanting a closer look, Ethan pulled up the collar of his leather jacket, lowered his head, and began weaving down the alley like a misbegotten drunk. His nostrils flared as he staggered into brick walls, cursing up a blue streak in the belligerent way fellows who've had a few too many often do, and mumbled to himself as he neared the truck.

Two men clad in black overcoats stood at the back door, supervising the loading of the containers, their breath coming out in cold puffs of air as they spoke. Ethan could tell by the cut of their coats and the sheen of their shoes that their garments were pricy — these were no ordinary shop employees. From a distance, he couldn't hear what they were saying, but it was clear that they were speaking either Russian or Polish — though he had no basis for feeling the way he did, something about that struck him as off. Had he been in Ukrainian village, or the Northwest side of Chicago, he might have felt differently, but here in the alley behind expensive boutiques, in the middle of the night?

Ethan did his best to make enough ruckus to draw their attention. The larger of the two, a burly, bald-headed type, broke off the conversation, frowned, and eyed him with suspicion. His right hand slipped beneath his overcoat — a telltale sign that his fingers now coiled around the barrel of a gun.

Bugger. That was a complication Ethan hadn't been looking for. It meant these bastards had something to hide which didn't bode well for Shark's little friends. *Son of a blooming bitch.* A little voice inside his head mocked him, telling himself that he should have left well enough alone, but it was too late. He was here and in too deep. He figured he might as well make the best of it and see if he could get a bead on what was going on. No time like the present to put on a good show.

"Hey!" Ethan grinned and waved both hands in the air, affecting his best New York accent. "Hey, do you think one of you guys can help me out?" He let his jaw go slack, rubbed the stubble on his left cheek and concentrated on making his eyes as unfocused as a man on a drunk. "I've gotten twisted around."

The bald-headed man barked out a stream of guttural Russian/Polish to his companion and approached Ethan with a menacing look in his eye. "What is it you are wanting? You have no business here."

"Business?" Ethan stumbled forward and clutched his belly as he laughed. "No business, not tonight." He let his legs propel him sideways where he laid a hand on a brick wall for support. "No, man. I was supposed to be meeting my friends at a gentleman's club after dinner." He winked and leered, finally getting the man's attention.

"A gentleman's club you say? How is it you are lost here?"

Ethan raised his hand to give the bald man a high five, dropping it when the man didn't respond. "Women," he sighed. "My girl called to check up on me, can you imagine that? She's not used to me being out of town. My friends went ahead without me and I don't know where the hell they are."

"Women," the man grunted in agreement. "They need to learn their place, no?"

"Yes!" Ethan pointed a finger in the air. "Damn straight." He lurched forward, slurring his words, "They don't understand sometimes we men need a little fun, to blow off some steam, you know?"

Baldy smiled, revealing a golden front tooth, and waved towards his companion to join them. "This man is looking for a gentleman's club. What is the closest one nearby? We help him get where he wants to go, yes?"

The smaller man scurried forward, hands stuffed in the pockets of his coat. The bald man narrowed his eyes, "You and your friends, you have a lot of dough?"

"Oh." Ethan nodded, "Yes, absolutely. They said this was a high class place, all the way."

"Not exactly downtown, but I am guessing you are looking for VIP's on Kingsbury Street — oddly enough a block or so off Hooker Street," the man snorted with laughter. "You will need to take a cab, my friend; it's not far from North Ave, which on a cold night is quite a walk from here."

Ethan knew the gig was up; he had no reason to hang around. He also had no reason to make the men suspicious. Putting on his best obnoxious tourist act, he backed up and pointed at the men with both index fingers. "You guys are golden. Thanks. I owe you one."

"Hey." Baldy's hand clamped on tight to Ethan's upper arm. He leaned in towards Ethan, close enough for him to smell the mint on the man's breath. "You go there, ask for Pepper. Tell her you get a lap dance and anything else you want on Vlad. Go. Have fun. Enjoy."

Ethan nodded. "Thanks. On Vlad. Thanks, man. Have a good one." He turned back the way he'd come and waved to the two men, anxious to get the hell out of there. Vlad. A Russian name. Did the Russian mob have a presence in Chicago? Who the hell could keep track of these things, certainly not him; he'd lived most of his life abroad.

He did know one thing for sure. There was an odd smell coming from the truck they'd been guarding, and it sure as hell wasn't from the scent of shoe leather being transported in the wee hours of the morning.

***

Sierra cracked open one eye. She was spent from hours of lovemaking and wished she could burrow into Skinbone's arms and sleep until morning. Tempting as the thought was, she couldn't rest, not with the picture of Melissa's friend haunting her.

Skinbone's arm clamped tight around her waist. She eased herself out of his embrace and scooted out of bed, careful not to disturb him. Sierra knew him well enough to know that he would try to talk some sense into her, and he was probably right. But how could she sleep when a girl's life was hanging in the balance?

She grabbed her robe and hurried out of the room, walking on tiptoes so she wouldn't wake him. Breathing a sigh of relief, she took the stairs two at a time to the third floor where Shark had a suite of rooms. A light glowed beneath his door, she didn't bother to knock knowing that Shark was using his cyber magic to try to locate Melissa's friend.

She turned the doorknob and poked her head into his room. "Any luck?"

Shark glanced up and pushed his black-rimmed glasses up where they'd slid down his nose. "Though it pains me to say so, I believe my luck has run out."

Sierra walked inside, pulled up a chair, and sat beside him at his desk. "I don't follow, what do you mean?"

"I foolishly thought the task would be a simple one, a matter of retrieving videos from the city's surveillance cameras."

"You hacked into the Chicago Police Department?" her voice rose an octave.

He shuddered. "As I've said before, hacking is an ugly word, but I digress. I did indeed see the fair Cherie enter the shoe store Melissa mentioned. By the time stamp indicated on the video, she arrived at four fifty-four, six minutes before the shop closes for the day."

"How long did she stay?"

"That's the problem. Footage from every camera, including those belonging to adjacent shops went dark between four-fifty-nine and five o-four. At first I suspected foul play, but a quick check of Com Ed's records indicate there was indeed a five minute power outage in the area do to icing on the wires. At five thirty-five, as you can see, an average height male, dressed in a black overcoat exits the shop and locks up for the night. Nowhere, on any camera, is there another glimpse of young Cherie."

Sierra sighed and leaned back in her chair, raking her fingers through her hair. She bit her lip and stared at Shark's computer screen. "A girl doesn't just vanish at that time of day on a crowded street. Somebody would have seen something if she'd been snatched."

"My thought exactly. I took the liberty of checking to see if anyone reported a disturbance during that period. There was not a single call to the police or to 911."

"Shark," she sighed in exasperation, "do you know what will happen to you if you are caught hacking into police department mainframes?"

He grinned. "I do. Which is why I will never get caught."

"So you hope."

"So I know." He took off his glasses and rubbed his eyes. "But for now, I've hit a dead end. Short of questioning the shoe store employees, there's not much else I can do."

Sierra's eyes narrowed. "Nine minutes."

"Excuse me?"

"If Cherie left before the power outage she was in the store for less than nine minutes. Could she have purchased shoes that quick?"

"From what Melissa said, she knew exactly what she was looking for."

Sierra shook her head. "Even so, she'd have to find the shoe on display, show it to the clerk who in turn would need to get it from the back room. Then she'd have to try both shoes on to make sure they fit, walk around a bit, and trust me, a teenage girl would spend at least a minute or longer admiring them in the mirror. If, in fact, the first size fit her, and she didn't need to try on a half a size larger or smaller. After that, the clerk still had to box them up, ring up the sale, bag them and Cherie would have needed to leave the store and be at least a block or two away not to show up on any of the camera's when the power came back on. I'm assuming you also checked the surrounding area?"

"Yes, of course, every camera leading back to Melissa's house."

"All of that in less than nine minutes. Doesn't that seem a bit impossible to you?"

"What are you saying? You think she never left the shoe store?"

Sierra shrugged. "I'm saying we need to be careful if we intend to question the clerk. We also need to know more about this older boyfriend. For all we know he could have been in on it and called Melissa as a smoke screen or to give himself an alibi. If she had her heart set on a particular pair of shoes, she may have mentioned it to the boyfriend. He could have been waiting outside the store for her and she wouldn't have thought twice about getting in his car."

"You make some excellent points."

"The least we can do is check these things out. If nothing comes of it then we'll advise Melissa to go to the police. By that time, Cherie's parents will no doubt be involved." She frowned. "I do feel bad about keeping them in the dark. They should know that their daughter is missing."

"I tend to agree, but at this point, all they could do is worry. The police won't consider this a case until the girl hasn't been seen or heard from in forty-eight hours."

"A stupid, damn law. It leaves too many hours for a trail to go cold." She stood up to leave. "Tomorrow, find out what you can about the boyfriend. I'll wait to see what you come up with and then I'll take the shoe store. Maybe I can charm some information out of the clerk."

"Sounds like a plan."

Sierra nodded, pausing before she shut the door behind her. "Oh and Shark? One last thing. Let's keep this between us. Skinbone doesn't need to know what we're up to. He worries about me too much."

"Only because he loves you, dear Damsel."

"I know he does," she smiled, "but that doesn't mean I want him loving me to death. He forgets sometimes that I'm more than capable of taking care of myself."

***

Ethan stamped his feet against the chill, hoping to get the circulation back in them. He fitted his key into the lock and eased the door open, hoping his gaggle of housemates were still abed for the night. He was luck. The house was dark and nary a peep echoed from any of the downstairs rooms. Just as well. He wasn't in the mood for company.

He unzipped his jacket, thought better of it, and decided to keep it on. This infernal Chicago cold was going to take some getting used to, same as the niggling conscience he was developing.

"What to do, what to do?" he muttered as he headed towards the wet bar, searched in the dark for the bottle of Makers Mark and poured himself a stiff one. The whiskey spread through him, taking a bit of the edge off. He slammed down the rest of his drink and poured himself another before taking refuge in an easy chair to think.

Something rotten was going on in the back alleys of Chicago's Gold Coast, he was certain of it. Vlad and his counterpart were no ordinary blokes. The question was did any of it pertain to Fishy boy's young friend. Shark, he corrected himself, the man's name was Shark, and he was part and parcel of the new family Ethan was now a member of. He would do well to keep reminding himself of that. He'd be dead right now if Sierra and her odd assortment of companions hadn't spared his blackened soul.

The question was, what was he willing to do for them in return? He had no blasted idea if the shenanigans in the shoe store had anything at all to do with the missing girl. If he spoke his piece, a cloud of suspicion might turn towards him and rightly so. He didn't need that kind of blame or aggravation; especially since this once, he didn't deserve it. But if he kept mum and the girl ended up dead or worse, the blame would surely land on his shoulders.

He crossed his legs and nursed his drink, conscious of his right foot shaking as he pondered his predicament. "Bloody son of a bitchin' hell."

The night seemed to drag on as he finished a second drink and then a third. Somewhere along the way, he shed his jacket and felt the heat rushing to his head. Bolstered by alcohol, he made his decision. The Fish — Shark — had been the first to extend a welcome by offering him a drink. The least he could do was help the lad out and put a bug in his ear. It would be far less awkward than confronting Sierra or his adopted brother Skinbone. Ethan sensed correctly, there was no love lost there.

Skinbone was going to reserve judgment until Ethan proved his worth and he was protective of those he loved. Skinbone had been given a chance at a normal life, whereas Ethan had been condemned to a hell not of his choosing. Spilt milk between brothers. Ethan couldn't afford allowing that to mess things up.

He drained the last of his whiskey and set the glass down. Since he hadn't yet had the chance to explore his new quarters, the house was a maze. From what he understood, he and Luke occupied the ground floor, Sierra and Skinbone had their own set of rooms on the second, and Shark's residence was on the third.

With a groan, Ethan slapped his thighs and stood, not relishing the trek up three flights of stairs.

***

Sierra dropped her robe on a chair and pulled back the covers, careful to ease back onto the bed. She scooted under the blankets and laid her head on the pillow, suddenly exhausted.

Skinbone's hand clamped around her wrist and he shot up in bed. "Did Shark make any headway on the missing girl?"

She blinked, feigning surprise, too tired to get into a discussion tonight. The yawn was real. "I don't know," she murmured sleepily. "I was a little restless and went downstairs to have a cup of tea."

"Why don't I believe that? I know you, sweetheart; you aren't going to let this rest. I'll help with whatever you need."

Sierra groaned and rolled over. "There isn't much we can do." She explained about the surveillance videos and the blank spot when the cameras went black. "Shark is going to see what more he can find out about the boyfriend."

"And let me guess, you're going to talk to the people at the shoe shop."

She pushed back a strand of hair back that had fallen across her face. "Can't hurt to talk to them. That's the easy part. I'll just show them her picture and see what they remember. What could go wrong?"

Skinbone reached out and caressed her cheek. His touch was warm against her skin. "Would it make you feel better if I went along with Shark to lean on the boyfriend and see if we can shake any information out of him?"

"You would do that?"

"Of course I would. I'm not going to turn my back on a kid in trouble." His expression turned grim. "I'm also thinking that if questioning the boyfriend turns out to be a bust, someone should speak to the parents and inform them what is going on. I somehow don't think a petrified teenager is the best candidate for the job."

"Some badass you turned out to be," she chuckled.

His eyes twinkled. "I was a badass in my former life, before you torpedoed your way into my world and gave me reason to want to stick around for a good long while."

She felt a warm glow deep inside, and knew how lucky she was to have found a man like Skinbone. Sierra wrapped her arms around his neck and studied his face, memorizing every feature. "Have I mentioned that I love you?" she whispered, leaning in to kiss him.

"You have, but that's the one thing I will never get tired of hearing." He drew her close; she rested her head on his chest, listening to the sound of his heartbeat as she drifted off to sleep.

***

Ethan rapped on Shark's door, uncertain of what he was going to say. He wasn't used to camaraderie, having spent most of his life as a lone wolf, bent on revenge. He wasn't quite certain his two cents would be welcome and wondered again, why he was inserting himself into the situation.

What did he know, really? The woman he saw being dragged could have just as easily been a mannequin as a person, and the two dubious types that were loading the shipment at night might have been the shops owners pulling long hours to make the high-end bucks. It stood to reason shipments to and from Europe could arrive and depart at odd hours, especially if they were selling counterfeit designer shoes and handbags, a growing trend in America.

The booze was causing his logic to ricochet back and forth. One moment he was certain he'd witnessed something of note and the next he was convinced he was jumping at shadows that didn't exist. Exhaustion after his long flight was kicking in. He knocked a second time and stared at the door. No light seeped out from beneath the crack in the doorway and no sounds came from within.

Shark had probably done the smart thing and gone to bed, unlike himself, who'd spent the night prowling the streets to solve a mystery he'd fabricated, all thanks to the histrionics of a frightened teenager. No doubt, the girl's friend had turned up by now and was fast asleep as well.

He decided to push the entire nonsense from his mind and hit the sack, glad that he'd been spared the embarrassment of making a total ass out of himself.

**

They hadn't counted on the inconvenience of dealing with kids still in school. Skinbone and Shark had caught up with Melissa before she left for class and got a better handle on the boyfriend, but were forced to wait until he was finished with classes before they could question him. They had no jurisdiction to pull him out of school.

Sierra wasn't faring any better on her end. She'd decided to have Melissa accompany her to the shoe store — the time frame in which Cherie went missing still bothered her — she wanted Melissa to point out the pair of shoes her friend had been so desperate to purchase and to find out Cherie's size. A minor detail, but one that would prove whether or not the shoes were in stock. For all they knew, Cherie had hurried out of the store in hopes of finding the same pair somewhere else and disappeared along the way.

It was her intention to mirror Cherie's actions from the moment she entered the shop until she left and to time the process from start to finish. If nothing else, it would set her fears to rest that something had happened to the girl inside the store.

She shivered as a cold blast of wind hit the back of her neck and wound her scarf tighter against the chill. Winter seemed to come earlier each year. Sierra glanced at her watch and back at the imposing structure and wondered why all girls Catholic High Schools seemed to bare an uncanny resemblance to prisons —or maybe that was just her own experience talking. The strict environment didn't serve to keep these girls out of trouble.

For the tenth time in as many minutes, she regretted not bringing her car. Considering the temperature, it would have been worth shelling out the thirty bucks it cost to park near Own Your Sole. At least then, she wouldn't have been at risk of turning blue. She almost sobbed in relief as the heavy school doors finally swung open and she spotted Melissa racing down the steps.

"Have you found her?" the girl gasped, out of breath.

"No, I'm sorry." Sierra shook her head, "But you can help me try to figure out what happened to your friend."

"Anything," Melissa's expression was earnest. "I'll do anything I can. She's been my best friend since grade school. I can't bear the thought of anything bad happening to her, and knowing that part of it is my fault."

Sierra felt for her. She wrapped her arm around the girl's shoulders. "You probably shouldn't have lied for her, but this isn't your fault, you understand me? With or without your help she would have found a way to sneak out with this boy. When you're young and in love, people take all kinds of crazy risks. Let this be a lesson to you, no boy is worth it. Especially one that has to be kept a secret from parents. That's bad news all the way. If you can't bring him home, he's not the sort of boy to be alone with, got it?"

Melissa's head bobbed up and down. "Yes, ma'am, I've got it."

"Good." They started walking in the direction of the shoe store. "Could you just do me one more favor, please?"

"Yes, of course."

"Don't call me ma'am."

***

Steven Anthony Peters was a cocky S.O.B., but after an hour of grilling, Skinbone Harris was convinced the preppy twerp had no part in Cherie Monroe's disappearance.

The kid was slick, but he was no kidnapper. He didn't even have the balls God gave him to keep from wetting his pants during Skinbone's inquisition. That didn't win him any sympathy. The little bastard didn't even have enough brains to get over himself. He kept whining that Cherie had stood him up, and that he'd endured a night of needling from his frat brothers who no longer believed he was dating a rich, hot, prominent black chick.

It made Skinbone want to pound the shit out of him. If Shark hadn't been there, he might have introduced the kid to his fist. Growing up, he'd always hated punks like Steven Anthony Peters. His distaste for the type hadn't tempered with age, he had no patience for white bread, entitled assholes who thought the world owed them a foot kissing.

Skinbone jerked his head towards Shark. "Give me a minute."

To his credit, Shark didn't bat an eyelash. He straightened up, cleared his throat, and said, "Take all the time you need."

Skinbone grunted his response, grabbed the kid by the collar, and threw him against the wall, making sure the punk felt his hot breath on his face. "When we find Cherie, and we will, you stay out of her life. You are not to approach her, talk to her, text her, or even look in her direction. If I hear one *hint* that you've contacted her, you're gonna have me to deal with. Are we clear?"

The kid was sweating bullets. "Yeah, okay, we're clear."

Skinbone kept hold of the boy's collar and tossed him towards the floor. Steven Anthony fell to his knees and cowered in the face of Skinbone's rage. "She's history. I won't have anything to do with her, I swear."

He glowered down at the kid until he was shaking.

"Never again. I promise."

"Make sure that's a promise you keep."

***

Ethan woke up on edge. It didn't help that he'd slept half the day away. He pulled on jeans and a T-shirt and headed out of his room in search of coffee. The pot was still on, but the house seemed oddly cold. Not in temperature, but in the fact that he seemed to be alone.

He poured himself a steaming cup and threw caution to the wind. "Hello? Is anybody here?" he bellowed. "Anyone? Someone?"

Silence greeted him.

"Come on now, is this any way to treat a bloke on his homecoming?" He took a sip of the strong black brew and wandered around the place. When no answer was forthcoming, he sighed. "Apparently so."

Ethan had hoped for better, but this was the lot he got. So much for a hearty welcome. Left to his own devices, he grew bored by the time he finished his first cup. He rubbed the scruff on his chin and looked around. "What the bloody hell do people do around here?"

His stomach rumbled in response. All he'd had to eat in the last twenty-four hours was a ten-dollar sandwich composed of dry turkey on a stale roll during the plane ride to Chicago. He strolled over to the fridge and peeked inside. The shelves were crammed full of food, but he wasn't much of a cook. He let the door swing shut and headed back to his room where he pulled on a sweater and grabbed his jacket and scarf.

There had to be somewhere decent to eat in this town.

Sierra gave Melissa an encouraging smile. "All I need you to do is show me the shoes Cherie wanted to buy. I'll take it from there."

Melissa returned the smile. "Whatever you say. Thank you for helping me."

"Let's just hope this gets us somewhere." She swung open the door and they both stepped inside. Sierra got a bad feeling as soon as they entered. Her eyes swung to the left and to the right, taking in the trashy displays and the scantily clad mannequins. There was one other patron in the store, a middle-aged woman clinging to youth, with a tightly pulled face, and a skirt peering out from her opened coat that was too short to be appropriate for her age.

In one corner, thigh-high boots sat comfortably displayed alongside handcuffs and whips. In another, six inch stilettos lay on their side nestled against red lingerie with peek-a-boo bra's and crotchless panties. This obviously was not your Momma's shoe store, and Sierra was puzzled how a shop like this occupied prime retail space on Chicago's Gold Coast until she picked up several pairs of shoes and read the designer labels.

Her first instinct was to hustle Melissa out of there until she remembered the girl had been here before. Blinking back her shock, she gripped Melissa's arm and asked her to point out the shoes.

Melissa glanced around the store, nonplused by her environment. "Umm. They moved the display. Give me a minute."

Sierra glanced at her watch. Cherie would have had the same reaction, needing a moment to find her coveted pair of shoes.

"Over there, I think." Melissa headed towards a far too early Christmas display complete with a racy looking Mrs. Claus clutching a pair of decorative Christmas balls in a highly compromising manner.

Sierra swallowed her disgust, pondering whether a call to channel seven's eye team was in order. This store was better suited to Broadway and Clark, a neighborhood that catered to adult kink. Melissa forged ahead and picked up a pair of shoes in triumph. "These are the ones!"

A clerk materialized from the back room. She could tell in an instant that he was European. What concerned her was the way his eyes slid over their bodies. To hell with timing a shoe shopping event, she wanted to get Melissa out of there.

"I don't think so," she said loud enough for the clerk to hear. "They're a little too old for you."

"But I thought…" Melissa protested.

"Forget what you thought," Sierra snapped, hoping Melissa would follow her lead. "You're not getting them and that's final."

"But?" Melissa squinted, confused.

"But nothing." Sierra pushed Melissa forward. "We're leaving and that's that." Instinct kicked in, or maybe it was her unhealthy curiosity. She paused at the doorway and met the clerk's gaze head on. The blatant look in his eyes chilled her to the bone, but she forced herself to return his look with a knowing smile and a wink.

Two-seconds later and sweating bullets, Sierra steered them out of there. It was time to take Melissa home. She'd come back a little later, without the girl.

***

A full belly greatly improved his mood. Ethan braved the cold and decided to walk a bit — starting over with a new life was going to take some work — but at the moment he had nothing else to do. At some point, he was going to have to make amends, sit down with each of his new housemates, and apologize for the harm he'd done. It still amazed him that the lot of them could be so forgiving.

Blokes stood on almost every corner collecting for charities and scores of shoppers bustled through the streets oblivious of the fact that there was a recession.

He marveled at the spirit these folks displayed and wondered if he'd ever feel normal. By all rights, he should have been in prison after taking the lives of Sierra's nearest and dearest, a prime example of the power of forgiveness.

With that thought in mind, he decided that if he'd ever gain acceptance as normal, he was going to have to act the part. He couldn't recall a time or place where he'd ever shopped for gifts, but there was no time like the present. He owed people and a small token of appreciation was in order.

The bloody hell of it was the idea of gift shopping made him almost cheery, another sensation that was foreign to him. If he was going to cement the changes inside him, there was no time like the present to get started. And if his shopping excursion led him past the shoe store, there was no harm in taking another look at things.

***

Skinbone clenched his jaw. He'd been holding out the hope that the boyfriend had a hand in Cherie's disappearance. With that theory now turning to rubble, his mind raced with all the horrific fates a young girl like Cherie could fall victim to.

A kid with everything to live for didn't just vanish off the streets of Chicago, not without a helping hand. The hell of it was they didn't have much to go on.

"What now?" Shark asked. "Do we talk to the parents?"

Skinbone slid inside the car and slammed the driver's side door shut. "Not yet. Do you have your computer with you?"

"I do indeed, as always."

"Let's see if we can find out a little more about Cherie, or if her parents had any enemies. Not everyone is a fan of the good minister."

Shark's mouth dropped open. "You think she was kidnapped?"

Skinbone's voice lowered to a growl, "I'm pretty damn sure she was taken." He sighed and leaned back against the headrest. "I hate to say this, but maybe we should hope for a kidnapping. At least that way there's a small chance we'll get her back alive."

***

Sierra had enough of freezing her ass off. Luck was on her side when she found metered parking two blocks north of the shoe store. She dug through the bottom of her purse for three bucks in quarters — the cost to feed a parking meter for an hour. It would be easier to swipe her credit card but she'd be damned if she was going to add insult to injury by paying interest for the privilege of parking at a curb. Still it was better than the thirty dollars she'd have to pay to self-park in a lot.

She shook her head at the exorbitant fees and bent her face against the bitter cold. The windchill near the lake dipped into the lower teens, causing her to shiver. It wasn't even Halloween yet, but white Christmas lights glittered from bare branched trees and it seemed a few stores were already busy setting up Christmas displays. Considering the weather, it almost seemed appropriate.

Her footsteps slowed as she reached the shoe store. Sierra hesitated, looking inside before she opened the door. Despite the cold, her palms were sweating. She pulled off her gloves, stuffed them in her coat pocket, and wiped her hands on the soft fabric.

It was now or never. Sierra took a deep breath and walked in. She'd timed her arrival to coincide with Cherie's from the day before. The same clerk who had been there earlier simply stared at her from behind the cash register. She found it disconcerting that he made no move to greet her, or acknowledge that he'd seen her there a mere two hours before.

Sierra pretended to look around for a few minutes before making her way to the display Melissa pointed out that afternoon. She picked up the strappy, silver platform shoe and turned it over in her hand. It reminded her of the styles from the late seventies and early eighties. She glanced towards the counter in search of the clerk and jumped when he spoke from directly behind her.

"May I help you?"

She forced a smile and held out the shoe. "I'd like to try these on in a size seven."

"Certainly. Please have a seat and I will be with you in a moment."

She placed the shoe down on the display and exhaled, realizing she'd been holding her breath. Sierra waited until he vanished into the back room, sat down, and unzipped her purse to make sure she had the picture of Cherie. No matter how uncomfortable the clerk made her, she was going to have to show him the picture and ask for assistance in retracing the moments before the girl went missing. Not that she expected him to be much help; there was something odd about the man.

Sierra checked the time. A little over four minutes had passed since she'd entered the store. It was becoming clear that Cherie could not have made a purchase in less than nine minutes. They were at five minutes and counting before he emerged from the back room with two bright pink shoe boxes in his hands.

"One more moment please," he said without setting down the boxes or glancing her way. His face was devoid of expression as he walked towards the front door and clicked the lock in place. He checked the door to make sure the bolt was secure and pulled a shade down over the glass.

"Closing time," he explained in a monotone voice. "But we are in no hurry, are we?"

His manner caused the hair on the back of her arms to stand on end. Instinct screamed for her to get the hell out of there. She told herself she was being paranoid, to calm down and see things through.

"I don't want to keep you. I can always come back another time."

"You are here now and I can tell by looking at you that these shoes were designed especially for you."

He still hadn't cracked a smile. She snuck another peek at her watch. Eight minutes.

"Someone is waiting for you?" he asked.

"No," she tried to keep her tone light. "Silly habit, I suppose, always checking the time."

"Yes. Quite silly." He set the boxes down beside her, pulled a short stool in front of her, and sat down on it, blocking her exit. His eyes never left her face as he took her foot in his hand, unzipped the suede boot she was wearing and tossed it across the floor.

His behavior bordered on rude. First, he'd agreed she was silly, and now he was throwing her boots aside with no regard to her property. And she didn't like the way he was staring at her. The hell with it, she wasn't sticking around. Without warning, the lights dimmed, plunging the shop into near darkness. There was no longer any doubt in her mind that something had happened to Cherie and that she was staring at the prime suspect.

Sierra swallowed hard, not wanting to tip her hand and reveal her suspicions. If they had any chance of finding out what happened to the girl, she had to play it cool.

"You know, I need to be somewhere. I don't mean to rush you but I am sort of in a hurry."

He scooted the stool closer, still keeping a firm grasp on her foot. "You said no one was waiting for you."

Now she was getting pissed off. "I said I need to *be* somewhere. If you'll excuse me…"

He was pulling a shoe out of the box, a multicolored stiletto that wrapped around the foot and buckled up the front.

"That isn't what I asked for," she said with an edge to her voice.

"Perhaps not, but this shoe will take you where you need to go."

Sierra tried to twist her foot away, but he jammed the shoe over her instep, in a single deft move, pulling the strap tight. She cried out in a mixture of pain and shock as something sharp penetrated the tender sole of her foot and plunged deep inside.

"Jesus Christ, get that off me. Something is stabbing me."

"Must be a nail inside." He yanked her foot upwards and forced it beneath his thigh, trapping her leg on the stool. He pushed the other shoe onto her left foot and a searing pain ripped through her instep as he fastened the shoe on her.

Fury replaced the shock of unexpected pain. She hurtled herself off the chair, pushing him with every ounce of strength she had, knocking him off balance. The throbbing and stabbing in her feet was excruciating but she stepped down hard knowing she had seconds to get out of there before he recovered and came after her.

She snatched up her bag and ran to the door when she came to a grinding halt. Her vision blurred and the single doorway danced before her eyes, multiplying with each second that passed until she couldn't tell which was the real door and which were hallucinations. She grabbed onto a door handle, staggering forward when her hand touched nothing more than air. Sierra whirled in panic, desperate to escape. The clerk stood in the center of the store, watching her piteous attempt to break free. His face popped out at her in 3-D images, floating through the room like balloons. A second man appeared seemingly out of nowhere, his bald head reflecting the dim light from the ceiling fixtures. They watched her stumble through the shop, clawing the air as she struggled to find the door.

Her chest heaved as it grew harder to breath and her body simmered with heat, drenching her in a cold sweat. She thought of Skinbone, and Shark, and Luke, the new "family" she'd grown to love. Her knees buckled and she fell to the floor and still the two men stared at her without a flicker of emotion in their eyes. Tears ran down her cheeks, the only part of her body that wasn't betraying her, as her limbs froze and paralysis crept up through her body like an insidious disease, rendering her helpless.

She murmured Skinbone's name with her last gasp of breath and prayed that he knew how much she loved him. Her eyes were the only part of her body capable of movement and she screamed in silent terror as she watched the two men advance on her.

***

Skinbone paced the living room like a caged animal. "It's seven o'clock. Where the hell can she be?"

The day hadn't gone well. No solid leads on the missing girl had turned up and the conversation with the minister and his wife resulted in a fresh set of problems. Fearful that their daughter was a kidnap victim, they begged him to stay on the case. Like many in similar situations, they were concerned that police involvement might get their daughter killed and placed their hopes in Skinbone facilitating her safe return.

Damn it, he never should have agreed to it.

"I need to look for her. It's not like Sierra to vanish into thin air." He tried to settle the queasy sensation in his stomach. Sierra was clever and resourceful, he'd never met a woman like her, but it weighed on his mind that she'd gone looking for clues in Cherie's disappearance and was now missing herself.

"I saw her…earlier." Ethan spoke up from behind the bar. "I had some time on my hands and was doing a little shopping and exploring and I saw her venture into that shoe store with the girl who was here last night."

"When was that?" Skinbone almost jumped on him.

"I didn't look at my watch, but I'd guess around three o'clock."

"Sonofabitch." Skinbone slammed his fist into the wall. "Did you see them leave?"

"I didn't think it was my business to hang around and watch them." Ethan left out the part where he's swung through the alley and circled back to glance inside the store. He didn't feel the need to stir the pot of worry brewing in Skinbone's brain. He'd done what he'd thought was right by checking up on them, but the girls hadn't seemed to be in any trouble so he went on his way.

"That was four goddamn hours ago. Where the hell could she be? Shark," he bellowed, "Call Melissa — she if she's home or if Sierra told the girl her plans."

He raked his hands through his hair, imaging the worst possibilities. "The GPS on her phone and her car, track them."

Shark flipped open his computer and grabbed his cell. "I'm on it."

Skinbone glared at Ethan from across the room. "I can't lose her. I won't lose her."

***

Sierra woke with a start and plunged into a deep state of panic. Her mouth was sealed shut with tape and her captors had bound her hands and feet. That wasn't the worst of it. She squirmed, eyes darting back and forth, as she examined her surroundings. They'd placed her inside a container, confining her within a small space from which she couldn't escape.

Her heart beat in terror. They hadn't killed her, or raped her, so what the hell did they plan to do with her? She struggled against the ropes, feeling them bite into her skin. Lack of air and the drugs they'd given her made her woozy. She searched the carton for some sign of air holes and struggled harder against her restraints when she didn't spot a single one. There was only so much oxygen inside the container, she couldn't use it up by giving into fear.

Sierra squeezed her eyes shut and willed herself to remain calm, reminding herself that she'd been in far worse predicaments and survived. She just needed to keep her wits about her. It took a great deal of effort but she managed to slow her breathing.

The men in the shoe store hadn't gone through all this trouble just to suffocate her in a box. They had other plans for her — and Cherie. As long as she drew breath, she had a fighting chance of getting out of this alive. She had to find a way to outwit her captors and keep them from pumping her full of drugs. With that in mind, she flexed her fingers, relieved to find the paralysis had worn off. She was careful not to move her feet, for fear of injecting herself with more of the first drug they used on her.

The fact that she could move her limbs should have been a relief but it served to bring on a fresh wave of anxiety, making her wonder how long she'd been out cold. Hours must have passed if the drug had worn off, which meant her kidnappers were confident they could subdue her in other ways.

There was no chance in hell of that happening. They caught her off guard the first time. She'd be damned if she gave them that opportunity again.

She bit back a scream as she felt the carton lift. She was tossed around inside like an overused rag. Her ears perked up as she heard a series of guttural grunts and a stream of Russian, and then the box was slammed down on a surface and pushed forward.

Her body went still, absorbing both the physical and mental shocks. The bruises she suffered would heal but she feared she was up against an untouchable adversary. If her suspicions were correct, she was now a captive of the Russian Mafia.

That didn't bode well for her.

"Melissa confirmed that Sierra walked her home at around three thirty." Shark's face creased with worry. "She said Sierra hustled her out of the store before they could speak to the clerk and that she seemed distant and agitated on the way home, but assured Melissa that she was going to go back to the shop on her own later."

"I don't like the sound of that. What the hell was she agitated about and why insist on going back later, alone?" Skinbone rubbed his face. "I should have been here, damn it. I should have been here and gone back with her myself."

An alarm sounded on Shark's computer. He rushed to check the monitor and pumped his fist in triumph. "I just got the GPS results. Her car and her cell phone are at the same location, a couple blocks north of the shoe store." Shark announced, voice brimming with excitement. "That means she's okay. She's probably doing surveillance."

"The hell she's okay," Skinbone snarled, hitting the speed dial on his phone and listening to it ring. "If she was okay, she'd be answering her damn phone."

"Well don't bite his bloody head off. The Shark is just trying to help." Ethan poured a few fingers of whiskey into his glass and leaned across the bar casting a dark look Skinbone's way.

Skinbone almost choked on his surprise in hearing Ethan Wilde jump to Shark's defense. For some reason, it angered him. "Which is a hell of a lot more than you're doing," Skinbone shot back with a scowl.

"Well if my girl was in danger, I'd make it a point to be around instead of playing hero for a complete stranger."

"You sonofabitch." Skinbone balled his hands into fists and leapt towards the bar.

"Gentlemen, please," Shark stepped in between them. "This is no time to fight. The important thing here is dear Damsel." He ripped a sheet of paper off a notepad and scribbled an address. "This is where she is, I say let's go find her and bring her home."

Skinbone snatched the paper from Shark's hand, making no secret of his contempt for Ethan. He raised a finger and pointed it at the younger man. "This isn't finished between us."

"I'd say as far as you're concerned, it's barely even begun." Ethan raised his glass. "But at some point we will have to make peace for the old man's sake. But the Shark is right. You should be focusing on your lady."

Shark laid a hand on Skinbone's shoulder. "You may not be fond of Ethan but he's right, Sierra is our priority. We should go."

Skinbone took a deep, ragged breath and met Shark's gaze. "Yeah, I hear you, but I'm going alone."

"I care about her too, you know."

"I know you do, and I owe you for keeping her safe in the past, but it won't do any good for both of us to go chasing a GPS signal. You should stay here in case she comes home," Skinbone's voice broke. "And to see if you can worm your way back into the Police Department's surveillance videos for this afternoon. You'll be a much bigger help staying here. Call me if anything turns up."

Shark nodded once and tried to twist his face into a smile. "Godspeed then. I hope you find her."

***

Sierra's nerves shattered when she heard the sound of a door slamming shut. It reminded her of the creaking sounds a garage door made as it shuddered closed. For some reason the idea of being locked inside somewhere was even more terrifying than being in a box. There was a sense of finality that came with the sound and she struggled to push back her tears. She needed to breath, and wouldn't be able to if her nose was congested. If she had any chance of surviving this ordeal, she had to gather all her strength.

A second sound caused the ground beneath her to rattle and her box to lurch forward. She listened carefully, trying to identify it. A motor. She could hear the gears grinding and felt every bump as the vehicle began its journey.

She twisted her head around so that her mouth lay on the floor and began to jerk her face back and forth against the bottom of the box in the hope she could rip off the tape they'd used to gag her. She ground her teeth in frustration when it didn't work and rolled onto her back, staring at the sealed top. There had to be a way out of here, there just had to be. She pushed herself into a sitting position and tried to raise her hands and her legs to see if she could break free, but the bastards had strung a rope between her wrists and feet and there wasn't enough slack for her to reach the top.

Sierra cried out in agony when the vehicle hit a pothole and her teeth pierced her tongue. Anger replaced the fear running through her veins. She grabbed onto the rage, using it to stoke her hatred against the bastards who thought they could take her. She'd been through far too much in her life to die now. There was no way in hell she was going to let these goons take away everything she'd worked so hard for, not while there was breath left in her body. She swallowed down a mouthful of blood and focused on coming up with a plan.

***

Skinbone weaved in and out of traffic, ignoring the honking horns of the other drivers. Sierra was in trouble, he knew it in his gut, and he'd promised to be there for her if she ever needed him.

She needed him now.

He slammed his hand against the steering wheel, pissed off at himself for leaving her alone. He should have known better and would never forgive himself if anything happened to her. Beads of sweat dotted his forehead. If someone had kidnapped or hurt her, he'd kill the bastards with his bare hands.

Skinbone spotted her car and hit the brakes, causing the car to come to a screeching halt. He double parked beside her car and raced out of his vehicle, praying she was inside. A parking ticket fluttered on the windshield and he felt a stabbing pain in his chest. Sierra would have fed the meter; she was a stickler about such things.

He punched the driver's side window and grimaced in pain. Her cell phone lay on the passenger side floor, it must have fallen out of her bag. Leaving his car double-parked, he broke into a run, racing towards the shoe store. All he could feel was white-hot desperation as the reality of the situation kicked in. He hit the disconnect button in his mind and focused on the facts. Two women were missing, first Cherie and now Sierra. The only thing that connected them was the goddamn shoe shop.

How in the hell did that make sense?

Skinbone reached the entryway and sucked in a lungful of air. Emotion could cloud judgment and cause a man to make sloppy mistakes. He couldn't afford either. The store was locked up tight for the night but that didn't stop him from whaling on the front door. He hadn't expected anyone to open it but disappointment sliced through him just the same. He wanted this all to go away, to be terrible mistake, to find Sierra with her head together with the shop owners, trying to piece together what had happened to Cherie.

No such luck. He pressed his hand against the store window to shield the glare of the streetlights. A bubble of fear burst inside him as he recognized Sierra's purse laying haphazard on the floor. His insides turned to ice.

She would never have left it behind.

It took him a full minute to regain his bearings. He jammed his hand into his coat pocket, pulled out a set of lock picks and went to work. The alarm system was one he was familiar with, and easy to disable. Skinbone bared his teeth and imagined blowing Sierra's abductors brains out.

He prayed he'd get the chance.

***

Ethan Wilde held his glass up to the light and studied the pure amber color of the whiskey. It was a diversion. He was trying to choose his words with great care.

Shark sat with his laptop balanced on his knees, mumbling, as his fingers raced over the keyboard. Ethan hated to see a good man waste his time and he'd come to conclude that Shark was indeed a good man, far better than the rest of them.

He sighed. And Sierra was a good woman. He couldn't let them twist in the wind if there was even a small chance in hell that he could help. Ethan set down his glass and walked around the bar, perching on an ottoman across from Shark.

He cleared his throat. "Shark, my good man, a moment of your time?"

Shark glanced up, a bemused expression on his face. "I'm rather busy right now. Can it wait?"

"I'm afraid it can't." Ethan shoved his hand into his jeans pocket and withdrew a tiny slip of paper. "I *may,* and I stress the word *may*, have information that might help."

Shark frowned and eyed the paper. "What kind of information?"

"A license plate number. It's from a truck I saw in the alley behind the shoe store late last night. Two Russian hard asses were supervising a shipment as it was being loaded. At least I think they were Russian. It doesn't matter. I didn't get the impression the dudes were on the up and up, and in light of what's happened with Sierra, I think it's worth looking into. For what it's worth, both men seemed to possess a greater than average knowledge of gentlemen's clubs. Not sure if that means anything or not but it seems worth mentioning."

Shark stared at Ethan without blinking and reached out a hand. "Give it to me."

Ethan obliged and felt a weight lift off his shoulders. "Can you do anything with it?"

"Oh, yes, I can indeed." Shark went to work and then glanced up at Ethan. "I don't understand, why would you have this? And why were you checking out the shoe store after you advised us to go to the cops?"

Ethan clasped his hands on his lap and hunched forward. "I had my reasons, peculiar as they might seem, but I suppose I should fill you in."

***

The vehicle slowed to a stop. Sierra pursed her lips behind her gag and planned her attack. She had no idea when or if the opportunity would present itself, but she knew the best she would get would be one chance to confront her abductors and she had every intent of making that chance count.

To her advantage, her captors didn't strike her as very clever. They seemed more intent on purpose than precision. It didn't take a genius to drug a woman and cart her away. The drawn shade and locked door provided them with a safety net in carrying out their plans. Though it made her shudder to think so, their crimes appeared to be based on opportunity and body count and not much more than that.

They were thugs. Hired hands sent to do the dirty work. A puddle of mud in place of brains between their ears.

Sierra closed her eyes and prayed. All she needed was a single chance to outwit them. She refused to acknowledge the obvious. Bound and gagged, she didn't have much of a shot. Neither had Cherie.

She cleared her mind of everything besides the girl's picture. A young woman, her whole life still ahead of her, who wasn't yet old enough to strike out on her own and know what it meant to really live. These bastards planned to take that option away from Cherie, the same way they intended to take her away from everyone she loved.

Like hell they would.

***

Skinbone picked up Sierra's purse and bit back his emotions as he held it between his hands. He had to think positive. He winced as he glanced around the store, unimpressed with the displays, which included props that were blatantly sexual, unable to imagine what type of clientele they attracted in this high-scale neighborhood.

He couldn't imagine female executives or other professionals shopping in a place like this. A pair of metal handcuffs dangled from a shelf near a collection of thigh-high boots adorned with chains. He grabbed them off the shelf and stuffed them in his pocket on the off chance they might come in handy.

The setting reminded him of some of the sleazier music videos he'd come across targeted at the younger generation. His eyes narrowed as he realized that was exactly who the shop owners wanted to attract, the *daughters* of upscale professionals who frequented the area.

But to what end? The last known place Cherie Monroe visited was this shop; there was nothing to indicate she'd vanished elsewhere. Yet the Monroes hadn't received a ransom demand, so on the surface her disappearance didn't appear to be a kidnapping.

He felt a sinking in his gut. It was highly unlikely the store was a front for a kidnapping ring. Too many young girls going missing in the same area would raise a red flag.

Unless no one knew they were shopping here. The minister and his wife certainly hadn't known and kids were notorious for keeping secrets and telling lies. He swore under his breath. He needed a contact in the

Chicago Police Department. One who could pull missing persons reports and determine how many unsolved cases they had in the general area and see if a pattern emerged. But that would take time and that was the one thing he didn't have.

A bright pink shoebox lay discarded on the floor inches from where he'd found Sierra's purse. It struck him as odd, the only thing out of place in the store, as if the clerk had left in a hurry and couldn't be bothered to return it to the stock room. Skinbone crouched down beside it, flipped the lid open, lifted out one of the shoes, and began to examine it.

He didn't have a clue in hell what he was looking for, but he'd learned long ago to trust his gut. Did Sierra pose as a customer and ask to try on the shoes? The strappy, multi-colored stiletto didn't seem like her style, but he supposed it didn't matter. She might have picked up the first pair she saw…

His head snapped up. The shop was a boutique. They didn't have an abundance of merchandise, and this shoe wasn't on the display. A quick second look around the shop confirmed that neither was this particular brand. A nightlight illuminated the counter. He knew he was wasting precious time but he wanted a better look at the shoe —or maybe — he admitted to himself, he just wanted to hold onto the last thing Sierra might have touched.

This was no time for sentiment. Not if he was going to find Sierra and Cherie. He had to try to disconnect, approach this like he would any other case and examine all the evidence on hand. He set the shoes on the counter and started tearing through drawers. The store didn't do a hell of a lot of business. In fact, they were in the red. Nothing jumped out at him until he came across a pricy receipt for diesel fuel. Why would a shoe store pay for gas unless they owned a truck, and considering the receipt, it had to be a large one.

Based on their books, the owners were going to have a tough time meeting next month's rent. Owning a truck seemed like a ridiculous and unnecessary expense. Unless they were transporting something more valuable than shoes — something they couldn't trust to a common carrier.

Skinbone cracked his knuckles. A store like this had to have a safe, a place where they'd keep extra cash, incorporation papers, business licenses, and maybe even a second set of books. He swung around the counter, intent on searching the back room and stopped cold. He'd placed the shoe directly under the light and caught sight of a something glinting inside the shoe. He rammed his hand inside and swore when he pricked his finger. He stared at the drop of blood on the tip of his index finger and creased his brow at the warm sensation he felt flowing through his hand.

"Sonofabitch." It took less than a second to make the connection. He cracked the shoe in half with his bare hands, chest heaving with cold-blooded anger. There was a goddamn needle inside the shoe and it sure as hell wasn't a sewing needle. A packet of liquid lay just beneath the sole, where the ball of the foot would rest.

When pressure was placed on that point, a stream of the liquid would activate, which in turn flowed through the needle's tip and straight into an unsuspecting customer's blood stream.

The bastards were drugging and abducting women.

But what the hell were they doing with them?

Rage overpowered him. They'd had Sierra for hours. Who knew what they were doing to her? He tipped the counter over, taking grim satisfaction at the crashing sound it made.

Shattered glass and splintered wood were nothing in comparison to what he'd do to the sonofabitches when he found them.

***

Shark's face was impossible to read. Ethan kicked the bar and poured another drink. He'd messed up in a royal way by playing things too close to the vest.

Bloody son of a bitch, it wasn't all his fault. He'd warned the lot of them to give the missing girl case a wide berth and turn it over to the police. They hadn't listened and now the shit was about to hit the fan.

"Have you turned up anything?"

"Not yet. I'm working on it."

Ethan glanced at his watch. Whatever Shark was doing was taking a damn long time. "Can't you go any faster?"

Shark turned to him with ice-cold eyes. "If I'd had this information earlier, we wouldn't have this problem."

"Oh, that's right, turn this all on me. You know, I'm the outsider here, and I have a lot to prove. If I'd told any one of you this story, would a single one of you have believed me?"

"Sierra would have. For some reason, whether you know this or not, she seems to be your champion."

Ethan sank down on a barstool. "Yeah, I've gathered that and I'm well aware that I don't deserve her compassion. Just what the hell are you doing anyway?"

"I'm penetrating files the general public doesn't have access to."

"So you're hacking."

"If I were you, I wouldn't use that word or push your luck. Dear Damsel is the glue that holds us all together, in point of fact, she is the one who *brought* us all together. If anything should happen to her..." Shark broke off, too emotional to continue.

Ethan tapped his fingers on the bar. "Well, we aren't going to let anything happen to her. You still never answered me. What the bloody hell are you doing?"

"The vehicle is registered to a Vladimir Sidorov and Dmitri Petroven. If the license plate has ever been captured by any of the city's surveillance cameras, I can access the GPS. In case that's too complicated for you, I'll be able to tell where it's been and where it's going."

"I'm not a blathering idiot for God's sake. I know what tracking a GPS means."

"Then you'd better sit there and pray I can do it."

"You really think God would be on my side? Really? You think he would listen to me?"

"In this particular case, yes I do. Now shut up and pray."

***

Sierra found herself on the woozy side of consciousness. She had no idea how long she'd been confined to the small space her box permitted, but she was aware that the vehicle transporting her had made several stops along the way.

At one point, she'd felt the air getting thin. Petrified that she'd run out of oxygen, she went against her better judgment and used the heel of her shoe to poke a few holes in the carton. Her efforts were rewarded by a blast of near unconsciousness. A fate she could ill afford.

She had to keep her wits about her. Had to remember she was a captive of the hired help. Whatever had happened to her so far was bound to be a cakewalk in light of what she was facing.

You can do it, she coached herself, *just stay strong.*

And if you're interested, I have the Brooklyn Bridge to sell you.

The drugs were getting to her. She tried to shake off her delirium by imaging a blast of cold air. She'd been in the box too long and was losing her grip on reality.

The truck, she had to assume it was a truck, rattled to a stop. The door shuddered open, the same way it had two or three times along the way. Her muscles were starting to cramp. She inhaled through her nose and forced herself to remain still. No need to give the enemy a heads up.

She heard a spatter of Russian and the sound of crates skidding against the truck's floor as they were unloaded. They'd reached their final destination.

Sierra had no idea what that meant, or what was in store for her. One chance, she reminded herself and concentrated on pushing the fog from her brain. She thought of Skinbone and all she had to live for and gathered her resolve.

Minutes or hours might have passed. Time ceased to have meaning. The box she was trapped in bumped along, shoved by human hands, and tipped onto a dolly. She grit her teeth and dug her nails into the palms of her hands.

Whether she lived or died, whatever happened next was on her. She intended to survive.

***

Skinbone armed himself with the information he needed. He raced back to his car, panting and out of breath. He couldn't shake the shock out of his system or calm himself into breathing easily. Not until he brought these bastards down.

He headed towards the pier and punched Shark's number into his cell.

Shark answered without preamble. "I'm on it. We'll meet you there."

Skinbone exhaled a sigh a relief. Backup was on the way. Whether it came in the form of Shark or Luke, he was grateful for it. It wasn't everyday he went up against the Russian Mafia. He had no idea how many thugs would be guarding the truck or boat, but he swore he would take every last one of them down, if that's what it took to get Sierra back.

He sped through the cold, dark night feeling as if his life were on the line. And in a way, it was.

Sierra had turned his world inside out and breathed fresh hope into him. If a woman of her caliber loved him, he couldn't be half bad. He needed her and counted on her. There was no way in hell he was going to lose her.

He peeled rubber as he turned into the pier. Skinbone hit the brakes and slowed his car to a crawl. The demons were working overtime tonight. His gaze honed in on the semi parked along the dock. Corrugated containers were being unloaded one at a time.

Skinbone curled his fingers around his steering wheel and checked for his Glock. He'd wait a few minutes and if Shark and his backup didn't arrive, he was going in alone.

***

Sierra's head slammed against concrete, dazing her. She fought down a wave of nausea and focused on her plan. This once, she couldn't think about Skinbone,

Shark, or Luke. Her survival depended on putting herself first, and finding a way to survive.

Her bruises ached and she held herself rigid, careful not to inject any more of the drugs into her system. That's probably what they were counting on, drugged, dazed, compliant women. Those words weren't even in her vocabulary, but if need be, she could play the part.

She fought a wave of nausea and wished she could hold on to something as she felt the carton wheeled forward and she was slammed from end to end, igniting fresh pain to her already tender bruises.

Sierra's wrists and ankles were bloody and raw from the struggle to escape the ropes and her feet throbbed where they'd been stabbed with the needles. She was slick with sweat, hair plastered across her face covering her eyes, and the clothes she wore clung to her body like glue. There was almost no air left inside the box despite her efforts to make holes in the container.

Without warning, she pitched forward as the carton tilted off the dolly. Her head smashed against the ground and she whimpered in pain. These bastards knew what they were doing. They wanted to break her spirit, to numb her with fear. If that was their plan, it was working, but she refused to give in to it, and focused on her anger instead.

She could hear the men's footsteps and wished she could see what was going on outside her tiny prison.

"Start to unload them," a man barked in heavily accented Russian. "He will want to inspect them before we put them with the others."

Others? Sierra's mind raced. *How many others?* She'd been worried about saving herself and Cherie. What would she do if there were dozens of other women? The noise drowned out her thoughts, cartons ripping open, muffled screams and the unmistakable thud of bodies hitting the ground.

She squeezed her eyes shut and prayed for strength. All thought flew from her mind as a knife sliced into the box. It was a hell of a thing to try to stay strong when staring up at the sharp end of a blade. The top flaps opened and a blast of cold air slapped at her face. So did the awful reality of her situation. Left for hours in a small bleak space to nurse her anger into a full-fired fury, it was easy to imagine overpowering her attackers. Now that the moment had come, she yelped in terror behind the gag. Two meaty hands appeared and the knife plunged into the box stopping inches from her body. A sob tore from her throat as she shivered in terror.

Damn it, the bastards were winning. She was afraid.

One of the hands grazed her body. The knife swung closer. The man reached for the rope that connected her wrists and ankles together and sawed it in half. The air rushed out of her lungs. If they'd intended to kill her, they would have done it by now. And that meant, no matter how impossible, she still had a chance.

The man tossed the knife; she heard it clatter to the ground near the carton.

Okay, she tried to calm her breathing, *he's unarmed, there won't be a knife at my throat.*

The hands reached for her next, sliding under her armpits with a cold hard grip, strong enough to break her neck and maybe even a few bones. He pulled her out of the carton, using his boot to break down the sides and threw her to the ground hard enough to knock the wind out of her.

"That's the last of them." He kicked the mangled carton aside. "You want I should put them with the others?"

Sierra took the opportunity to look around. They were on a large boat; she could feel it sway beneath her, heard the kick of the waves licking at the sides, and could smell the lake air. A second man came forward. She recognized his voice in an instant as belonging to the clerk from the shoe store.

"Take a break. Go have a smoke. He will want them chained up in the back, so that when the buyer comes onboard he will see the whores, strippers, and illegal's first. That will whet his appetite for more. Then we show him the good ones, no? The ones we drug and take from the stores. He will pay a good price for them, top dollar, which means bonuses for us. With any luck, we have a few virgins in this batch. It's too bad they go for so much money, there's a few here I'd like to sample for myself."

"You can buy just as good with the money we make. Maybe better. I go to smoke. You call me when he is ready for me to move them below."

"Take your time. Enjoy. He will want to look them over good. Vlad is smart man, good with the business. He will choose the best to show the buyer last."

The men laughed.

"Okay," Meaty Hands said. "And then we drink to our good fortune."

"Dlya schast'ya."

Sierra's blood ran cold as she listened to the exchange. They were being sold into white slavery…or worse. The moment the boat set sail was a death knell. She had as long as it took for someone to smoke a cigarette to figure out a way to survive.

***

"Don't park near the front bow. Head towards the back." Ethan directed Shark. "Human nature. People tend to look forward but rarely look behind."

"So now you're a philosopher too?" There was an edge to Shark's voice.

"You know I *am* trying to help. It wouldn't hurt for you to lose the sarcasm."

"Dear Damsel is in great peril. You provided a license plate number. I did the rest."

"Oh, Geez, really? We're going to quibble over who has the biggest balls?"

"I'd prefer to refrain from any conversation that includes mention of your privates."

"Uh-huh. Tell me, Shark, if you're such a hero, who was it again who froze his *balls* off last night creeping around back alleys in this peculiar town?"

"And if you would have shared that knowledge, we might not be in the position we now find ourselves in — which is trying to figure out a way to get Sierra off that boat before any harm comes to her."

Ethan threw up his hands. "There is just no winning with you people."

"Maybe you should have considered that before you tried to kill us all."

"Walk a day in my shoes before you judge. I wouldn't wish what had been done to me to Lucifer's legions in hell but that was the straw I drew. I wasn't born a monster, I was turned into one and you have no idea of what I've gone through this past year to reverse all the damage done to me as a child. Do you really want to get into all of this now when your precious Dear Damsel's life is hanging in the balance?"

Shark jerked the car to a stop. "What's our plan?"

"You have a map of the boat?"

"You watched me print it out," Shark snapped, reaching towards the back seat. He handed Ethan the paper and fumbled beneath the car seat for a square black box.

"What the hell is that?"

Shark pressed a series of buttons. "It's where I keep my weapon."

Ethan raised his brows as Shark withdrew a shiny and undeniably new Glock. "Have you ever fired that thing?"

"At the shooting range. I'm a pretty good shot."

He couldn't help but notice the way Shark's hands shook. A weapon would come in handy — but not in the hands of a computer wizard. Ethan narrowed his eyes and gave Shark a considering look. The kid had pluck and heart, he'd give him that, but it was doubtful that he had it in him to blow someone's head off.

"Can I see that a moment?"

"Why?"

"I just want to look at it."

Shark placed the gun in his lap. "We're wasting time. We need to storm the boat and get Sierra back." Shark exhaled as if he was imaging his role in all this and was taking the time to muster up his courage.

Ethan seized the opportunity and reminded himself that what he was about to do was for the best. A woman's life was at stake. He grabbed the gun from Shark. "I don't think so, mate."

Before Shark could react, he brought the gun down on his head and knocked him out cold. "Sorry, chum, but I can't have you mucking up my plans."

***

Skinbone swore and slammed his car door shut. He could have used backup but he wasn't about to waste any more time. He'd found enough incriminating evidence to know his adversaries were in the slave trade. He could run the risk of the boat sailing off before he rescued his woman.

The sonofabitches had stores scattered all through the city. It was no wonder the cops hadn't caught on. They'd managed to create enough of a diversion and were smart enough not to take too many women from the same location.

The Russian Mafia had no compulsion and no restrictions. They were a rough group, deadly and cold as vodka on ice. At least when the Italians ruled the city they had a bit of class and grace. They'd wine and dine you before putting a bullet through your head. Women and children were off limits. Not so with the Russians. They'd kill first and laugh later.

And Sierra was their captive. So was Melissa's young friend, Cherie.

Skinbone reached for his gun and approached the boat.

He intended to get them out of there alive.

***

Sierra lay still. A pair of gleaming spit polished black shoes walked past her. Vladimir, she assumed. The men switched to Russian, making it impossible for her to follow the conversation. It didn't matter. She was waiting for the opportunity to make her move.

The unexpected commotion felt like a thousand tiny pins and needles pounding into her skin. A woman shrieked. The last time Sierra had heard cries so horrific was when her ex-fiancée was burning alive. Memories came crashing back, paralyzing her for a terrifying moment. She pushed them aside, instinct kicked in and she knew she had to focus on the here and now.

She twisted her neck to see what was going on. One of the girls was fighting the situation hard. The shoe store clerk was holding her up as Vladimir ripped at her clothes, pawing her as if she were an animal.

The girl bashed her head into Vladimir's face. He escaped the worst of the blow but there was cold fury in his eyes. He hauled off and smashed his fist into her face. She fought like a wild thing, attempting to kick out with bound legs, grunting with effort as she tried to break free of the arms that held her.

Vlad used both his hands, reining a series of blows to her head and torso. His bald head sweated with effort. He grabbed the girl by her hair and rammed a curled fist into her eye. Sierra winced, feeling every blow the girl was enduring, but that wasn't the worst of it. Before Vladimir had the chance to turn the girl's face to pulp, Sierra had gotten a good look at her.

The fighter was Cherie Monroe.

Sierra tried to swallow, but her throat had gone too dry. Cherie's resistance proved fighting was futile. She was going to have to try to outsmart them another way.

***

Ethan shoved Shark's gun into his pants at the small of his back and crouched as he made his way towards the boat. There was no time to waste. He grabbed the rung of a ladder and hauled himself up.

Shark had found a way to get "ears" on the boat by manipulating a thing or two. Something to do with radio frequencies or some such thing. Ethan wasn't about to pretend to understand the capabilities of a cyber/geek/wizard/hacker, but he sure as hell appreciated the man's skill.

Courtesy of The Shark, he now had a cover and he intended to milk it for every possible advantage. He only hoped it wouldn't come back to haunt him. He already had enough explaining to do.

His leather jacket was ill protection against the bitter chill coming off the lake. He grit his teeth and leapt onto the boat. His chosen point of entry was deserted. He brushed himself off and straightened to his full height, assuming a swagger.

There was such a thing as timing and another like presentation. Both were on his side. With any luck, he'd make quick work of his mission and come out on the other end of it richer for his efforts.

***

Cherie fell to the floor in a bloody heap. Vlad bared his teeth, snarled, and delivered a savage kick to her side.

"She is damaged goods now. What you want me to do with her?" It was the man who'd posed as the shoe clerk.

Vladimir spit on the sobbing girl. "You exaggerate, Dmitri, my friend. The cuts and bruises will heal before we deliver the merchandise. It's a long boat ride to where they are going. Tell Victor to make sure all the other girls below get a good look at her. A good reminder of what will happen to them if they misbehave."

Sierra dug her fingernails into the ground, remaining as still as possible as Vlad strolled down the line of girls, pawing at each of them with rough hands or using the tip of his boot to turn them over to get a better look. She kept her eyes sealed shut and braced herself for her turn.

Vlad crouched beside her and grabbed her by the hair, rolling her over onto her back. She could smell the stink of his breath and knew at any moment, his hands would be on her, probing and pinching her body as he inspected her. She swallowed her disgust, wishing he would get it over with, she didn't know how long she could lie, forced to wait for him to inflict indignity on her.

His hand fastened around her chin. He tilted her head back, exposing her throat until her muscles screamed in protest. Vlad laughed, aware of the strain he was putting on her body. He tightened his other hand around her neck and squeezed hard, cutting off her air supply. Her body twitched in panic and her eyes bugged open wide. Gurgling sounds came from her throat and her heart pumped so hard she was sure it was about to explode.

He laughed again and pinched her nostrils shut. She knew she was going to die. Minutes, seconds, it didn't matter, he was choking the life out of her, and it amused him. Her life was going to end to provide a sadistic bastard an instant of pleasure.

The scream started in her belly, and caught in her throat. Without warning, he released his grip on her and stood up. Her head slammed into the ground for a second time that night, leaving her dazed.

"Dmitri," he called. "This, one, the one who was snooping around in the shoe store — take her to my office." He leered down at her. "There is no mistaking this one for a virgin, eh? Not at her age. She will be keeping me company until I figure out what to do with her. She will find out soon enough how persuasive I can be in making someone talk. If she is a smart girl, she will tell me what she knows. If not?" He shrugged. "She can amuse the crew once I am done with her until the ship is far enough out to dump her overboard."

Dmitri laughed and elbowed his partner. "Let me know if you want me to take a stab at her while you get your rest."

Vlad slapped his friend on the back. "That is a good one, take a stab at her. I like your humor."

Sierra's nostrils flared as she listened to their exchange. They'd have to kill her before she'd submit to what they had in mind for her. Dmitri grabbed her by the ankles and began to drag her towards Vlad's office.

Unless she figured out a way to kill them first.

The two men were pure evil. They took pleasure in inflicting pain, and treating women like cattle. The bastards felt they were entitled to speak freely about using and beating a woman and tossing her overboard once they finished with her. The horror sent her mind into overdrive, the lighthearted camaraderie between them as they laughed and joked about her death.

Slivers of wood pierced her buttocks and back as Dmitri dragged her along like a bag of trash. Hatred beat a steady rhythm within her and there was no turning back.

Sierra wanted to watch the life flicker out of their eyes. They were the ones who needed to die.

***

Skinbone approached the boat. He'd watched a man exit the ship and hurry down to the pier where he lit a cigarette and sucked on it as if it were air. He smoked it down to a stub, lit a second, and pulled a cell phone from his pocket.

The man waved his cigarette and was in the midst of an excited conversation, laughing and stamping his feet. Skinbone didn't understand a damn word the man was saying, but he could read body language. The man had reason to celebrate. He tossed a butt into Lake Michigan and lit a third cigarette while finishing his call, and then pulled a flask from his coat pocket and took a deep, long drink.

He never heard Skinbone come up behind him, not until the barrel of Skinbone's gun tapped the back of his head.

The Russian had good reflexes, but Skinbone's were better. The man's body tensed and his hand dove into his pocket. In a flash, he whirled and brought his own weapon up, attempting to aim it between Skinbone's eyes.

It was too bad for the Russian that Skinbone anticipated his move and shot the gun out of his hand.

The man yelped in pain staring in shock at his decimated right hand and peeled off a stream of Russian expletives.

"Cut the bullshit," Skinbone growled, grabbed the man by his collar and placed the gun against his temple. "I know you speak English and unless you want your brains blown out you are going to tell me how many men are on this boat, their positions, and where I can find the women you just brought on board. You got that? Two-seconds or you're fish food. It's your choice, man. Tell me want I need to know, you walk away. You're free to go to a hospital and see about getting your hand fixed. Or stay silent and get shot dead. Up to you. The clock is ticking."

***

Ethan preferred the element of surprise. He glanced around, flinching at the ungodly odor emanating from the ships bowels.

He grimaced as he breathed in the foul air. It was quite clear to him that Sierra and the abducted girl were new arrivals. There were other women aboard, kept here long enough to stew in their own waste, enough women to earn more than a pretty penny from selling them abroad. A lucrative living if you had the stomach for it.

Ethan's stomach was cast iron. He'd done much worse in his past. These men were no match for him as they were soon to find out.

His ears perked at the sound of a gunshot. He reached for Shark's gun and tensed, listening for sounds of trouble. All was silent beyond the howling wind and waves slapping the sides of the boat. He really needed a better jacket to combat the infernal wind chill of Lake Michigan.

Satisfied that he was not about to walk into a round of gunfire, he crept onboard, let his feet drop to the ground, and took a moment to get the lay of the land. No guards rushed forward to question his arrival — quite a sloppy mistake in his opinion. He would never run things that way.

Ethan turned up his collar and assumed a cocky stance. Go ahead, he dared the unseen, try and stop me. Question me and see what happens. Anyone bold enough to try and do just that would never have the time to live to regret it.

***

Sierra expected more. It was her life at stake and it was worth more than being a pawn in a sick and twisted game. Dmitri hauled open a door, yanked her inside, and slammed it behind him. She heard a lock click in place and the sound of his footsteps walking away.

For all their bullying tactics, the men weren't very smart. Or maybe the women they'd dealt with in the past were too terrified to put up much of a fight.

Sierra used her legs to scoot her body towards the single desk in the room. She grabbed onto its edge and pulled herself up. They'd bound her hands in front of her, a foolish mistake on her captor's part. She ripped the tape from her mouth and sucked in two lungs full of air. She was going to need all her strength for what came next.

There wasn't a moment to waste. She jerked open drawers until she found a pair of scissors. Not knowing how much time she had, she went to work on her ankles and cut the ropes free. She flexed her numb feet and was about to go to work on her wrists when the doorknob turned.

Sierra slammed the drawer closed and scurried to the center of the small room, keeping her head lowered. A key fitted into the lock and Vlad swung the door open. She'd decided on a plan and prayed that it worked.

The goon stepped inside and belched, swinging the door shut behind him.

One chance, she reminded herself, and she had to make it a good one.

He ignored her and went to a cabinet where he pulled open a drawer and reached in for a bottle of vodka. Vlad unscrewed the cap and took a swig before turning ice-cold beady eyes towards her.

"So," he said, "it seems we have a bit of a problem." Vlad reached inside his pocket and tossed down the picture of Cherie that she'd hidden in her purse. "You will tell me why you were looking for her and who else you might have told."

Sierra didn't risk moving, for fear of drawing his attention to her unbound feet. One shot. She knew what she had to do but to make it work she had to piss Vlad off first.

"I asked you a question. Answer now, girlie, or you will find yourself very, very sorry."

She kept her eyes lowered towards the ground. Whatever happened next was going to be bad, but not as bad as dying.

"Stupid bitch, I asked you a question." His spit flew across her face. He grabbed her by the hair and looked her in the eyes with a penetrating gaze. "Answer me."

Sierra pressed her lips together and remained mute.

She could almost feel the blow before he pulled back his fist and aimed for her jaw. Sierra waited until the hair on his knuckles brushed her face and pretended to fall to the floor, screaming in agony.

The force behind his fist propelled him forward, making him lose his balance when she ducked before his hand slammed into her jaw. He snorted, face red with rage, as he staggered and bellowed like a rutting bull.

"Bitch! You will pay for this! No one makes a fool of Vladimir Sidorov."

Sierra panted in fear. One wrong move and she was a dead woman. She knew she only had seconds before he came at her again. She swung her legs to the side, twisted her shoe off her foot, and held it by the instep, so that the heel pointed away from her body. Sierra flashed back to her childhood and remembered what her mother used to say. *If you're out alone, keep your keys in your hands. If anyone ever tries to grab you or attack you, aim your keys at their eyes.*

"Thank you, Momma," she whispered, and coiled her body so that she would have enough strength to attack from her position on the floor.

Vladimir grabbed a chair and flung it across the room. She winced at the sound of splintering wood, felt her heart pump in fear as he broke off a loose chair leg, and turned towards her.

She froze, watching in terror as he laughed, slicing the air with the stick. *Dear God*, her eyes widened as she realized he meant to beat her with it.

He sneered at her, revealing gold teeth. He dropped the arm holding the chair leg and towered above her. His face twisted into a mask of hatred, but she saw a glint of pleasure in his eyes and knew he was going to enjoy hurting her.

***

Ethan strode across the ship's deck with purpose, making no effort to conceal his presence aboard. He itched to come across the bastards who'd taken the girls, to get in their faces and make them squirm. In addition to kidnapping, they'd mucked up his homecoming and placed him in a precarious position with his housemates. It was also thanks to them he'd spent his entire time in Chicago freezing his damn ass off, which in of itself was enough to sour his mood.

He spotted a Russian in a pea coat and cap leaning over the railing and talking on his cell.

"You," he called out with a tone of authority startling the man into dropping his cell. Ethan picked it up and shoved it in his pocket. "Where is Vladimir?"

"Who the hell are you?" The man demanded in heavily accented English.

"I'm the man paying his salary. Take me to him."

The man looked skeptical. "You are American."

Ethan sighed. "And you are a low-life brute. Now that we've gotten better acquainted, I'm going to ask nicely one last time. Take me to Vladimir."

The Russians cheeks puffed out in anger. He lunged at Ethan, "I take you to him all right with both your arms broken in half."

Ethan sidestepped the man's clumsy attempt to overpower him and brought the gun up to the man's Adam's apple. He smiled as the man's eyes bulged in fear. "There's one more little detail you should know about me. I'm deadly."

Skinbone hurried across the ship's gangway in search of steps that would take him to the lower deck where the Russians were keeping the girls locked in a cabin directly above the boiler. He prayed it wouldn't be hard to find. Skinbone knew nothing about ships or their design.

The night provided excellent cover but he had no idea what waited below. He drew his gun and raced down the flimsy steps, pressing his back against the wall at the sound of voices coming from just up ahead.

His brow creased as he listened. He identified two male voices though he couldn't understand a damn thing they were saying. Skinbone felt the blood in his veins harden to ice as the men guffawed, laughing, he assumed over a comment one of them had made. For the crimes they were committing, they deserved skewering over hot coals instead of being free to stand around cracking jokes while Sierra and countless other women were ripped from their families and stowed in cramped quarters to await being sold into slavery.

Skinbone clenched his jaw and slipped unnoticed around the corner. The men sat at a makeshift table in front of a metal door that they'd padlocked and bolted from the outside. They were gnawing on chicken wings, tossing the bones into a cardboard box and washing them down with Russian beer.

Both of the men were heavily armed. Skinbone's stomach twisted as he noticed a heavy baton and a cattle prod propped up outside the door. The baton had blood and hair on it. He was guessing one of the girls hadn't survived her abduction and was at the bottom of Lake Michigan. His face turned to stone. *Please God,* he begged, *don't let it be Sierra.*

He was alone with the guards. There was no judge here and no jury. And no witnesses. Skinbone curled his lips into a snarl, raised his weapon, and stepped out into the open. His finger curled on the trigger. He cleared his throat once, to get their attention. He wanted them to remember his face.

The thinner of the two men bolted from his chair and reached for his gun.

"It's too late for that," Skinbone growled. "There's a reservation in hell with your names on it."

***

Vladimir flexed the fingers of his left hand while tapping the chair leg against his thigh with his right. "Get up off the floor, bitch."

Sierra crouched in position and waited for her chance.

"I warn you one last time. Stand up and get on top of the desk. First, I tie you to it, and then I beat you. How bad a beating you get depends on how fast you obey me."

She tightened her fingers around the shank of the shoe. *One chance,* she repeated, *make it count.*

"Miserable, bitch," he spat. "You've tried my patience for the last time."

He swooped down on her, grabbing her shoulder with an iron grasp. She shrieked to distract him, brought her legs up, and aimed for his windpipe kicking hard. He clutched his throat and fell backwards, squealing like the pig he was.

Sierra leapt to her feet and straddled him. He bucked hard to try and throw her off. She slammed her palm across his nose and brought the heel of the shoe down as hard as she could, burying it into his eyeball. She gagged at the sickly squishing sound and the liquid substance spraying across her hand.

His hands went for her throat. The sonofabitch was too mean to die. She lifted the shoe a second time and plunged it into his remaining eyeball, shuddering at the crunching sounds it made as she used both hands to push the five-inch heel deep inside his head.

Vladimir's body twitched and spasmed. She rolled off him, still clutching the shoe in her hand. The heel was sticky with bits of brain and bone. Sierra stared at it in shock. The horror was too much to process. She'd killed Vladimir with the shoe he and his henchman used to drug and kidnap her. She was sickened by what she'd just done, but felt no remorse. There was no doubt in her mind that he would have beaten her to death. She did what she had to in order to survive.

There was no sweetness in her victory. She'd murdered a man, and it wasn't the first time. In both cases, it was self-defense, but it was still something she had to live with. That wasn't the worst of it. There were other men on this boat, others she would have to get past if she was going to save herself. And she had to do it fast if she had any hope of rescuing Cherie and the other poor girls who were on the ship.

The adrenaline rush that came over her during her battle with Vlad was gone. Her body sagged with exhaustion. Sierra averted her eyes so that she didn't have to look at the corpse and pulled out a chair. She sank down on it and buried her face in her hands. What she needed was a gun, a way to level the playing field in her favor. Vlad probably had one on him. She was going to have to search his body.

Sierra took a deep breath and forced herself to sit straighter. She knew what she had to do. The problem was, her feet didn't want to move.

***

Ethan tucked the Russian's gun inside his waistband. A few hours earlier, he'd been unarmed, now he had two weapons. It was getting to be a damn tough thing in this town to walk the straight and narrow. Could be, coming here had been a mistake.

Or maybe he just wasn't meant to be good. On the other hand, if he rescued Sierra and the other girl, some might call him a hero. It seemed there was a blurry distinction between right and wrong.

He pulled the Russian chap's hat down low on his forehead and added a swagger to his step. Ethan had a feeling the shit was about to hit the fan which meant he had to act fast and make quick work of this caper. He just didn't need Vlad or his henchmen recognizing him too soon in advance.

He was coming up to the front of the boat. The man's back was to him but he recognized the black overcoat. It was the smaller man from the alley, and he was leaving a blistering message on someone's phone.

Ethan's eyes narrowed. He was going to have to rethink his strategy. A dozen or so girls with their hands and feet bound, laid on the floor of the deck inches from where the Russian stood. There was a good chance Sierra was among them. He couldn't run the risk of any of them getting hurt in the crossfire.

**

Skinbone searched the bodies of the guards for the keys to the metal door. He found them hooked to the chubbier man's belt, clutched them in his fist, and prayed hard. He had to get the women off the ship safe and in one piece. If he acted in haste, he could be putting their lives in jeopardy.

There were other men on this ship of the dangerous and lethal variety. Men who would think nothing of opening fire on the women if they knew the gig was up and they wouldn't turn a profit by selling them.

He looked at the door and weighed his options. The need to know if Sierra was inside burned a hole in his gut, but he would never be able to live with himself if his actions got her killed.

Damn it, this is why he needed backup. Shark promised it was on the way, where the hell was he? A headache settled between his eyes. He raked his hands through his hair and paced the tiny hallway. Whatever he did, he had to get it right the first time. One wrong move and he'd have innocent blood on his hands.

***

Shark rubbed the bump on his head and winced in pain. The egg size lump on his noggin was nothing compared to the hit his pride had taken. He'd allowed himself to believe Ethan Wilde's earnest appeal and offer of help in rescuing Sierra. The end result should not have included being knocked out cold, which meant whatever Ethan was up to stank of no good.

He'd been on the wrong end of Ethan's treachery once before, and wasn't about to let it happen again. Shark blinked until the double vision cleared from his eyes. Ethan might think he had the upper hand, but Shark had learned a thing or two since the last time they'd met.

He squared his shoulders and popped open the trunk of his car. The Glock Ethan had stolen wasn't the only weapon he had available. He wasn't about the let any harm come to Dear Damsel, not when he had the power to stop it from happening.

***

Ethan slowed his pace and with stealth, he didn't know he possessed, crept up behind the man in the overcoat. He raised his arm, pushed the gun against the back of the man's head, and released the safety.

"Take me to your leader." He wrapped his left arm around the man's neck and laughed. "Damn, I've always wanted to say those words."

The smarmy bastard tried to go for his own gun. Ethan jerked the man's head back. "I wouldn't do that if I were you. You'll be dead before you can reach the handle."

Dmitri let his hands fall to his side.

"That's a good boy. Now give me what I want and there is a slight chance I'll let you live. Any chance is better than none, wouldn't you agree?"

"Who the hell are you and what do you want?"

"I'm crushed that you don't recognize my voice. I'm the bloke from the alley last night. You remember, don't you? The cheery lost drunk looking for strippers."

"Your accent has changed."

"Very astute. I hail from the other side of the pond, far, far away from New York."

"And that matters why?"

"It doesn't matter at all. I only mentioned it because you brought it up first. The important thing is that I have a gun to your head, and trust me when I tell you I have killed far better men. You are nothing more than a bug on the windshield of life and I wouldn't lose a wink of sleep over your death."

"I ask you again, what do you want?"

"See now, here I give you credit for being astute and then you go and ask me a stupid question. I want Vlad, but first you and I are going to take a look at these girls. You and your boss have done some sloppy work. You made the mistake of taking two girls that matter to me."

"Two girls is what you want? Take them and go. Then you and I, we can call ourselves even."

"You think it's that simple. Really? How you've managed to get away with this so far is beyond me when it's obvious you have piss for brains."

"No need to hurtle the insults."

"Wrong again. Insulting you gives me so much pleasure. Now shut the hell up and walk."

Ethan kept the gun pressed against Dmitri's head. One of the captive's bore a resemblance to the girl Shark's friend had been worried about, but her face was too swollen and bruised to be sure. There was however, something he was certain of. Sierra wasn't among them.

"Where the hell is she?"

"Who? I don't know what you're talking about."

"You'd better figure it out quick. I want the last one you snatched. The blonde, in her thirties. Last seen going into your store."

"No idea who you mean."

"Is that your final answer?"

"Yes. Final answer."

"Alrighty then. I'll take you at your word." He shoved Dmitri towards the railing and bent him over it. "Then it seems I have no further use for you. One shot and you go over the railing. I hear the water is cold this time of year."

Dmitri twisted in his grasp. "Wait. Wait. Maybe I do know something about the woman you described."

"I'll give you one-second to start talking."

***

The doorknob turned, rousing Sierra from her stupor. She wasn't ready. She hadn't had enough time to formulate a new plan. The knob rattled a second time. She shot up from her chair and snatched the shoe off the table. The chair leg would be a better weapon, but there wasn't time to grab it from beside Vlad's body. There also wasn't any place to hide. With no time to consider her options, she ran towards the wall that ran parallel to the door. When the door swung open, it would conceal her behind it. If luck was on her side, she had a fifty-fifty chance of escaping before someone grabbed her.

A key turned in the lock. She brandished the shoe like the deadly weapon it was. Fate was giving her one more chance. If opportunity presented itself, she would take it. The door flung open, almost smashing her against the wall. It banged into her head, delivering a fresh wave of pain.

That was the last straw. She'd had it with these perverted creeps. They should all be rotting in hell. She screamed like a banshee and hurtled her body from behind the door, throwing herself on the intruder. They both went tumbling down, but she had the upper hand, landing on top of him. He lay on his side, stunned by the unexpected attack.

Sierra raised the shoe high above her head, brought it crashing down into Dmitri's ear canal and pressed on it in hard with the heels of both her hands. No more, she thought, he was never going to have another chance to kidnap unsuspecting women. Not if she had anything to say about it.

Tears flowed down her face. This was too much. All too much. She pushed herself off his body and staggered backwards, covering her mouth with her hand.

"A shoe as a deadly weapon. Nice touch. I never would have thought of it myself. Well done."

She knew that voice. Her eyes flew to his face and her mouth dropped open in shock. Sierra bent at the waist, yanked the shoe from Dmitri's ear, and held it in front of her, waving it like a crazy woman. She trembled from head to toe, and tried to make sense out of what Ethan Wilde was doing here.

***

Skinbone recoiled. He'd seen a lot of bad things in his life, done enough bad himself, but nothing prepared him for what waited beyond the metal door.

"Sierra?" he yelled, horrified by what he was looking at. The inhumane treatment these girls were enduring was evident by the stench alone. Chained to the floor and packed together without so much as an inch to spare between them, they were wallowing in their own filth. There were at least two hundred women crowded into the small hot space and not a single one was willing to meet his gaze.

His body shook with an anger that ran deeper than any he'd ever felt. He couldn't imagine his Sierra chained and tortured, forced to breathe this putrid air, left to rot here like an animal. Once he found her, he was going to choke the life out of every last man responsible.

He had to find her and get her out of here. Why the hell wasn't she answering him? "Damn it, Sierra, talk to me. Say something. Say something, damn it, so I can find you."

Skinbone was getting frantic. He screamed her name again, and felt like a bastard for scaring the other girls. Most of them cowered, some sobbed, many had a look on their faces that was so vacant they bordered on catatonic. By the looks of things, a whole lot of them had been here for a good long spell, for weeks, or maybe a month even.

He wanted to reassure them, to tell them they were safe now, but he couldn't make that promise. Not yet, but damned sure would once he knew the bastards who'd done this to them were rotting in hell.

He covered his nose and stepped further inside; figuring out pretty quick there wasn't any more room to walk. He knew in his gut it didn't matter. If Sierra were here, she would have answered him. She wouldn't go down without a fight and that's what worried him most of all. These men wouldn't hesitate to kill.

Skinbone backed out of the room and choked on his agony. Pain fueled his rage. He grabbed the makeshift table the guards had been sitting at, flung it against the wall, and bellowed loudly. "I'm going to kill you bastards, do you hear me? I'm coming for you."

A red mist blurred his vision. He gnashed his teeth and raced up the stairs, taking them two at a time. He spotted a man on the upper deck. The asshole had to be blind, deaf and dumb not to have heard all the noise. Skinbone charged across the deck, falling on the man like a rabid dog. He went for the man's throat and bashed his head to the floor a time or two and then Skinbone let go and pulled out his Glock.

The Russian cried like a baby and tried to scurry away like the cockroach he was. Skinbone grabbed him by the collar, shoved the barrel of his gun into the man's mouth and watched his eyes fill with terror.

"You got two choices," Skinbone informed him with deadly intensity. "You can either eat this bullet, or you can show me where I can find the girls you brought on board tonight. I'm going to take this gun out of your mouth. You have one second to start talking."

***

Sierra backed further into the room, staring at Ethan in shock. "I don't believe this. You were in on this all along, weren't you?" she gasped.

He gave her a blank look and took a step forward. "No, Sierra, you've got it all wrong."

She shook her head. "I don't think so. This is why you agreed to come to Chicago, isn't it? Because you're behind the kidnappings. My God!" She raked her hand through her hair. "You'll never change, will you? That's why you tried to talk us out of looking for Melissa's friend, and told us to turn it over to the cops. You figured you could make a clean getaway before they caught you. And then I screwed up your plans and you couldn't have that, could you? You had to get rid of me, just like you wanted to before when you were trying to bring down the Kepler's and Foxtrot and you thought I was in the way."

Ethan flinched at her accusations. "No, luv, I'm telling you, you've got this all wrong. I came here to rescue you, not to kill you."

"Don't you dare call me, luv," she spat. "And don't you dare take one step closer."

"Okay, I'll stay where I am." He raised both his arms at his sides and let the gun dangle from his hand. "I'm trying very hard not to get angry, you're hysterical, and in shock, with good reason, I might add. God knows what these animals did to you, and you've just killed two men."

"Don't patronize me. I'm not hysterical and I'm not in shock. I know what I saw."

"Damn it, you have no bloody idea what you saw." He dropped his arms and started to pace. "This is exactly what I was afraid of." Ethan turned to face her, shaking his head and laughing in disbelief. "I should have known better than to get involved. This is the thanks I get for risking my neck and putting my life on the line. I might have expected this type of reaction from Skinbone, but you? I never would have expected it from you."

Her eyes narrowed. He was giving a good performance of being the injured party, good enough to pique her interest.

He walked to the table and pulled out a chair. He set the gun down in front of him and looked her straight in the eye. "If I wanted you dead, would we be having a conversation right now? I could have killed you before you had a chance to finish Dmitri off. I had a goddamn gun to his back and I forced him to take me to you. I'm the one who pushed the door open and shoved him into the room. You saved my life once Sierra, is it so wrong to think I might return the favor?"

She was starting to believe him. "How did you know where to find me?"

"Does it even matter? If you're that willing to think the worst of me, I don't have a bloody chance in hell of fitting in with you people." He dropped his head to his hands and groaned. "Especially after what I did to Shark."

"What did you do to Shark?"

"I knocked him out cold and stole his gun. He wanted to come onboard with me. I didn't think he could hold his own in a shootout with the Russian mob so I cold-cocked him."

"Really?" she raised a brow.

"Look, maybe my actions were a bit harsh, but Shark is a good kid. I didn't want to put him in danger."

"So you assumed that because Shark is a cyber genius, he can't fire a gun."

"Something like that, yes."

"Shark is a crack shot, better than Luke, maybe even better than Skinbone."

"You're putting me on."

"No, I'm not." She sighed. "You're missing my point though. You made a judgment call based purely on appearance."

He looked at her in confusion. "I don't see what that has to do with anything."

"I rushed to judgment the instant I saw you standing in the doorway."

He cracked a smile. "I take it that's a backhanded way of admitting you might be wrong?"

"Something like that, yes."

He sprung out of the chair and snatched his gun off the table. "Then what are we waiting for? Let's get you home."

"We can't leave. We need to find Cherie and get her to the hospital, and we need to save the other girls."

"Let me handle that. I want to get you off this boat before any more of Vlad's goons come sniffing around."

"You promise to come back for them?"

"I give you my word. Shark should be coming to about now. I'll take you to the car, but I'm not sure if he'll be all right to drive. What about you? Do you need to be checked out by a doctor?"

"I think I'm okay."

***

Skinbone stopped when he recognized Cherie. One of her eyes was swollen shut and her face was caked with blood. "Sonofabitch."

He kneeled beside her, swallowed his anger, and sliced the ropes from her wrists and ankles. Her limbs were bound so tight that her hands and feet were turning blue. "It's okay, you're going to be okay. Melissa sent me to find you."

"Melissa?" The girl croaked through puffy lips. She started to sob.

Skinbone cradled her against his chest and spoke in a soothing tone. "Your friend was very worried about you. I've got you and you're safe now, but I need your help. The bastards who did this to you have someone I love. She should have been here, with you, but I can't find her anywhere." He reached into his pocket and pulled out his wallet. Inside was a recent picture of Sierra. "I need you to look at this and tell me if you've seen her. I need to know where they've taken her."

***

Sierra's legs bucked before they made it halfway across the deck. Ethan caught her before she fell.

"Hang onto me, we've just got a bit further to go."

She nodded. It was all catching up to her. Sierra wrapped her arm around Ethan's waist and held on. "Sorry. I'm not usually so helpless."

"Helpless? Now that's the understatement of the year. You brought down two key players in a white slavery ring, members of the Russian Mafia, no less, and with your hands bound. I think you're allowed a little leeway."

"When you put it that way." She smiled and took a few more steps. Her legs gave out a second time.

"I need to rest a minute."

"You probably need to get your circulation going again. They tied your feet for quite a long time. You also need to be home in your own bed with that surly bastard you insist on loving, taking good care of you."

"Skinbone is not a surly bastard," she protested.

"So you say. I still haven't met his good side."

"Give it time. You will."

"Meanwhile." He bent at the waist and swooped her into his arms. "I'm getting a bad feeling about being on this boat. Hope you don't mind if I carry you the rest of the way."

***

By the time they reached Vlad's cabin, Skinbone was frantic with worry, terrified that Sierra was badly injured...or worse.

"I think this is it." Cherie mumbled against his shoulder. "I think this is where I saw them drag her."

Skinbone's eyebrow twitched. He set Cherie down a few feet from the door and drew his gun. The door was open a crack. He kicked it open the rest of the way and charged in with both hands on his weapon.

He stumbled over Dmitri's body, feeling his stomach leap into his throat. He braced himself before he looked down, afraid he would see Sierra's lifeless eyes staring up at him.

Skinbone almost collapsed with relief when he saw it was one of the Russians. He spotted Vladimir's dead body in the middle of the room and tore the place apart looking for Sierra. He glanced at the broken chair and the cracked-off leg inches from Vladimir's hand.

It wasn't hard to connect the dots. He knew how the man planned to use it. The entire situation was a colossal nightmare and his emotions were spinning into overdrive. He had no idea if Sierra managed to escape or if the bastard beat her to death. Was it possible she killed the Russians, or was he grasping at straws in order to keep his desperation at bay?

He couldn't take much more of this. The woman he loved had vanished for a second time. He rubbed his brow and tried to figure out his next move. Every time he thought he was close to finding her, he came up empty.

It seemed there was nothing more he could do, but he wasn't ready to give up. Not until he found her. He'd get Cherie off the boat, call an ambulance for her, and begin his search again. It was possible there were still Russian's on board and that they were hiding her somewhere.

His shoulders slumped as he left the room.

"Did you find her?" Cherie asked.

He shook his head and leaned over to help her up.

She took his hand and leaned on him for support. "I've got some feeling back in my legs. I'd like to try to walk if that's okay."

"Sure," he answered, but his mind was elsewhere. Cherie's injuries forced them to walk at a slow pace, he didn't mind as it gave him time to think. They walked along the length of the cabin and made a gentle turn.

Skinbone jerked to a stop and stared ahead in disbelief. Sierra was being carried off the boat by another man. A man with a familiar walk and an unmistakable jacket, one he'd seen just last night.

Ethan Wilde had Sierra. The sonofabitch was rotten to the core. He'd never reformed, the rehabilitation fiasco was a sham. There was no doubt in Skinbone's mind that Ethan had been in on the white slavery ring all along. Why else would he be here? How else could he have ended up on this boat?

He motioned for Cherie to stay quiet and yanked his gun out of its holster. He couldn't get a clear shot, not from this angle and not with Sierra in his arms. He moved with the stealth of a tiger, stalking its prey.

Ethan never heard a thing, Skinbone made sure of it. He crept up behind his so-called adopted brother and rammed his gun into Ethan's back. "Put her down, and walk away."

Ethan froze. "Lower the gun first. I'm not doing a damn thing until you lower the gun."

Sierra twisted in Ethan's arms. "No!" she cried out.

Skinbone misunderstood her fear. His gaze wavered for an instant, gut clenching at the terror he saw in her eyes.

"I'm done chasing demons, Ethan. The fact that could you do this to Sierra after she saved your sorry hide proves you're not fit to live. Put her down and you die easy. Make me wait and you die hard."

"Skinbone, wait!" Sierra twisted again, struggling to break free. "Don't shoot."

Ethan tightened his grip and tried to reason with him. "Listen, mate, this looks bad, but things aren't always what they seem. Listen to the lady and put the gun down."

"Not until I put a bullet through you." His eyes blazed with the heat of anger. He just needed a clear shot, one was all it would take.

"Stop," Sierra screamed. "Both of you. Ethan hasn't hurt me. He's not responsible for any of this."

"He'll never believe you," Ethan spat. "You're wasting your breath trying to get him to listen."

Skinbone's lips tightened into a thin hard line. Sierra had a soft heart. Even after all she'd been through, she was still looking for reasons to trust. "Give me one reason why I should believe you. It's stretching coincidence a bit much don't you think?"

"The hell with this, we're wasting time. I'm taking Sierra and we are walking off this godforsaken boat. I know you, brother. You won't shoot while I'm holding onto her. When we get to shore we can discuss this like reasonable men."

"Don't you dare make a move." Skinbone bared his teeth and cocked his gun. Ethan wasn't going anywhere with his woman.

A gust of wind blew in from the east. The boat swayed. Ethan's feet slipped, his grip on Sierra loosened.

Cherie let out a chilling scream.

***

Sierra felt Ethan losing his balance. He tried to steady himself by grabbing hold of the railing. Her legs swung to the ground, her heart pumped in terror. Skinbone was in a blind rage, there was no time to convince him of Ethan's innocence, not when she'd jumped to the same guilty verdict herself.

For a moment, it seemed that time stood still. Ethan broke away from her. The deck was wet and he was losing his battle to regain his balance. Skinbone let out a bloodthirsty howl, her breath caught at the murderous look in his eyes.

There was no time to think. Sierra couldn't give Skinbone a clear shot at Ethan. He would never be able to live with himself if he killed an innocent man. *She* wouldn't be able to live with herself if Ethan's death was on her hands.

She threw herself forward, towards Ethan, putting herself between him and Skinbone's gun. Cherie let out a bloodcurdling scream. A gunshot blasted through the night. Sierra felt the heat of the bullet as it whizzed past and opened her mouth in a silent scream. Blood and gore flew across her face. Her eyes met Ethan's startled gaze. The front of his leather jacket was soaked with blood.

The boat rocked. Ethan staggered forward. Sierra's gaze flew to Skinbone's face. He wasn't looking at her and he wasn't looking at Ethan. His stance rigid, he'd turned away and was looking behind them.

Sierra heard the sound before it registered, the ship's ladder, clanging against the side of the boat. She turned in time to see a pair of legs swing over the railing and a man drop down onto the deck.

She looked from the man to Ethan, and grabbed onto Skinbone's upper arm. "Look."

Shark grinned and wiped his brow with the back of his arm, holding a semi-automatic in his right hand. "Whew!" he said pointing his gun at the Russian who had been sneaking up behind them. "That was a close one."

Caught up in the drama playing out before them, none of them had been aware that one of the ship's men had been advancing on them, aiming for a straight shot at Sierra's head.

"Good thing I showed up when I did. No thanks to you," he motioned at Ethan with the barrel of his gun.

Ethan stared down at his blood-soaked jacket and then back at Shark. "Bloody hell, you blew that man's brains out from *that* distance? For God's sake, mate, your bullet whizzed right past our cheeks. If either Sierra or I had moved…"

"I chose my moment with great care." Shark rubbed the lump on his head. "Unlike some people."

"I guess I owe you an apology for that — but by the looks of things, you owe me a new jacket."

"Saving your life wasn't enough?"

Sierra tore her gaze away from Shark and Ethan. Skinbone stood alone, a faraway look in his eye, a stricken look on his face. She reached out and rubbed his arm.

"It's over," she whispered. "We can go home now."

Skinbone shook his head. It was clear he was rattled. "I almost shot him. I almost shot Ethan. I didn't listen to you when you told me he wasn't guilty. I let my anger and rage get the best of me."

"But you didn't shoot him."

"I would have, if it wasn't for Shark."

"It was a complicated situation," she tried to sooth him. "I thought the same thing when I saw him myself."

Ethan must have overheard their conversation. He walked over to Skinbone and held out his hand. "My past has given you reason to doubt me, and Sierra's right, it was a complicated situation. I don't know how I would have reacted had I been in your shoes. We seem to share more than Luke as a father, we share trigger tempers and the ability to kill. Makes for a dangerous situation between us unless we leave the past where it belongs and agree we are the same side. What do you say, mate, a truce?"

Skinbone's expression was unreadable. Sierra held her breath, waiting to see what would happen next. A foghorn blew in the distance. He holstered his gun, accepted Ethan's hand. "Truce."

Sierra breathed a sigh a relief. Skinbone turned to her and gathered his face in her hands. "I was afraid I'd never see you again. You scared the living hell out of me."

She nodded, tears of joy running down her face. "I was scared too."

Shark stamped his feet and cleared his throat. "I'm all for happy reunions, but what say we blow this place." He jerked his chin towards Cherie. "I'll be happy to assist that young lady off the boat."

"There's other girls," Sierra said.

"That job is too big for us to handle." Skinbone shook his head, a sad expression on his face. "They not only need medical care, they've been severely traumatized. They need professionals looking after them."

Ethan reached into his pocket and withdrew a cell phone. "I took this off one of the Russians. We could call it in from the car; give them an anonymous tip, save ourselves from answering a lot of questions."

Sierra felt Skinbone's arm tighten around her. She glanced up at him. "I would like to go home. I'm sure Cherie would too."

As they made their way to solid ground, snow started to fall. Ethan paused and glanced up at the sky.

Sierra caught his look. "It's beautiful, isn't it? When it's fresh and brand new?"

He seemed to ponder her words. "On a night like this, it's almost bloody inspiring."

Shark smiled and craned his neck in Ethan's direction. "It almost feels like Christmas, the season for miracles. And good cheer, we can't forget the cheer."

Ethan's laugh split the air. "So what does that make us, a merry band of oddballs?"

"And crack shots," Shark joked. "Just a reminder to give credit where it's due."

"If you think your gunshot was impressive, did I mention how Sierra brought down the Russian Mafia armed with a shoe?"

"Wait. What?"

"I'm telling you, mate, you should have seen her. She killed two blokes with the flick of a wrist and a wicked high heel."

"You're kidding me."

"I couldn't make up a story like that. But I still say you owe me a jacket. Your crack shot ruined this one. Look at all this blood."

Sierra smiled at their banter and slowed her pace. She glanced up at Skinbone. "Are we okay?"

Skinbone came to a stop and wrapped his arms around her as the snow fell gently upon them. He tipped her chin back with his hand and smiled down at her. "We are more than okay. I don't know what I would have done if anything happened to you," his voice was husky with emotion.

"Let's hope you never have to find out." She stood on her tiptoes and kissed him on the lips. "I love you, Skinbone Harris, even if you are a stubborn ass some of the time."

"And I love you too, Sierra Montgomery, despite your penchant for running headlong into trouble and putting your life at risk."

She grinned. "I guess we both have our faults."

He shrugged. "Could be, but I know one damn thing for sure. Loving you isn't one of them."

"You say the sweetest things," she teased, peering up at him from under her lashes.

He pulled her into a rough embrace. She felt the warmth of his kiss straight down to her toes.

***

The inspiration for this story by author, Lori Gordon:

The inspiration for this story sprang from a conversation with fellow author Stephen Penner — and the idea of using a shoe as a deadly weapon. The discussion took on a life of its own and soon other authors were involved in a lively debate about killer shoes and the stories we could tell about them.

When it came time to sit down and write the actual story, it seemed a perfect fit for the characters I first introduced in my debut novel, State of Panic. And where better to find killer shoes than in a shoe store located on Chicago's Gold Coast? But I needed motive, means, and opportunity for the story to unfold, and a worthy adversary for Sierra Montgomery. I chose the most ruthless characters I could imagine who would also have the resources to use shoe stores as a front for something far more diabolical. Mix in a missing teenager, a reformed killer trying to turn his life around, and the far too real issue of women sold for profit and I had all the ingredients I needed to build my story. Hope you enjoyed it!

We hope you've enjoyed reading the Dead Shoe Society Anthology. You can learn more about the authors by visiting the Dead Shoe website at www.deadshoesociety.com.

Made in the USA
Charleston, SC
17 December 2011